SUSPICION OF MURDER

"I'm sorry about your aunt. Even though we'd just met, I could see what a special lady she was."

"Aunt Mary was one of a kind." Paul spoke slowly; his words were heavy with sadness. "She had so many wonderful friends and everyone who knew her felt the same way you did. That's what makes this whole thing so hard to understand . . ."

"I'm sure the fact that it happened so unexpectedly didn't help," I said gently. "Was it a heart attack?"

"No, although that's what everyone thought at first. It was a natural assumption. Aunt Mary had some medical issues related to her age, but she wasn't mortally ill. Yesterday morning, I had every expectation that she might live for another decade.

"But after . . ." He cleared his throat, then continued, "The director at Winston Pumpernill called the medical examiner. I gather that's standard when things like this happen. I thought it was just a formality. But when I called a few minutes ago to make arrangements for the funeral home to come and pick her up, I was told that the body wasn't being released. Apparently, there's a suspicion of foul play . . ."

Books by Laurien Berenson

Published by Kensington Publishing Corporation

A Melanie Travis Mystery

Raining Cats & Dogs

LAURIEN BERENSON

KENSINGTON BOOKS
KENSINGTON PUBLISHING CORP.
http://www.kensingtonbooks.com

1

"I'll tell you the secret to happiness," said Aunt Peg. "It's this: Never grow old."

I looked at my aunt, who'd turned sixty-three on her last birthday. From my vantage point three decades younger, that seemed pretty old to me. I resisted the impulse to say what I was thinking, but my discretion didn't help. Aunt Peg was able to read minds, or something close to it.

And not just mine, either. Peg always seemed to know what her big black Standard Poodles were thinking. She had six of them, all retired show champions, all related to my two, Faith and Eve. Now she gazed pointedly in my direction and lifted a brow.

Faith, who was lying under my chair with her long muzzle resting on my foot, cringed slightly and turned her face away, as if maybe she didn't want to witness what was coming next. I think she can read minds, too. When it came to psychic ability, I seemed to be the only one who had gotten left out.

"Age," Aunt Peg said loftily, "is merely a number on a calendar. What matters is how you feel inside. The enthusiasm and curiosity with which you greet each new day. The boundless energy you devote to the things that interest you."

"Boundless energy?" I repeated. I may have sunk lower in my chair. The mere notion of trying to muster such a thing seemed like entirely too much effort.

We were having this conversation at five o'clock on a Thursday afternoon. I'd already put in a full day of work, attending to my job as a special needs tutor at Howard Academy in Greenwich. My eight-year-old son, Davey, was at spring soccer practice. My new husband, Sam, would be picking him up and bringing him home within the hour. I was supposed to be cooking dinner.

Instead, I was planted at my kitchen table, hands wrapped around an oversize mug of fully caffeinated coffee. Aunt Peg had her usual tea. Sprawled on the floor around us were five Standard Poodles of various ages. My two plus the three Sam had brought with him when he'd moved in three weeks earlier. My house was small and cozy. There wasn't nearly enough room to accommodate five large dogs, not to mention an extra adult. No matter how badly Davey and I both wanted him there.

So far, Sam's and my marriage—which had begun with a spur-of-the-moment elopement to Vermont over spring break—had all the elements of a three-ring circus: thrills, chills, laughter, and suspense. Oh, yes, and great sex.

Okay, so maybe it was better than most circuses I'd been to.

Still, it was a challenge to comprehend how this

was all going to come together. And combining two households might prove to be the least of our worries. I was thirty-four and had been a single parent for most of the last eight years. Sam was two years older, previously divorced, no children. Both of us were accustomed to living life on our own terms, keeping to our own schedules, and, for the most part, answering to nobody but ourselves. Both of us were willing to compromise; we just hadn't figured out yet how to make everything work.

And the cramped living quarters, which had the eight of us—Poodles included, naturally—constantly tripping over one another, weren't helping.

"All right, maybe not boundless," Aunt Peg said. She peered at me closely. "And here I thought marriage to Sam would be good for you. Are you sure you're getting enough sleep?"

There we were, I thought, back to that great sex thing again.

"I'm fine," I chirped, straightening in my seat. "Quite fine. Positively fine."

"Well, if you don't mind my saying so, you look like hell."

As if my minding would have stopped her. As if my objections to anything Aunt Peg proposed ever slowed her down for even a minute.

"No, I'm just regrouping," I said. "Conserving my energy for later. Faith and I are going to our first obedience class tonight."

"Oh, really? I'd forgotten all about that."

Aunt Peg thinks she's a good liar. At one point in my life, when I knew her less well, I had thought so, too. Now, however, I can spot her ulterior motives a mile away. And this impromptu chat, occasioned by Peg showing up at my door with a box of cinnamon buns in her hands and an innocent expression on her face, had all the earmarks of an inquisition.

"Tell me again," she said casually, "why you decided Faith needed a second career in obedience."

This would be after the Poodle's first career as a show dog. Faith, like Aunt Peg's Standards, was a show ring champion. She had also recently become the dam of a champion when Peg had finished Zeke, a puppy from Faith's first litter. Eve was Zeke's littermate, and she was working toward her championship as well. So far, she had amassed twelve of the fifteen points necessary to earn her title. With luck, I would have her finished by summer.

"Instead of something fun," Aunt Peg continued, "like say . . . agility?"

Agility—dogs and their owners racing pell-mell around a course of obstacles, trying to beat the clock while running through tunnels, in and out of weave poles, and over jumps—did look like fun. It was also currently all the rage. Obedience trials, on the other hand, had been around for decades. That sport was more disciplined and exacting. When done correctly, it did not involve any running, or yelling, or fits of helpless laughter.

Aunt Peg was doing agility with Hope, Faith's sister. And, as always, she expected me to follow in her footsteps.

Except that, for the first time, I was putting my foot down.

"Obedience," I said firmly. "Faith and I are going to have a great time."

"But she's already obedient. For one thing, she's a Standard Poodle, which means that she was born knowing ten times more than your basic retriever or terrier."

You'll have to forgive my aunt. She loves all dogs; she truly does. But in her heart of hearts, she's totally Poodlecentric.

"Plus, the very fact that she was a show dog means that she's already learned to do all sorts of things: she comes, she stands, she stays. She walks beautifully on a leash."

I nodded in agreement. "That's why we're not starting in the beginner class. I spoke with the instructor about it when I signed up. Even though Faith and I don't have any background in obedience, Steve was fairly confident that being in the novice group would bore us silly. Tonight's class is for the more advanced dog and handler teams, those who already know the basics and are working toward a degree. We'll have to play catch-up, obviously, but since Poodles are such quick learners, Steve was sure that after a couple of weeks we'd fit right in."

"You'd fit right into my agility class, too." Like a foxhound on a fresh scent, Aunt Peg hated to give up.

"But that's just it. It would be *your* agility class. And once again you would have excelled at something before I even had a chance to try."

It wasn't that I resented Aunt Peg's success in the dog show world. Quite the contrary, I was in awe of all she'd accomplished. Her Cedar Crest Standard Poodles were known nationwide for their wonderful quality, their superb temperaments, and their excellent health. For three decades, she had produced and managed a line of dogs with which anyone would have been proud to be associated.

More recently, Aunt Peg had turned her hand toward judging, and with assignments coming in from all over the country, she was quickly making a name for herself in that arena, too.

In the dog show world, most people knew me first as Margaret Turnbull's niece. Even though I'd worked hard for the things I'd accomplished, I knew there were competitors who felt that I'd never paid my dues, that my success was due to Aunt Peg's influence. And the worst part was, I wasn't sure that the critics were entirely wrong.

Faith, my first Poodle, had come from Aunt Peg, after all. She wasn't the medium-quality dog most beginners have to contend with, but rather, a beautiful Standard Poodle who'd finished her championship easily, despite my inept handling. Aunt Peg had steered me toward the better judges and told me which ones to avoid. She'd taught me how to clip and blow-dry, then set the lines on Faith's trims, and cleaned up my fumbling attempts at scissoring.

I was enormously grateful for everything Aunt Peg had done for me. But where Poodles and dog shows were concerned, I'd been standing in her shadow from the very beginning. It was time for me to try something on my own—an enterprise where Aunt Peg's name wouldn't open any doors or smooth my way along, where Faith and my success or failure would be based solely on our own merits.

"Obedience," I said firmly.

Aunt Peg looked surprised by my conviction. That made two of us. Or three, if you counted Faith. She glanced up at me, then placed her muzzle back into position on my foot. Nothing like a gesture of support from the peanut gallery.

And the decision was made.

* * *

Which didn't prevent me from having to defend it once again over dinner. I'd had a pot roast sitting in the crock-pot all day while I was at school, so coming up with the rest of the meal was pretty easy. Aunt Peg left just as the men in my life were arriving home. I'd invited her to stay for dinner, but she declined. Having lived alone except for her Poodles since her husband, Max, had died several years earlier, I think she found the chaos inherent in our current living situation to be a little overwhelming.

Unfortunately, she wasn't the only one.

Sam and Peg greeted each other at the door, then he walked her outside to her car. Davey, predictably, raced straight for the kitchen. Since he was still wearing cleats and shin guards, the clatter he made on the wooden floors got Sam's three Poodles—who weren't used to living with a child yet—up and barking. Faith and Eve knew full well there wasn't anything to get excited about, but bowing to peer pressure, they joined in anyway.

A full minute passed before the din quieted and I could even get a word in. "How was soccer practice?" I asked, directing the question to my son's back. His head was stuck in the refrigerator.

"Great." Details weren't Davey's forte. He didn't bother to turn around. "When's dinner? I'm starving."

"Soon. Wash your hands and set the table."

"If I do, can I have a sticky bun?" His eyes lit on the remains of Aunt Peg's bounty, sitting on the counter where she'd left them behind.

"After dinner," I said.

"What's after dinner?" Sam asked. He walked up behind me and slipped his arms around my waist.

I leaned back into him and our bodies fit together effortlessly.

It had always been that way between us. Right from the beginning, there'd been that frisson of awareness, that undeniable attraction, whenever we were together. It had taken us three years, one broken engagement, and a host of other complications before we'd managed to get ourselves married.

Looking back, I wondered what had taken us so long.

"Cinnamon buns," I said, prudently neglecting to mention that I'd already eaten two myself. "Aunt Peg left one for each of us."

Sam and Davey quickly set the table while I prepared the plates. The Poodles milled around our legs in a happy state of confusion. All of them, Sam's and my dogs alike, knew better than to beg for food. But that didn't stop them from wanting to be on hand in case something should happen to fall on the floor.

Like the humans in their house, the Poodles hadn't had quite enough time yet to meld into a cohesive pack. Sam's three had to be wondering about their change of abode, which had brought with it cramped living arrangements and the necessity of sharing their person with others. Faith and Eve were accustomed to having Sam around. They just weren't entirely sure about welcoming three canine interlopers into their space. But Poodles are nothing if not adaptable, and so far, the crew was making do with typical élan.

Sam and I had already begun house hunting; finding a more appropriate home for our blended family had been the first thing on our agenda upon our return from Vermont. Sam's house was bigger than mine, but it was also half an hour north in Redding. With Davey happily ensconced in a nearby Stamford elementary school, and my job in Greenwich an easy commute away, it had seemed the best decision was to wedge ourselves into Davey's and my small cape for the time being.

It was a decision I was trying not to regret more than once or twice a day.

"Don't forget I have class tonight," I said, when the pot roast had been served and eaten and we were all munching happily on warm, gooey cinnamon buns. Sam and Davey had been discussing whether there'd be time to fit a game of Scrabble in around Davey's homework.

"That's dumb," my son said.

"What is?"

"I'm a kid. I have to go to school. But why would anybody want to go to classes if they didn't have to?"

"They're for Faith," I told him. "It's obedience school. We're going to see if she can earn a Companion Dog degree to go along with her championship."

"Of course she can." Davey licked his fingers, a breach of etiquette both adults at the table decided to ignore. "Faith is the smartest dog ever."

The accolade was pretty much true. Until I'd become a Standard Poodle owner, I'd had no inkling of the scope of the breed's intelligence. Poodles didn't just learn by rote, they thought and reasoned things through. They also possessed a tremendous desire to please, as well as an unexpectedly well-developed sense of humor, all of which combined to make their temperaments nearly irresistible. Living with a Poodle wasn't like owning a dog, it was akin to adding another member to the family.

"Too bad Tar is still in hair," said Sam. "He could probably benefit from a few obedience classes."

As one, our gazes went to Sam's big black male Poodle. Asleep and snoring softly, he was lying flat out on the kitchen floor. His spine was pressed up against the pantry door, probably because he remembered that that was where I kept the biscuits. The profuse hair in his topknot—kept long and thick for the show ring, and confined at home in protective, colored, banded ponytails—had flopped forward over his face. They rose and fell with each breath he took.

The most notable thing about Tar, however, was that somehow he had managed to get comfortable on the floor, and then had fallen asleep with one of his hind feet resting in the water bowl. The fact that his shaved paw and the bracelet above it were wet and cold had apparently made no impression upon him. At least, I noted, he hadn't tipped the bowl over.

Not yet, at any rate.

Tar was an undeniably handsome Standard Poodle. His show career thus far had been stellar. Having recently won his fourth Best in Show, he was currently one of the top Non-Sporting dogs in the Northeast. What Tar wasn't, poor thing, was brilliant.

Oh, tell yourself the truth, I thought. Tar wasn't even terribly smart. In a household where most of the dogs' IQs approached that of the human inhabitants, Tar was an anomaly. A sweet dog, to be sure. A loving dog, even a trustworthy one. One who always tried his best to please, however limited that effort might be. Tar was a Poodle who meant well, but he couldn't think his way out of a dark corner.

When I'd only seen Tar at dog shows and at Sam's

house, his limitations hadn't been that obvious. But now that I lived with him full-time and dealt with him on a daily basis, it was hard not to compare him with his more intellectually endowed peers. And to see that he came up short.

"Tar is very sweet," I said slowly. I knew how I'd feel if someone insulted one of my Poodles, so I chose my words carefully. "But I'm not sure that obedience would necessarily be the right option for him."

"I'm not saying he would be a star," Sam said. "But taking a few lessons might teach him how to deal with new things. You know, he could learn how to learn."

"Or how to think," said Davey, shaking his head. "Because that is one dumb dog."

So much for not insulting the new family members.

To my relief, Sam chuckled. "I wondered how long it would take you two to notice. I don't know when was the last time I had a Poodle that was so lacking in brain power." His hand waved in the direction of Raven and Casey, his older females. "Those two know everything. If you told them to cook you breakfast in the morning, they'd ask how you wanted your eggs. But Tar . . . well, what can I say? Everyday he wakes up to a whole new adventure, because nothing he learned the day before ever seems to stick."

Hearing his name, Tar lifted his head. His weight shifted, and his leg moved. His sodden foot slipped off the rim of the water bowl and landed on the floor with a soggy thump. Cold water splashed up onto his close-clipped hindquarter. Expression quizzical, clearly confused, Tar turned to see what had caused the spray.

"I don't think obedience would help," I said.

"Maybe agility," Sam mused.

The thought made me laugh. "I've seen Tar get lost coming down the stairs. And twice so far, I've had to untangle him from Davey's swing set. Something as fast-paced as agility would probably send him into shock."

"You're probably right," Sam admitted. "I bet Faith would be good at it, though."

"Don't even start," I said. "I just had this conversation with Aunt Peg—"

Abruptly, Tar leapt to his feet. He crossed the kitchen in a single, athletic bound, barking ferociously as his front paws slammed against the back door hard enough to make the glass rattle. Immediately, the other Poodles were up and on alert. Their outraged voices joined his. I spun in my seat and looked to see what had caught their attention.

The Poodles had all been out in the fenced backyard earlier; the outside lights were still on. Silhouetted in their glow, a large orange cat was clearly visible through the window above the sink. He must have been standing balanced on the windowsill; his yellow eyes calmly scanned the room.

Tar was a mere few feet away, barking so hard now that the effort bounced him up and down on his hind feet. The cat cocked his head in Tar's direction but didn't retreat. The Poodles' raucous ire at his invasion of their space didn't seem to faze him one bit. His fluffy tail lifted high in the air and swung slowly from side to side. A gesture of disdain if ever I'd seen one.

"I didn't know you had a cat," said Sam.

"I don't. He must belong to one of the neighbors, though I've never seen him around here before."

"You'd think a cat would have more sense than to come here," said Davey. "This place is like Dog Central."

"Maybe he's lost," Sam said.

I looked again and the cat was gone. Now that he'd removed himself from their sight, the Poodles quieted. They were beginning to look rather sheepish about their outburst. I stood up, walked over, and peered out the window. The cat had disappeared.

"Wherever he came from, he's gone now," I said. "And speaking of which, Faith and I have to go, too."

"Go ahead," said Sam. "Davey and I will clean up. Then after that, we'll hit the books."

He made it all seem so simple, I thought as I dug out Faith's choke chain and leather leash. No need to arrange for a babysitter. Or worry that if I took Davey to class with me, his homework wouldn't get done. Marriage might not be the easiest thing I'd ever done, but it definitely had its perks.

2

According to the brochure I'd picked up at the New Canaan YMCA, Steve Barton had started the South Avenue Obedience Club in his backyard. A longtime competitor in obedience trials, he'd become frustrated and ultimately outraged by the number of pet dogs that routinely ran free through his suburban neighborhood. Eventually, he'd come up with the idea of holding beginner obedience lessons once a week for anyone on his block who cared to attend.

Over time, the classes' popularity had grown, and as of the previous year, Steve's lessons were offered under the guise of adult education and held in the basement of the YMCA. Beginners went on Tuesday nights. The advanced sessions, in which Faith and I were to take part, were held on Thursdays.

For seven o'clock on a weekday night, the parking lot of the Y was surprisingly full. Faith was sitting beside me on the front seat as I pulled in and parked. The big Poodle was accustomed to going places with me, but Eve usually came with us, too. I could tell that Faith was excited by the prospect of an outing where she would have my undivided attention.

I twisted in my seat and slipped the choke collar over her head, placing it so that when Faith was on my left side, as she'd be for most of the obedience lessons, it would release quickly and correctly. Faith stood up on the seat and shook her head experimentally. The collar rattled around her neck, then settled back into place, nestled into the thick hair beneath her ears.

Poodles that are being shown never wear collars except when they're in the ring, because the constant friction causes the oh-so-important mane hair to mat and rub away. Faith had been retired for more than a year, and I'd long since clipped off the elaborate continental trim she'd worn to attain her championship. But somehow I'd never gotten around to putting a collar on her. As the Poodle dipped, then raised her head, flipping the choke chain into place once more, I knew she was wondering what was up.

The parking lot was well lit, and I could see several people taking their dogs for one last walk on the stretch of grass that wrapped around three sides of the building. A Doberman Pinscher, a Cairn Terrier, and a Papillon all walked sedately at the ends of their leashes, sniffing the ground as they looked for a likely spot, but still keeping one eye trained on their owners. Each ignored the distraction caused by the other dogs. I snapped the six-foot leather leash to the ring on the end of Faith's collar and got out to join them.

The three dog owners, two women and a man, had been talking among themselves. As we ap-

proached, their gazes shifted in our direction.
Being dog people, they looked at Faith first, appraising her quickly before lifting their eyes to me.

"You must be the newbie," said the woman holding the black-and-tan Doberman. She looked every
bit as sleek and strong as her dog. Leash already in
her left hand, she extended her right for me to
shake. "I'm Julie Hyland. Jack, sit."

Immediately, the Doberman's hindquarter sank
to the ground. He stared at Faith curiously. She
stared right back. I placed myself between them
and shook Julie's hand.

"Melanie Travis," I said. "And this is Faith. How
did you know I was new?"

"Steve told us we'd be adding a Poodle to the
group," said the man with the Cairn. His smile revealed a small gap between his front teeth. "And
your girl certainly fits the bill. I'm Mark Terry.
Nice to meet you." His terrier sauntered over to
touch noses with Faith. We all watched until both
dogs wagged their tails.

"Don't forget us," said the third member of the
group. She was fortyish, plump, and had blond
hair that was fading to gray. Despite her words, she
didn't look like the kind of person who would allow
herself to be overlooked for long. "I'm Stacey. I
won't even bother giving you my last name. You'll
meet so many new people tonight you'll never remember them all anyway. And this is Bubbles."

I almost laughed but caught myself just in time.

Stacey nodded at my reaction as if she'd seen it
before. "I know, the name's entirely lacking in dignity, even for a small dog. But Bubbles was a rescue, and that's what she came with. After all she'd
been through, I figured the least I could do was let
her keep her own name."

The Papillon cocked her head to one side and gazed up at us. Her ears, large for her size and covered in long, silky hair, flicked back and forth. "You hear your name, don't you?" Stacey cooed, pursing her lips and making kissing sounds. "What a little sweetheart you are. How anyone could have been so cruel as to abandon you by the side of the road—"

"Maybe you'll have time to tell Melanie the story later," Julie broke in, sounding exasperated. "But now, if we don't get moving, we're going to be late for class."

"Oh, right. Of course. Wouldn't want to be late, would we?" Stacey leaned over and scooped Bubbles up into her arms, then hurried toward the back door of the Y.

"She means well," Mark said as the three of us followed more slowly. "And Stacey couldn't be nicer to her dogs. But she does tend to talk."

"A lot," Julie added. I saw that Jack had automatically taken up a heeling position beside her left leg. "In fact, if there's anything you want to know about our little group, just ask Stacey. I'm sure she'll be happy to tell you everything."

Julie, I noticed, didn't sound entirely pleased about that.

"Maybe you can tell me one thing. When I signed up for these classes, I was told that the first session was going to be held tonight. Yet now I get the impression that all of you already know each other and have been doing this together for a while. Am I starting in the middle?"

"That's the thing about Steve's obedience club," said Mark. "Once you've graduated from the beginner session, the classes just sort of run continuously. There's no real beginning."

"And no end either," Julie said with a smile. "We tease Steve about that all the time. There's a core group of us—diehards, I guess you might say. Or maybe fanatics. We just keep coming back week after week. Nobody even keeps track of whether we're starting another session or not. It's all the same to us. All I know is, if it's Thursday night, Jack and I are at class."

"But . . ." I sputtered, glancing down at the impeccably behaved Doberman. "What happens when you run out of things to teach him?"

"Hasn't happened yet. Maybe it never will. Jack got his C.D. last year, and his C.D.X. six months ago. He won all three of his Open classes and was High in Trial twice. Now we're training toward his Utility Dog degree. I won't compete him, though, until he's perfect. In the meantime, we come here every week and sharpen up his skills."

"And to make the rest of us insanely jealous," said Mark.

In contrast to Jack, Mark's short-legged Cairn wasn't practicing his obedience at all. Instead, the smaller dog's nose was still to the ground, his thoughts clearly centered on the enticing smells in the yard. Every so often he'd stop walking to sniff at something, and Mark would have to snap the leash to get his attention.

"Reggie, behave!" he said with exasperation on the third such occasion. Unrepentant, the little terrier simply lifted his head and scurried to catch up.

"How long have you been coming to class?" I asked.

"At least as long as those two." Mark nodded toward Julie and Jack. "Quite possibly longer. Actually,

I think I'm in denial about the whole thing. I've simply blocked the timetable from memory."

"And is Reggie progressing?"

"In a manner of speaking. At least he has his C.D. now, though it took us nearly a dozen tries and we just squeaked through by the skin of our teeth." Mark lowered his voice and added confidentially, "Training a terrier is different, you know. It's not anything like working with a Dobie or a Poodle."

"That's what Mark would like you to believe anyway," said Julie. She'd reached the door and pulled it open. "Another way of looking at things is that some of us are more dedicated trainers than others."

"True." Mark's tone suddenly had a sharper edge. "Because some of us have lives and jobs and families to attend to. Our entire existence doesn't revolve around our dogs."

I'd expected Julie to be offended by the comment, possibly even insulted. I hadn't expected her to laugh.

But that's exactly what she did as she held the heavy door and ushered us in ahead of her. "Welcome to obedience class," she said.

Faith and I followed Mark and Reggie down the narrow hallway, with Jack and Julie bringing up the rear. A door at the end of the hall stood open and I could hear the babble of conversation from within. As we passed through the doorway into a large, brightly lit room, Mark and Julie were already shrugging out of their jackets. A row of metal chairs lined the wall nearest the door. When the other two threw their coats onto a pile that had already been started there, I pulled mine off and followed suit.

Julie immediately headed for a group of people and dogs clustered on the mats in the middle of the room. I hung back for a minute. I supposed I ought to find Steve Barton and check in, but while I'd been expecting an introductory session that would explain the goals of the course and what would be expected from us, everyone else already seemed to know what they were doing.

I jumped slightly as Mark came up behind me and placed a hand on my elbow. "That's Steve over there," he said, pointing to a man standing off in a corner, talking to a woman who was unpacking a set of scent articles from a canvas bag. I was too far away to hear what the two of them were discussing, but the Standard Schnauzer sitting at the woman's side was watching their conversation with rapt attention. His ears were pricked, and his head swiveled back and forth between them as they spoke.

"Thanks," I said. "I'll go introduce myself."

Faith followed me across the room, her feet padding softly on the rubber mats that had been spread across the floor to give the dogs traction. The Poodle had been to numerous dog shows and knew how to conduct herself in company. But although she kept one eye on me at all times, I could tell she was fascinated by all the new and different dogs, many of which were romping together at the end of their leashes as their owners waited for class to begin.

We were still a good ten feet from the pair in the corner when the sound of Steve's raised voice reached me. Faith, I imagined, had heard him even sooner. "I said no, Minerva, and that's final," he was saying. "This is my class and my decision. I'll run things the way I see fit."

"Then maybe I should think about finding a different class—" the woman retorted. But when the Schnauzer pressed up against her leg turned to watch Faith approach, she looked around as well. Her features were attractive, but the sour expression on her face lessened their appeal. Her mouth snapped shut in an angry line. She glared at Steve as he left her side and came to greet me.

"You must be Melanie." Steve held out his hand. "Thank you for coming."

I offered my hand and it was shaken firmly and released. Everything about Steve Barton, from his close-cropped brown hair to his stiffly erect bearing to the fine crease in his khaki pants, made me think of the military. All at once, I found myself wondering if I'd signed Faith up for the canine equivalent of boot camp. I knew that obedience was an exacting discipline, made up of exercises where seconds and inches counted, but I'd joined the class hoping that Faith and I would have fun learning something new. If Steve's discussion with the Schnauzer woman was indicative of the way he ran things in general, we might not last any longer than the first session.

"Don't mind Minerva," Steve said. "She tends to get a little pissy when things aren't going exactly her way."

The woman dropped the canvas bag onto one of the chairs and brushed past us. My eyes followed her as she joined the group in the middle of the room.

"I hope there isn't a problem?"

Steve barked out a laugh. "Where she's concerned, there's always a problem. But, please, don't let that ruin things for you. Other than Minerva, we're a generally happy bunch. The rest of us, including Coach, have learned to cope with her little tantrums, I'm sure you will, too."

"Coach?"

"Sorry, I forgot you weren't introduced. Coach is the Schnauzer, Minerva's near constant companion, and the soul of patience if you ask me."

"I met some of the other participants on my way in," I said. "Stacey, Mark, and Julie?"

"Good people. They've all been with me a while."

"So I gathered. I hadn't expected that. I thought everyone else would be just starting out like I am."

Steve shook his head. "Maybe I should have explained things better when we spoke on the phone. For most people who are into dog training, it's a real avocation. A hobby, of course, but also much more. You'll see, it can be almost kind of addictive. You start out thinking maybe you'll put a C.D. on a dog, and next thing you know that's done and you had some fun, so a C.D.X. begins to look like a workable goal. Many of the people you'll meet tonight have been coming to my classes for several years. Some aim for higher degrees and better scores. Others just keep starting new dogs and working them through the system."

The more he spoke, the more out of place I began to feel. I'd never put an obedience degree on any dog. As a matter of fact, I'd never even devoted much time to watching the obedience dogs at the shows. And what little training Faith had had couldn't begin to compare with the structured discipline her classmates would have been expected to adhere to.

"I think I've made a mistake," I said. "Faith and

I don't know any of this stuff. We're just starting out. I'm sure we must be in the wrong place."

"I don't think so," Steve said. He squatted down on his haunches so that he was eye level with Faith, who was sitting at my side waiting to see what was going to happen next.

"Nice to meet you, Faith." Steve held out his hand for the Poodle to sniff. Once she'd done that and remained where she was, her demeanor relaxed and merely curious, he scratched her under the chin, then reached down with his fingers to lift the chain collar out of the thick hair at her throat. After a brief inspection, he let it fall back into place and rose to his feet.

"Faith may be lacking in formal obedience training, but the two of you are much too advanced for the beginner class. You have to understand, those classes are often chaotic. Despite the detailed instructions I send out ahead of time, most people arrive with the wrong equipment. If they have purchased a choke chain, it's often the wrong size and almost certain to be on upside down.

"Not only that, but in the beginning, half the dogs are just running all over, dragging their owners around the room. Some are barking uncontrollably; a few are usually snarling. It's not unheard of for me to have to break up a fight. The beginner classes tend to be as much about getting the dogs socialized as they are about learning specific exercises. Faith may not know how to heel perfectly yet, but she understands how to focus on you, which is the basis for everything that comes after. I see she can sit and stay. And I'll bet she comes, too?"

He looked to me for confirmation and I nodded.

"In the basic twelve-week course, I'd be happy if half my graduates were as well behaved at the end as she is right now. So don't think for a minute that you're not ready to join the advanced group. Obviously you've done some good work with Faith already. As long as you're dedicated and practice what we do here at home, I'm sure the two of you will catch up in no time."

That made me feel better, and why wouldn't it? Who doesn't like to hear their dog's behavior complimented? Of course, I didn't dare tell Steve that Faith's calm and obedient demeanor was due to the fact that she was a Standard Poodle, and had little to do with any exceptional training skills on my part.

Nor was there time for me to demur, as Steve was already looking past me toward the door. "Great," he said. "Here come our other first-timers. Kelly and Paul are both recent graduates of the beginner class who got bit by the obedience bug and wanted to continue their dogs' training. Excuse me while I go make them feel welcome."

Kelly had an Akita at the end of her thick leather leash. The dog was brindle in color, large and powerful looking, and its small, dark eyes surveyed the room with disdain. Kelly was probably about my size, but she seemed small standing next to the Akita. Fleetingly, I found myself wondering whether she'd gotten such a large dog for protection.

It seemed like an odd thought, and after a moment, I realized why it had crossed my mind. All the other dogs in the room were at least somewhat attuned to their owners. Not the Akita in the doorway. His back was to Kelly and he was looking out and away, almost as if he thought he was on guard.

She'd wrapped the leash around one of her hands and was gripping it firmly with the other. It looked like she might have trouble controlling the big dog. I wondered if that was why she'd decided upon obedience lessons.

In contrast to Kelly, who looked tense and hesitant, Paul walked into the room with a smile. A sable Cardigan Welsh Corgi with big ears and a long tail cavorted at his side. Paul, I noted, was careful to keep himself and his dog at least a leash length away from the pair that had preceded him.

Good call, I thought.

The group standing in the middle dispersed, scattering before the newcomers. Julie sidled over to stand beside me. Jack was staring hard at the Akita that was standing at the edge of the mats. When he lifted one side of his lip and exposed his teeth, Julie reprimanded him with a stern look.

"It looks like the gang's all here," she said under her breath. "Let the fireworks begin."

3

You know me. I can never leave well enough alone.

"Fireworks?" I repeated. "Are you talking about Kelly or the Akita?"

Julie sent me a speculative glance. "What makes you think I'm not talking about Paul?"

Oh.

Stacey materialized beside us. As soon as the Akita had entered the room, she'd taken the precaution of lifting Bubbles up into her arms. Now the Papillon was cuddled snugly against her shoulder. "That Akita's name is Boss. Kelly also calls him Boss Man sometimes. Not that anybody asked me, but that is *not* the sign of a healthy relationship."

Nobody'd asked me either, but if they had, I probably would have agreed.

I gazed back at the doorway. "I thought Steve said those two were newcomers like me. How come you know them already?"

Julie looked like she might have replied, but

Stacey beat her to it. "Paul and Kelly are new to the advanced class, but they started training in the beginner group over the winter. In the past, the two sessions haven't mixed much, but the reason Paul started bringing Cora—that's the Corgi, by the way—to class was because he has a great-aunt living at the Winston Pumpernill Nursing Home. You know, over in Greenwich?"

I nodded. Everyone knew Winston Pumpernill; it was a local landmark, a skilled nursing facility that had been around for more than forty years. The institution was located on thirty acres, the site of a former estate, in backcountry Greenwich. I'd driven past the large brick edifice many times but had never been inside.

"Anyway, Paul had read some article in a magazine about therapy dogs. You know, the ones that go to visit people in nursing homes or homes for the aged. It's really a great thing. If I was going to be stuck in a home like that, I'd probably go stir-crazy without any canine companionship. Wouldn't I, Bubbie?" Stacey paused to make chirping noises in Bubbles's face. The Papillon responded by licking her on the mouth.

Julie grimaced slightly, but I think it was the baby talk that had offended her, not the shared kiss.

"Paul wanted to take Cora to go visit his aunt and some of the other residents in the home, but the article said there were guidelines for dogs and owners who wanted to get involved. It recommended that they start with basic obedience training, which was what brought Paul to class in the first place."

I could see why Julie had said that Stacey liked

to talk. She'd been working on this explanation for two or three minutes and had yet to answer my original question.

Luckily, when Stacey paused to take a breath, Julie stepped in to help out. "Long story short, Paul was so enthused about his idea that he got Steve interested in it, too. Steve mentioned it at one of our classes, and nearly half of us volunteered to go with him. It was right around Christmas, and I guess we were all feeling that 'good will toward men' vibe."

"It was a real eye-opener for me," said Stacey. "Before we went, I didn't have any experience with nursing homes or managed care at all. It was more that I had the afternoon free and thought, what the heck? But you know what? The whole thing turned out to be a great experience."

Julie nodded. "It was fun, and very satisfying in a way that perhaps none of us had expected. Kelly was one of the first to join the group. That was how we met her."

"And Boss"—the name stuck in my throat for some reason—"does okay in a situation like that?"

"Well, he hasn't done anything irredeemable yet. And Steve, thank God, keeps a pretty close eye on things."

"I expected everyone to slack off when the holidays were over," Stacey said. "But it hasn't turned out that way at all. Instead, we have a group that gets together regularly on Sunday afternoons. The home has even written our visit into the weekly schedule. We're right on the calendar and everything."

"You might want to think about joining us," said Julie.

It did sound like an interesting idea. "Faith and

I are so new to all of this. Do you think she would qualify?"

"Don't worry about that," said Stacey. "We're not part of an official Therapy Dog program. This is just an informal arrangement Paul worked out with Winston Pumpernill. I bet you two would fit right in."

"Okay people!" Steve stepped out into the middle of the mats and clapped his hands loudly. "Time to get to work. Social hour is over, even though I know that's what most of you *really* came for."

Laughter rippled around the room, and nobody bothered to disagree. They did, however, begin to take up their positions on the mats. Dogs and handlers formed a line that took up two sides of the large area. I assumed that that meant we were going to be working on heeling first. As I placed Faith next to my left leg and told her to sit, Minerva hurried Coach into the empty place behind me.

"Hi," she said, "we haven't met. I'm—"

The greeting was interrupted by her Standard Schnauzer, who leapt abruptly into the air. Steve had taken a red rubber ball out of his pocket and bounced it on the mat. Most of the dogs noticed; several dove for it, including Coach. He hit the end of his leash and fell to the ground. His owner, feet braced for impact, was barely thrown at all.

"I just wanted to see if anyone was paying attention," Steve said with a grin.

"Idiot," Minerva muttered under her breath.

"I'm Melanie," I said as she hauled Coach back into position by her side. "And you're Minerva, right?"

"It's Minnie, please. The only one who calls me

Minerva is Steve, and he only does it because he knows it annoys me."

She unbuttoned her sweater and pulled it off, revealing a tight, low-cut T-shirt underneath. Minnie's assets, hidden beneath the bulky sweater, were now admirably on display. Though it was only April, the heat in the basement was off and there was a distinct chill in the air. So I assumed she hadn't stripped down because she was too warm.

When several men in the group gazed appreciatively in her direction, and Minnie shot a triumphant look at Steve, who was standing in the middle of the room and looking everywhere but at her, I figured my guess had been correct.

"Sure, they're staring now," Minnie said. "But wait until we get started working. It'll heat up in a hurry. You'll be sorry you wore a turtleneck."

Frankly, with this much dissension going on, I was beginning to wonder whether I'd be sorry that I'd come at all.

Then Steve snapped out the command, "Forward!" and the line began to move. As one, the handlers instructed their dogs to "Heel" and strode out briskly. Each started left foot first to act as a visual cue, and I followed suit.

On the roster of basic obedience exercises, heeling was where Faith and I were the weakest. She'd certainly been trained to walk on a leash. But the kind of movement that was desirable in the conformation ring and the kind that was considered acceptable for obedience were two entirely different things.

For one thing, Poodles don't sit down in the show ring. Not ever. Whereas other breeds might take a brief rest while they're not being judged, the elaborate hairdo that Poodles wear when they're shown requires a copious application of hair spray to keep it in place. Once the topknot and neck hair are set, the dog needs to remain standing with his head *up*, otherwise everything will be pulled apart.

Faith had never been asked to sit when we were moving before. In fact, she'd been heavily discouraged from doing so. And yet now I wanted her to sit down every time I stopped. This required an adjustment on her part that we were still in the process of making.

The second difference would be even harder for Faith to come to grips with. In the conformation ring, Poodles are supposed to show off. One of the most endearing attributes of the breed is its happy, fun-loving temperament, and Poodles are expected to display that attitude while being judged. They tend to play and cavort at the end of their leashes, hopefully displaying their correct movement, but also having a good time while doing so.

Not so in obedience. For the purposes of the heeling exercise, Faith was supposed to stick to my side like glue. She was meant to turn when I turned, to speed up and slow down when the length of my stride changed, and, in general, to make no decisions for herself. Faith was intelligent enough to understand what I wanted her to do, but at the same time, that very intelligence caused her to question the wisdom of the restrictions I'd placed upon her.

Poodle ownership is often a learning experience. For Poodle and owner, both.

I discovered, however, that Minnie had been right. After fifteen minutes of heeling, the room felt as though it had warmed up considerably. Faith was panting and I was barely managing not to do the same myself. When Steve finally called a halt to the proceedings, several of the handlers simply sat down on the mats where they'd stopped. Others crossed the room to the chairs where they'd left their things and dug out thermoses and bowls to give their dogs a drink.

Now that I knew what to expect, I thought, next week I'd come prepared.

In the meantime, Mark beckoned me over. He and Reggie were standing with Paul and Cora. The Cairn and the Corgi had both finished drinking from a stainless steel bowl Mark had brought with him. The two smaller dogs were now sacked out side by side on the floor.

"I didn't think to bring water my first time either," Mark said as Faith and I approached. He refilled the bowl and passed it over. I set it down on the mat and Faith drank gratefully while Mark performed the introductions.

"So you're a newcomer, too," Paul said. He had broad shoulders and a thatch of brown hair that fell down over his forehead. "I'm glad Kelly and I aren't the only ones. The rest of these guys have been training together for so long it's like they're a private club or something."

We both looked at Mark, who didn't bother to disagree.

"I know you didn't come through the beginner's ranks here. Did you start over at Ox Ridge?"

"No, this is the first class we've ever been to. Obviously Faith and I are still a bit over our heads. But Steve seemed to think that since she's a Poodle, we could probably manage to keep up."

"Poodles." Mark snorted derisively, but I could tell by the laughter in his eyes that he was only teasing. "Not much challenge to training one of those, is there?"

"Like Border Collies," said Paul. "Or Dobermans. Those breeds are born trained, aren't they?"

Mark retrieved the dog bowl from the mat and set it aside. "I wouldn't try telling Julie that if I were you."

"Trust me." Paul laughed. "*I* wouldn't try telling Julie anything."

"How long a break do we get?" I asked Mark. Several of the handlers had left the room. I wondered whether they'd gone outside to grab a cigarette or to exercise their dogs.

"It varies depending on Steve's mood. As you've probably seen, things are pretty free-form around here."

"It's different in the other class," said Paul. "There's much more discipline for the beginners. And, wow, nobody ever made us heel for fifteen minutes straight. That's tough on a short-legged dog."

Faith had already recovered from the exercise. She was sitting down but looking around alertly, waiting to see what came next. Paul's slightly overweight Corgi, however, had flopped over on her side and was snoring softly.

"You'll get used to the pace in no time," said Mark. "And then when you actually go to show your dog, the exercises in the ring will seem like a breeze compared with what you've been doing here. I imagine that's why Steve works us so hard."

"That's fine for most of you guys," Paul replied. "But I don't have any aspirations toward the show ring. All I want is for Cora to behave well at home and be perfectly reliable on our visits to Winston Pumpernill so that the staff keeps inviting us back."

"Is there any question that they might not?" I asked, surprised. "Julie and Stacey were telling me about your therapy dog group earlier. They made it sound as though your visits had been very well received."

"In general, they have. But there have been one or two minor . . . incidents."

"Incidents?" Mark lifted a brow. "I don't recall anything like that."

"Well, of course, you haven't been there every single time. And nothing was allowed to get totally out of hand. But as you can imagine with a place that has the kind of reputation Winston Pumpernill does, the staff is very protective of their residents. And there's one person in our group—one of the most dedicated to the visits actually—who isn't always entirely in control of her dog."

As one, we turned and looked across the room to where Kelly and Boss were standing off by themselves waiting for the session to resume. Even standing quietly, the Akita was a study in leashed power. His head swung slowly from side to side, his small eyes taking in the activity in the room. He looked like a solid hundred pounds of barely contained energy simply waiting for his chance to show what he could do.

"Once it was just that he got away from her," said Paul, "and chased a departing visitor's car down the driveway. I imagine he must have given the driver quite a fright, but of course we were outside at the time, and none of the elderly residents was around. One of the administrators saw it happen, though, and it was the lack of control that bothered her more than anything else. It seemed pretty clear that if Boss got it into his head to do something, none of us would be able to stand in his way.

"The second episode happened last month in the sunroom. Boss was standing beside a woman in a wheelchair. She always likes seeing the bigger dogs, the ones she doesn't have to lean over to pat. Minnie and Coach were there, too, and I guess the Schnauzer got a little too close for Boss's comfort. He was feeling very protective of 'his' patient and growled at Coach."

"What did the woman do?" I asked.

"She laughed it off," Paul replied. "Said she liked her dogs the same way she liked her men, with a good dose of spunk. But I'm afraid my Aunt Mary wasn't nearly as amused. She feels some responsibility, you see, since I was the one who started the program. She complained, and Steve had to step in and smooth things over. That's why Kelly and Boss have joined this class. Steve told her if she didn't continue with Boss's training, she wouldn't be allowed to go to Winston Pumpernill anymore."

"She doesn't look entirely happy about it," I said.

"She doesn't have to be happy, she merely has to comply. There's no way we can include anyone in our group who runs even the slightest risk of endangering one of the patients. Obviously we want the residents to enjoy our visits without reservation, but aside from that, just think of the potential liability."

Steve strode to the center of the room. "Back to work, everyone," he said. "Time to see how much your dogs like you. Let's work on the recall next."

We pulled ourselves back into a semblance of

organization. Over the next forty-five minutes, Steve
ran us through the rest of the basic obedience exercises that would be expected of a dog competing
for its Companion Dog degree. After the recall, we
did two long stays—one with the dogs sitting in a
long row, then another one with them lying down.
We heeled in a figure eight pattern, then practiced
the stand for examination.

Due to her experience in the conformation
ring, Faith, who was clearly behind most of the
others in the majority of the exercises, was a star at
this one. So much so that Steve pulled us out into
the middle of the mats to demonstrate how it
should be done. I knew we weren't showing the
other handlers anything they hadn't already known
and guessed that the trainer had singled us out to
boost our confidence. Even so, it was nice to know
that we could do one thing exactly right.

The class, which was scheduled to last an hour,
ran closer to two. And as I was gathering up my
things, I saw that many of the participants intended
to stay even longer. Julie and Steve were pulling
equipment out of a corner to set up broad and high
jumps on the mats. Stacey had a petite, Papillon-
size dumbbell in her hand, and Minnie had gone
to get her scent articles.

Faith had a long way to go before she'd be ready
for the exercises they were about to work on. Still,
I was willing to bet they'd be fascinating to watch.
Another night, when Sam wasn't already expecting me, I intended to stay late and see how it went.

Kelly had headed straight out the door the
minute Steve declared the end of our part of the
class. But Paul and I ended up walking out together.

"That's a really nice Poodle," he said. "Is she a show dog?"

"She was. She's retired now."

"If you have any interest . . ." He paused, then frowned. One hand reached up and brushed back the hair that had fallen into his eyes. "When we were talking about the therapy group earlier, I hope I didn't give you the wrong idea. The staff at Winston Pumpernill really enjoys our visits. And so do the participants. Lots of the older people we see . . . well, they talk about Poodles. That breed was popular for so many years, it seems like half of them owned one at some point in their lives. You probably haven't given this any thought at all, and I don't want to put you on the spot, but if you'd like to come with us, I'm sure they'd all be delighted to meet Faith."

Actually, I'd been thinking about it since Julie had first mentioned the visits earlier. They sounded like something Faith and I might enjoy.

"Sure," I said. "I'd like that."

"Great! We'll be going again this Sunday. You should join us. Unless that's not enough notice for you. . . ."

"That should be fine. Let me just check . . ." I started to say "my schedule," then quickly amended, ". . . with my husband. I'll let you know, okay?"

Paul pulled out a piece of paper and scribbled his phone number on it. "Try to make it," he said. "You won't be sorry."

4

My husband. Talking to Paul wasn't the first time I'd tripped over the phrase. Even after three weeks, I was still getting used to saying the words.

But if I had trouble announcing our new status, Sam seemed to delight in blurting it out on any and all occasions. "I'll have what my wife is having," he'd say when we ordered dinner in a restaurant. Or when the phone rang and it was for me, "Let me get my wife for you."

Somehow he'd immediately adapted to the rhythm of our new relationship, whereas I was still struggling to come to grips with the change. Now that we were married and living together, it was as though somebody had raised the stakes when I wasn't looking. I suddenly realized how badly I wanted everything to work. With one failed marriage already, I was working with a track record that wasn't stellar. For all our sakes—Davey's, Sam's, and mine—I was desperately hoping to do better this time around.

When Eve wasn't entered in a dog show, Saturdays were my morning to sleep late. I loved not having to jump right out of bed and do something useful. Somehow, though, Sam didn't seem to have gotten the memo.

"Time to get up," he said, sitting down on the edge of the bed.

The mattress dipped in his direction and I rolled with it. I groaned, then deliberately lifted the pillow and placed it over my head. Even the Poodles could read that body language. It didn't deter Sam, though.

I'd been vaguely aware of him getting up twenty minutes earlier. I'd heard the dogs scramble down the stairs to go outside. Then the soothing sound of the shower running had lulled me back to sleep.

Now Sam was back, dressed and ready to go. His hand stroked the lump I made under the covers. I lifted one edge of the pillow and eyed the clock. It wasn't even eight yet.

"Go away," I mumbled.

"I can't. We have an appointment."

"Who would be so dumb as to make an appointment at eight o'clock on a Saturday morning?"

"Nine," said Sam. "Downtown."

Notice he didn't respond to the part about being dumb.

"We're meeting Marilyn."

Marilyn was our real estate agent. The one who had yet to show us the perfect house. In her defense, we'd only been looking for two and a half weeks. But it was seven-forty-five on a Saturday morning, and I was feeling cranky and not up to defending anyone.

"I thought we were seeing her later," I said.

"She and I talked yesterday and decided we

might as well get an early start. She's giving us all day."

"Yippee," I said. My tone might have lacked conviction.

"So that's why you have to get up."

I groaned again and rolled over on my back. Sam gazed down at me, looking impossibly cheerful. If my hands hadn't been tangled in the covers, I might have been tempted to slap him. Either that, I thought, looking at the mussed blond hair still wet from the shower and the laugh lines that creased either side of his slate blue eyes, or reach for his belt buckle and pull him toward me.

Unfortunately, I didn't get the chance to do either one.

"Hey, Mom," said Davey. He walked into the bedroom, cradling a mug of steaming coffee carefully between both hands. "Sam told me to bring this up when it was ready. He said you needed it."

I pulled myself up into a sitting position. Always in a hurry, I tended to buy whatever coffee was handy in the supermarket. Now that Sam was in residence, he'd been experimenting with all sorts of new blends. The coffee smelled heavenly. As if it might even be worth getting up for.

"Thanks, Sport. I do need that."

Reaching for it, I saw that Davey had already added a dollop of milk. What a kid. The first sip tasted every bit as good as it smelled.

Faith had followed Davey up the stairs. She slipped around him and jumped up onto the bed. She circled twice, then laid down across the warm pillow I'd just vacated. It was a conspiracy, all right. Even my dog wanted me to get moving.

"All right," I grumbled. "I'm going."

Sam was smiling.

"You," I said, pointing rudely. "Cut that out."

"Yes, ma'am," he said.

Fifteen minutes later, I walked downstairs into mayhem. Actually, I'd heard the Poodles barking as soon as I turned off the water in the shower. It was amazing how much louder five canine voices sounded than two.

Even more amazing was the fact that the Poodles continued to bark as I pulled on my clothes. Downstairs, the din must have been deafening. I wondered why Sam hadn't told the dogs to be quiet. Or, failing that, why Davey hadn't done the job.

Enforcing the rules with five dogs wasn't nearly as easy as it had been with two. But they were Poodles, after all, so they understood what was expected of them, even if—in these new and unaccustomed circumstances—they might be tempted to see what they could get away with. But while the Poodles worked on perfecting their pack mentality, I was working equally hard on asserting my position as alpha bitch. The house was simply too damn small for everyone in it to have a different opinion.

Then I reached the kitchen and realized why nobody had told the dogs to shut up: nobody was there.

Nobody human, that is. The five Poodles were very much in evidence. As was the big orange cat we'd seen on Thursday evening. He was, once again, peering into the kitchen through the window above the sink. And, as I discovered when I made my way through the pack of outraged canines, opened the back door, and slipped carefully through, leaving the Poodles behind to continue voicing their annoyance at maximum decibels, this time the cat had brought a buddy with him.

A second cat—sleek, black, and medium size— was sitting calmly on the back steps cleaning one of his front paws. The fact that five dogs—each of which outweighed him by at least fifty pounds and none of whom were pleased about his existence in their lives—were mere inches away on the other side of the door didn't seem to distress him in the slightest. It certainly didn't distract him from his bathing ritual. As I watched, he took the wet paw and dragged it up over his head, smoothing back his ears.

"Shoo!" I said.

Neither cat paid a bit of attention. After a moment, the one who'd been balanced on the windowsill hopped down and landed beside my feet. Back arched high in the air, he curled his body around my ankles.

"Go home!" I said, trying to sound menacing.

The cats looked at me as though I were daft.

Maybe I was. I'd never had a cat myself, but I'd always heard they were supposed to be smart. These two didn't seem to have a clue.

A dog, even a dumb dog, could take a hint.

Maybe they were deaf, I thought.

I leaned down and cupped my hands around the body of the orange cat. He was still pressed up against my legs. Long orange hairs stuck to my jeans where he'd rubbed. His tail was curled around my calf.

The cat felt firm and plump beneath my fingers; well fed, not like a stray who'd had to fend for himself. I tried to nudge him toward the steps. He tipped his head sideways, looked up at me, yowled loudly, and resisted.

That got the black cat's attention. He stood up and sauntered over to see what was going on. Now I had two of them circling my legs in unison.

"Stop it," I said. "No!"

Was there a dog in the world who didn't know what that meant?

Inside the house, the Poodles abruptly stopped barking. They must have thought I was talking to them.

I rest my case.

I reached down and picked up the orange cat. He weighed more than he looked like he ought to, and long, silky hairs immediately floated up to tickle my nose and eyes. He didn't threaten to bite or scratch, however, so I figured I should probably be grateful.

"Come on," I said. "You're leaving. Both of you."

But when I reached down to scoop up the black cat with my other hand, he squirmed away and shot down the back steps into the cedar-fenced yard. When I went after him, I saw that the gate around the side of the house was open. It was a good thing I hadn't let the Poodles out to deal with these feline interlopers, or the entire neighborhood would have been treated to a spectacle. A not entirely unusual occurrence around here, unfortunately.

"There you are," Sam said when I reached the gate.

He and Davey were standing in front of the house next door with a woman I hadn't seen before. She was younger than me by a few years and apparently brave enough to stand outside on a brisk April morning dressed in only a negligee and peignoir. In her arms was a third cat; this one buff-colored with black points. It looked like a Siamese.

The woman's fingers, nails painted shocking pink, were stroking the cat's long body. Even from where I stood, I could hear it purring. The cat hummed like a well-tuned motor. Since she was barefoot, I could see that the woman's toenails were also tipped in pink.

Until very recently, the house next door to mine had been occupied by an elderly Italian woman. Edna had moved out just after Christmas, however, and had gone to live with her daughter in Seattle. Her house had been on the market only briefly before selling. I knew the buyers were a young couple; and I'd heard from my friend, Alice Brickman, that a moving van had come and unloaded someone's belongings that week while I was at work. Presumably, then, the woman talking to my husband in little more than her underwear was my new neighbor.

Oh joy, I thought.

The black cat shot past me and wrapped itself around the woman's bare legs. Maybe they could cuddle together for warmth.

"Wonderful," she said brightly. "I see you've met Felix. You must be Melanie. Sam was just telling me all about you. I'm Amber Fine." She untangled one hand from the Siamese's sinewy body and held it out.

My hands were, of course, similarly occupied with the orange cat. And being accustomed to big animals, the kind that stood on their own four feet next to me, I didn't have Amber's skill at tucking a wriggling cat under my arm. Instead, I bent over to put him on the ground.

Felix, unamused by the change in stature, suddenly braced both hind paws against my chest and pushed away hard. He flew out of my arms as if I'd thrown him. The cat hit the ground and landed running—right back into my yard. Long hairs, left floating in his wake, drifted up to coat my lips and eyelashes. Before I could straighten, I was already sneezing.

And by the time I caught my breath I could hear the Poodles barking again. Felix, I realized, was probably back on the windowsill.

"Oh, dear," said Amber. "You're not allergic, are you?"

"I don't think so. To tell the truth, I don't know. I've never been around cats before."

"Never?" Her green eyes widened, and I realized that although Amber hadn't bothered to dress yet, she had had time to put on makeup. More than I wear in a month, actually.

"My mother didn't like pets," I said.

"How very sad for you." Now she was pouting. The woman had an entire arsenal of charming expressions at her disposal.

"And now I have dogs."

"So I hear."

Her tone hadn't been reproving, but I bristled anyway. Anyone who lives with multiple dogs in a neighborhood setting has to be aware of the necessity of keeping them quiet. And until recently, I'd had no problems in that regard. Things had become a little more complicated with the addition of Sam's three Poodles, but we'd been working them out.

Until Felix and cohorts showed up.

"My Poodles don't usually bark this much," I said. "Your cats have been coming over and teasing them. That's what's setting them off."

"Teasing them?" She laughed. "You must be kidding."

"No, I'm not. When Felix climbs up the back of my house and the dogs see him through the window, they bark at him." I paused—mindful of the fact that we'd just met and I was going to have to live next door to this woman—then added in what I hoped was a diplomatic tone, "Which is why he's going to have to stop doing that."

Amber drew in a breath. Her chest swelled with the effort. Sam, I noted, was carefully looking elsewhere.

"But cats are natural climbers," she said. "It's what they do. It's not as if anyone can regulate their behavior."

So much for diplomacy. Maybe blunt would work better.

"Of course your cats are welcome to do whatever they want." I smiled sweetly. "As long as they're on your property."

Sam reached out, took my hand, and squeezed. Hard.

"This certainly isn't something we have to settle right this minute," he said. "Amber's barely even moved in."

Oh, I thought snidely. Maybe that was the problem. She had yet to unpack her clothes. I did not, however, remove my hand from Sam's.

"In time," he continued, "I'm sure we'll be able to get everything worked out."

"Mrs. Fine is really cool," said Davey. "She has seven cats. That's even more than we have Poodles."

"Seven cats," I repeated. The phrase seemed to stick in my throat. "How unusual." Apparently my standards for what was cool and what wasn't were different than Davey's.

"Not really," Amber replied. "Many cat lovers tend

to be collectors. I certainly never started out to have this many. But the first one needed company, which meant adding a second. The third one sort of adopted me. The fourth was a rescue who turned out to be pregnant, so you can see how things just kind of snowballed."

I could, actually. And I'd seen plenty of dog owners do the same thing, adding just one more and then one more after that, until their homes were filled to bursting. Considering that I currently had five big Poodles living in my small house, I didn't have much room to complain. And I wouldn't have if Amber Fine had looked like she had even the slightest intention of keeping her feline population out of my yard.

Then I thought back to what Davey had said. He'd called Amber "Mrs. Fine." I brightened slightly and wondered if Mr. Fine was going to be joining us in his bathrobe some time soon.

"Your husband must like cats, too," I said.

"James?"

She made it sound like a question. If she didn't know what her husband's name was, I had no idea how she expected me to. I nodded anyway, just for the heck of it, and that seemed to be enough encouragement for her.

"James travels," Amber said. "He's on the road a lot. Business."

"What kind of business is he in?" asked Sam.

Amber shrugged and looked perplexed. As if these were hard questions we were asking. "It's, like, import/export," she said. "You know, he buys stuff in one place and sells it in another."

Supply and demand. Amber made it sound like a novel concept.

"Anyway, he's almost never home," she said. "Which is why I'm so glad I have all my kitties to keep me company."

By now the Poodles had stopped barking. I wondered whether that meant the orange cat was no longer sitting in the window, or that they'd simply grown tired of watching him ignore them. I would need to let the dogs out for a run in the yard before we left to meet the real estate agent. Maybe the sight of all five big black Poodles running loose on his side of the door would be enough to make Felix realize that he ought to find another house to visit.

Sam's thoughts must have mirrored mine, because he looked down at his watch. "Mel, Davey, we'd better get going."

"Sounds good to me," I said. "Nice meeting you, Amber. Welcome to the neighborhood."

"Thank you," she cooed. "This is such a cute little street. Much better than the apartment we had before. The kitties are going to love having their freedom here."

Sam still had my hand. He used that hold to spin me around before I had a chance to reply. Next thing I knew, we were striding back toward our house.

"That went well," he said. "Don't you think?"

I muttered my answer under my breath and shut the gate behind us.

5

So we went house hunting. Again.

All right, so we really hadn't been looking for that long—less than three weeks, and mostly on the weekends. But it felt like longer. I mean, how long should it take to find the perfect home?

I know, I know. Don't answer that.

So far, we'd managed to look at nearly thirty houses. We wanted to stay in North Stamford if possible, to keep Davey in the same school district and close to his friends. Not much was available in the surrounding neighborhoods, however, and the few places we'd seen had each been unsuitable for one reason or another.

So we widened our search. Greenwich, where Aunt Peg lived and I worked, was lovely, and also incredibly expensive. Old Greenwich was a possibility, but there was hardly anything on the market. The houses we had seen in Riverside and Cos Cob didn't have enough land for the Poodles. New Canaan and Darien were nice; still, we had yet to walk into a house and know, with certainty, that that was where we wanted to live.

And so we kept looking. The end of Saturday's search found us in northern New Canaan and Wilton, where my brother, Frank, lived with his wife, Bertie, and their new baby daughter. But to get to Howard Academy from Wilton would take a good chunk of time during rush hour. Plus, Davey would have to make all new friends. Sam already owned a house in Redding that was bigger than mine. He'd been planning to put it on the market. If we were going to live in Wilton, we realized be-latedly, we might as well live in Redding. It wasn't all that much farther away.

Luckily, Marilyn was a patient woman. When we parted company at her office just before five, she promised to check the new listings every day that week and comb again through the existing offer-ings to see if there was anything we might have missed seeing. Davey, to my surprise, was jubilant in the car on the way home.

"What's up?" I said, turning around in my seat to look at him. "I thought you were looking for-ward to moving to a bigger house."

"Yeah." My son's gaze slid sideways out the win-dow. You didn't have to be a teacher to recognize that kind of evasion.

"But?" I prompted.

"But I thought we'd be moving somewhere close to home. You know, so I could stay in the same school and everything."

"That's what we're hoping," said Sam. "That's definitely our first choice. But we need more room for the dogs."

"What we need," I said, thinking out loud, "is a house like Bob's."

Bob was my ex-husband and Davey's father. After going AWOL from our lives when Davey was just an infant, he'd reappeared unexpectedly several years earlier. Though he'd been living in Texas at the time, our reunion had been such a success that Bob had ended up purchasing a house in Stamford. Now he lived in a large colonial on a couple of acres of land only a mile or two from our own.

Davey brightened. "Do you think Dad would let us move in with him?"

"Uh . . ." I sputtered. Sam made a choking noise that sounded suspiciously like laughter. "That wasn't exactly what I had in mind. More like maybe something will come up for sale in his neighborhood."

"Yeah," said Davey. "That would be cool."

Cool, I thought. If we didn't perish from overcrowding in the meantime.

When we got home, I found that Paul Lennox had left a message on the answering machine about Sunday's visit to Winston Pumpernill. I carry a cell phone, but it drives me crazy having to field calls all day long, so I never give out the number. Paul didn't seem to mind not being able to reach me directly.

"I hope you'll join us tomorrow," he said. "Everyone meets at two outside the main entrance, and we usually have a pretty good size group. The staff will be expecting us, of course, and the residents will have gathered in the sunroom. So if you're going to come, try not to be late. I know Faith would be a big hit, so I hope you'll try to make it."

I'd already checked with Sam. He and Davey didn't mind being left to their own devices on

Sunday afternoon. I suspected they were going to do something manly together, like watch a baseball game. I called Paul back and told him to expect me.

Sunday morning, I clipped Faith's face, feet, and the base of her tail and gave her a bath. Because I keep her in a sporting trim now, her hair is relatively short. Even so, because of her size and because her coat is so thick, it took me more than an hour to blow her dry. Accustomed to the multi-hour grooming marathons it took to get Eve ready to go in the show ring, however, this seemed like a breeze.

When I loaded Faith into the car and she realized we were going to embark on another activity for just the two of us, she became even more animated. Eve, who'd never been an "only dog," seemed to mind the expansion of our canine population less. But Faith, who had been Davey and my sole companion for several years, definitely had had some moments recently when she seemed to be feeling rather put upon. I was happy to have found another activity that she and I could share by ourselves.

Paul had been correct I discovered when we pulled in the driveway at Winston Pumpernill: the outing had drawn a sizable crowd. Nearly all the dogs and owners I'd met at class were there. Steve Barton was talking to Minnie and Julie while Coach and Jack sat side by side in amiable company. Mark, Stacey, and Paul formed another group with their three smaller dogs chasing around their ankles.

The only ones I didn't see were Kelly and her Akita, Boss, which, I decided, was probably just as well. Since this was our first time, Faith and I would be feeling our way and trying to figure out what to do. Both would be much easier to accomplish without having to look out for that fractious pair.

I pulled my Volvo over to the line of cars and parked. Faith knew what to expect. She waited for me to fasten the leather leash to her collar before hopping out. Immediately, Paul and Steve strode over to greet us.

"Welcome," said Paul. "I told Steve you'd be coming. We're really glad you decided to join us."

"Wow." Steve gazed at Faith admiringly. "Did you give her a bath? She looks great."

Faith, who always knows praise when she hears it, gave him a doggy smile and preened from side to side so he could enjoy the full effect of her beauty.

"Just this morning. I figured she might as well dress up a bit for our visit."

"The residents will appreciate it. Many of them enjoy calling the dogs, even the bigger ones, up into their laps. They love to bury their faces in the dogs' fur. Trust me, you and Faith are going to be very popular."

Steve glanced at his watch, then turned back to look at the others. "It's just about time. Let's head inside, people. Is everyone ready?"

Paul fell into step beside me. Cora and Faith touched noses in greeting, then trotted along with us. "In the beginning, just stay with the group and do what everyone else does. There's no trick to it, really. Have you ever visited an assisted care facility before?"

I shook my head.

"This place isn't at all what you'd think of when you think of a typical nursing home. For one thing, we're in Greenwich, so the people who reside here are, for the most part, accustomed to living very well. You'll find there's sort of a country club atmosphere. And the monthly schedule sounds like something from a cruise ship. There are classes in art and yoga and poetry, not to mention bridge sessions, bingo games, and bowling.

"The residents are elderly, but most are still in pretty good shape. They had full and rewarding lives before, and they don't have any intention of changing that now. They get up and dress each morning as if they really had somewhere to go. It's not unusual to see the women in pearls and the men wearing sports coats. Sometimes I think half of them are really here for the social life." Paul stopped and smiled sheepishly. "Well, not really, but you know what I mean."

I did. "You have an aunt who lives here, right?"

"Great-aunt, actually. Mary Livingston. She's a hoot and a half. You'll love her when you meet her. Everyone does. Eighty-three years old and doesn't look a day over seventy-five. She's the one who got me and Cora started on visiting. She'd had dogs her whole life and missed their companionship terribly when she moved in. 'There's something therapeutic about petting a dog,' she told me. And you know what? She was right. Whatever happens when we visit here . . . it's hard to explain, but somehow it just feels like magic."

We'd reached the wide stone steps that led up to the front door, which was already being opened by a smiling woman in a blue shirtwaist dress and low-heeled pumps. As the dogs and handlers in the front of the group began to file inside, a horn tooted urgently behind us.

We all turned to look. A black Lexus sedan was speeding down the driveway. When it came closer,

I recognized Kelly Marx behind the wheel. Boss, the Akita, was sitting on the front seat beside her.

"Late, as usual," Minnie muttered. "Like she thinks the whole world ought to wait for her."

Beside me, Paul sighed under his breath. Julie looked annoyed. Mark was shaking his head.

"It's wrong of me, I know," said Stacey. "But every week I hope she'll find something better to do on a Sunday afternoon. Someday that woman and her dog are going to cause some real trouble."

We stopped to wait for her. I watched Kelly loop a leather choke collar securely around Boss's thick neck and head our way. "Surely Steve would make sure not to let that happen, wouldn't he?"

"Steve can't control everything," said Minnie. I noted that she and the rest of the handlers shortened their leashes and pulled their dogs closer to their sides as Boss and Kelly approached. "Even though he's anal enough to think that he can."

"Besides," Stacey added in an undertone, "it's Kelly."

The others nodded in agreement. I read between the lines and wondered if I was coming up with the right conclusion. Later, I should probably check on that.

"Sorry I'm late," Kelly chirped. "Traffic was beastly."

"On Sunday? In backcountry Greenwich?" said Julie. "How unusual."

Steve shot her a quelling stare. Julie ignored him, but the hackles on her Doberman's neck rose. Faith prudently retreated a step. I thought about following, but the group was already moving forward again. Dogs and handlers pushed through the open double doors and into a vast reception

area with gleaming hardwood floors and real art-
work on the walls.

Paul pulled me aside as I entered. He was standing with two women, one of them the blonde who
had opened the door. She was in her forties, tall
and spare, and far more stylish than I could ever
hope to be. "Melanie, I'd like to introduce you to
Catherine Stone. She's the Director of Therapeutic
Recreation. It's her office that oversees our visits
here."

Catherine shook my hand and introduced me
to her assistant, Lynn Stephanopolus, the Director
of Volunteers. Standing beside her boss, Lynn had
a tendency to fade into the background. Her skin
was surprisingly pale against very dark hair, and
her eyes appeared small behind thick glasses with
black frames. Faith was polite to Catherine, but
she warmed to Lynn immediately.

"I'm pleased to meet you," she said. "And Poodles
are always welcome here. She's a big one, isn't she?"

"Faith is a Standard Poodle. That's the largest of
the three varieties." It always amazed me how many
people seemed to expect all Poodles to be small
dogs.

"My family had a Poodle when I was little," said
Lynn. "A silver named Smoky." She held out her
hand about knee high. "He was only this big, but
he lived to be sixteen. What a great dog he was."

"They're all pretty great," I agreed.

"Let's head back to the sunroom," said Lynn,
stepping to the head of the hallway. "Everyone's already gathered there, and we have a good-sized
group today. I know they're anxiously awaiting
your arrival."

I joined the rear of the procession and looked
around curiously as one wide hallway joined into

the next and we made our way to the back of the building. Doors opened into rooms on either side. The first several were administrative offices. After that came a couple of common rooms. Then we were escorted down a series of residential hallways.

I'd expected the facility to look and feel like a small hospital, but I was quickly disabused of that notion. Instead, Winston Pumpernill resembled an upscale hotel. Apart from the fact that the floors were uncarpeted, the decor was reminiscent of those gracious old resorts that had once flourished on Cape Cod and in the Poconos. Nurses, identifiable by their name tags, wore soft-soled shoes and tracksuits in vibrant colors. The occasional residents we passed were dressed as though they might have been on their way to afternoon tea.

The sunroom was a large, open space in the rear of the building. Floor-to-ceiling windows looked out over manicured lawns and the woods beyond. Skylights added to the bright and cheery atmosphere.

It was a good thing Faith and I were at the back of the pack, because when we reached the doorway, I stopped dead. I'd been expecting a group of maybe a dozen seniors. Instead, the gathering looked more like forty or fifty. Most were already seated, some in wheelchairs, many in the armchairs and sofas that were scattered around the room. All gazed expectantly in our direction.

"Oh, my," I said softly.

Julie glanced back at me. "I know. It's a little daunting, isn't it?"

"I'll say. I had no idea . . . ."

"None of us did our first times here. But then you begin to think about what your life would be like if you had to live without dogs, and it makes perfect sense. Come on, don't hang back. The best part about this is that there's no way to do it wrong, because every single person here is absolutely thrilled to see us."

"Or our dogs, at any rate," Mark said with a laugh. He'd been listening in.

"What do I do first?" I asked. Minnie and Stacey, who'd been at the front of the group, were already approaching the closest of the seniors.

"Just walk in and say hello to somebody. Introduce yourself and your dog. After that, see what happens naturally and just go with it."

Julie and Mark headed off in opposite directions. I hesitated for a moment, observing the interactions between the nursing home inmates and the dogs. Everyone looked happy and comfortable, as if this were something they'd done a number of times before. Which, of course, it was.

My gaze was drawn to an elderly woman, who was sitting by herself on the fringe of the activity. While everyone else was looking at the dogs, she alone was staring out the window. Her gnarled fingers clasped and unclasped a lap robe that had been placed over her knees as she gazed off into the distance. I wondered why she was there with the others if she hadn't wanted to take part in the program.

As always, Faith picked up on what I was feeling. Striding out confidently, she headed in the woman's direction. Automatically, I followed along behind.

We'd almost reached her before the woman even turned around. When she did, she didn't look happy to see us. She arched one penciled eyebrow imperiously upward and demanded, "Well?"

The gesture and her tone reminded me so much of Aunt Peg that I couldn't help but smile.

The woman stared at me coolly.

"I just came over to say hello," I said.

"Hello." She nodded curtly. "Is that it?"

"I'm Melanie. And this is Faith."

"Now I suppose you want me to tell you my name."

Nearby, a card table surrounded by four straight-backed chairs sat empty. I pulled one of the chairs over and sat down. "If you like."

"What I don't much like," she said, "is dogs."

I glanced at the Poodle, who was standing between us. Catching Faith's eye, I patted the side of my thigh and said, "Sit." Faith circled away from the woman, nudged herself up against me, and sat.

"Even obedient ones," she said, though her voice seemed to have lost some of its starch.

"You're in the wrong place, then. At least for the next hour or so. Would you like me to find a nurse who can take you somewhere else?"

"No, I don't want to go someplace else!"

Oops. The imperious tone was back.

"I like it here, in the sun. I just have no desire to be bothered by a pack of dirty, slobbering canines."

"Okay," I said, pushing back my chair. That certainly made things clear enough. "I'm sorry Faith and I have bothered you."

"Cats," the woman said as I stood up to go.

"Pardon me?"

"I like cats. Always have. Nice, tidy creatures. Good hunters. Independent. Not always throwing themselves at a person begging for attention."

"I'm sorry," I said helplessly. This wasn't at all the way I'd expected things to go.

"What's that?"

"I said I'm sorry."

"About what?"

"I guess," I said, "I'm sorry I didn't bring a cat."

"Do you have a cat?"

"Actually . . . no."

"Well, then you would have had a hard time bringing one, wouldn't you?"

Good point.

"Nobody ever brings cats," the woman said. "Why is that?"

As if I looked like the kind of person who would have that answer.

"Maybe because they're afraid they'll scratch?" I ventured.

She sucked in an annoyed breath. "You really don't know much, do you?"

"Apparently not," I agreed. It seemed like the wisest course of action under the circumstances.

"Go." Her hand lifted from the lap robe and made a shooing gesture in my direction. I couldn't comply fast enough.

Then, unexpectedly, as Faith and I started to walk away, her voice stopped me. "Mrs. Ellis," she said.

I paused and looked back at her.

"Caroline Baxter Ellis," she said. "And you're Melanie. And that . . ." She lifted her hand, and her finger was shaking ever so slightly as it pointed at my Poodle, ". . . is Faith."

"Yes."

"Silly name for a dog," she sniffed.

6

We'd been dismissed again.

This time Faith and I made good our escape. In fact, we were walking so fast that it crossed my mind to head straight for the door and just keep going. I could find my way back to the car, and Faith and I would be on our way before anyone even had a chance to miss us.

Before I could put that plan into action, however, we were waylaid by Paul. He fell into step beside me, dropped a comforting arm around my shoulder, and steered me back toward the center of the crowded room.

"I see you met Mrs. Ellis," he said sympathetically.

I nodded.

"Sorry about that. I probably should have warned you. She doesn't like dogs."

Was it just me, or was it a little late to be telling me that *now?*

"I want to introduce you to my aunt," said Paul. "She's going to love you."

That would be a pleasant change, I thought.

"She loves everybody," he added brightly.

"Including dogs?"

"She adores dogs."

Paul's aunt sounded like an easy touch. Just what Faith and I needed.

In contrast to Mrs. Ellis, Mary Livingston was seated in the center of a long couch, right in the middle of all the activity. Friends sat on plump cushions on either side of her. I'd wondered where Paul had left Cora when he came to get me. Now I saw that the chubby Corgi was nestled happily in his great-aunt's lap. Cora was lolling on her back, tongue hanging out of the side of her mouth, stubby legs paddling in the air in time with the hand that was rubbing her stomach.

Mary Livingston used that hand to shake mine when we were introduced. "I hope you'll call me Aunt Mary. Everybody does. And pardon me if I don't get up. This little dog weighs an inordinate amount for her size." She gazed over at her nephew. "When it comes to keeping Cora in shape, I'm afraid Paul is entirely too soft a touch."

He looked amused. "Or maybe that has something to do with the liver treats that every dog here knows you keep in your pockets."

"Guilty as charged, I'm afraid."

Mary turned to her friends and made the introductions. On her left was Madeline Reeves, a kindly looking woman with smartly styled gray hair and a ready smile. She wore a silk dress and an elegant gold watch with a diamond-encrusted bezel. A pink cashmere cardigan was tossed jauntily over her shoulders for warmth.

Borden Grey sat on the other side. He rose when we were introduced and treated Faith and me to a courtly half bow. "It's about damn time somebody brought a Poodle to see us," he announced. As he sank back into his seat, he held out a weathered hand for Faith to sniff.

"Now, Borden, watch your language," Mary chided gently. "There are youngsters present."

Youngsters? Paul and I exchanged a glance. I supposed that meant us.

"You're a pretty thing, aren't you, girl?" Borden patted the cushion beside him. "Why don't you come on up here and sit down next to an old man?"

Faith looked at me, checking to see if she had permission. I looked at Paul, who shrugged.

"My dog's already on the furniture," he said. "I can hardly tell you not to let yours do the same."

"It's okay," I said to Faith. "Go ahead."

The black Poodle placed one front paw delicately in the space Borden had moved over to provide and leaped up gracefully beside him. She turned a half circle on the cushion, then sat down facing forward, just like her human companions on the couch.

Borden slapped his knee and laughed out loud. "Now that's a Poodle for you. They think they're just like other people. And who knows? Maybe they are." He looked up at me and winked.

"Well, I don't know why I'm sitting here getting short shrift," said Madeline. "Everybody has a dog but me."

"Maddy, dear, we wouldn't want you to feel left out. Let me lend you Cora for a while." Mary encouraged the Corgi to get up and shift from one lap to the next. The little dog walked two steps and plopped down again, ending up on the cushion between the two women.

"Now, Melanie," Mary invited, "why don't you

tell us a little bit about yourself? Aside from the fact that you own a big, beautiful Poodle."

A Poodle who was, as we spoke, leaning into Borden's side, resting her head on his shoulder, and staring adoringly into his eyes. What a ham.

"Paul is such a dear to bring all these dogs to come and visit us. And, of course, we love seeing them. But it's nice to meet new people, too. After you've been living here a while, you begin to feel like you know everything there is to know about everybody."

"How long have you been here?" I asked.

"Almost two years now. But don't you try to turn things around, young lady. I want to hear about you."

"There isn't that much to tell. I'm a special education teacher. I have an eight-year-old son." I paused, then added, "And I just recently got married."

"Oooh," Madeline said excitedly. "Now that's something." She held out her hand, fingers beckoning. "Let's see the rings."

They were beautiful, if I did say so myself. Sam had purchased the engagement ring a year earlier after unexpectedly inheriting some money. The center stone was a two-carat, emerald-cut diamond. Three weeks earlier, he'd added a platinum eternity band to it.

I took my left hand out of my pocket and held it forward. Madeline and Mary both had a look. Even Borden leaned over so he could see better.

"Well done," said Mary. "You must have found yourself a man with good taste."

"And a fat wallet," said Borden.

"Now, Borden, you just quit it." Madeline rolled her eyes for my benefit. "Don't you pay any attention to what that man says. We have to watch him every minute."

"You're a fine one to talk, Maddy. It's not as if one or two of your husbands weren't pretty plump in the pocketbook."

My gaze went to the gold watch on the older woman's slender arm. And although Madeline wasn't wearing any rings, there was a sapphire brooch on her left shoulder. Diamond studs the size of blueberries adorned her earlobes.

"I never said I didn't make out okay in the romance department. Best of all, I loved my husbands, each and every one of them. Would have helped if one or two had had stronger hearts, mind you."

Mary smiled gently. "Maybe not Milton, though."

"No, not Milton," Madeline agreed. "God rest his soul. I wasn't terribly sorry to see him go. Him and his wild ideas about everything. What kind of seventy-two-year-old man thinks he ought to go parasailing in Mexico? That's what I'd like to know."

"I'm sure I have no idea," I said. What had ever made me imagine that we would spend the visit talking about dogs?

"Nobody does." Borden shook his head. "That Milton, he was a highflier. Sorry, Maddy, no pun intended."

Madeline sighed. "No offense taken, Borden."

"This is my first visit," I said into the silence that followed. "So I'm not really sure how things are supposed to work. Maybe Faith and I should be mingling?"

"Did you hear that?" Mary laughed. "Here we are yammering on about people Melanie's never met and things that happened a long time ago and we've bored her senseless already. She wants to take her Poodle and go sit with someone else."

"No," I said quickly. "It isn't that—"

"Don't you worry a thing about it," Madeline said, waving a hand. "We're happy to have had you here for the time we did. Now you go see someone else. I think that nice lady with the Papillon might be headed our way. We always like to talk to her."

"Just so long as it isn't the other one," Borden muttered in an undertone.

I'd leaned over to motion Faith down off the couch. If I hadn't been so close, I wouldn't have heard him. Clearly, I wasn't meant to.

"The other one?" I asked.

The three elderly people looked guilty. I glanced around at Paul. He shrugged slightly. "Kelly," he said after a pause. "You know . . . and Boss."

That pair was at the other end of the room now, over by the windows. Kelly was talking with animation to an older man sitting in a wheelchair. The Akita was standing next to the chair, his massive head resting on the man's knees.

Steve, I saw, was standing close by, near enough to intervene quickly should the need arise. In fact, the entire time we'd been in the sunroom, Steve had been shadowing Kelly and Boss. I wondered if that was the way he normally conducted himself, and whether Kelly noticed how much extra attention she and the Akita received. She was young and very attractive, maybe she simply accepted it as her due.

"You go ahead and forget you heard me say that," Borden instructed. "We're just happy to have people come and visit us. None of us has any right to complain."

"Even if that dog does look like he wouldn't

mind munching on a person's arm for lunch and spitting out the bones," said Madeline.

The description wasn't far off. As always, there was an air of watchful tension about Boss. I loved dogs, and I'd never, for a minute, been afraid of one. But even to me the Akita didn't look like the kind of animal that I would want to cross—or meet up with in a dark alley.

"You go on now," Mary said, as Borden gave Faith a pat good-bye. "We'll see you again later."

Faith and I did as we'd been told. I'd expected the population in the sunroom to remain relatively constant during our visit; instead, people were coming and going all the time. Despite what Mrs. Ellis had said about wanting to sit by the windows, she disappeared shortly after I spoke with her. Her place was taken by a fragile-looking woman who leaned heavily upon a cane and was escorted to a seat in the sun by her visiting daughter. Both were no strangers to Poodles, and they enjoyed the opportunity to meet Faith and visit for a while.

After I was finished there, I joined up with Julie and Jack. A group of residents, clustered around the Doberman, had asked whether he knew any tricks. Julie had cleared a small area and was demonstrating how well her dog responded to the commands to heel, stay, and come.

Minnie brought her Standard Schnauzer, Coach, over to observe. "They asked for tricks," she said when Julie and Jack were finished. "Not an obedience demonstration."

Julie turned and glared. An older man who'd been watching the performance leaped to her defense. "She did just fine," he said. "That stuff looked pretty tricky to me."

Minnie looked at him and smiled. "Julie believes in classic obedience training. She likes to teach routines and patterns and specific exercises, the types of things that get rewarded in the show ring. Some of us like to have a little more fun with our dogs."

She led Coach out into the cleared area where Julie and Jack were standing. Minnie didn't actually elbow Julie aside, but she might as well have. It was clear she intended to steal the other woman's thunder, as well as her audience.

As Julie and Jack stepped back, Minnie raised her hand, giving Coach a silent signal to sit. The Schnauzer's hindquarter sank promptly to the floor. His dark eyes were riveted on his owner's; his stubby tail wagged back and forth. Clearly, this was a game he enjoyed playing.

Minnie lifted her hand again. Palm up, she wiggled her fingers. Coach lifted first one front paw, then the other. The third time he pushed off and raised himself up into a begging position. Balanced successfully on his hindquarter, he looked very pleased with himself. Several of the elderly residents clapped at the accomplishment.

"Not yet," Minnie said with a smile. "Wait."

She reached in her pocket and pulled out a biscuit. Taking two steps forward, she leaned down and placed the treat on the top of Coach's nose. The Schnauzer trembled with anticipation but waited for Minnie's signal.

She didn't make him wait long. "Okay Coach," she cried. "Get it, boy!"

The dog tossed his head, flipping the biscuit up into the air. Eyes never leaving the spinning treat, he jumped up after it and caught it on the fly. His strong jaw ground down on the biscuit, and he swallowed before he'd even landed. Coach hit the ground and spun around, tail wagging, face grinning, asking to do it again.

As the group of residents laughed and applauded, Minnie clasped her fingers together and held out her arms, fashioning them in the shape of a circle. Coach saw the hoop and dove for it. Minnie leaned down, and the Schnauzer leaped up. He sailed through her arms and landed on the other side. Skidding on the floor, he caught himself quickly, whipped around, and jumped back through.

By then, nearly everyone in the room had gathered around to enjoy the show. I saw Madeline and Borden, though Paul and Mary were no longer with them. Even some of the nurses who'd been passing by in the hall were clustered in the doorway.

"What a show-off," Julie said. She'd faded back out of the circle and brought Jack over to stand beside me and Mark. Now Minnie had Coach dancing on his hind legs.

"You're just jealous," Mark was grinning when he said it, but the words still had bite.

"Of *that?*" Julie tossed her head disdainfully. "I don't think so. Jack has entirely too much dignity to put on such a display. Minnie's got that dog prancing around out there like she thinks he's some sort of froufrou Poodle circus act."

It took her a moment to realize what she'd said, and in front of whom she'd said it. Then she swallowed abruptly and glanced at me out of the corner of her eye.

"Sorry. You know I didn't mean Faith. I was talking about those little Poodles that you see. You know, Toys and Minis that are dyed all sorts of pastel colors. The ones that run around with clowns and ride bicycles or play the piano."

"No problem," I said.

Over the years, Faith and I have heard pretty much the entire gamut of Poodle insults. Mostly, I realized, they came from people who weren't familiar with the breed. Because I'd never met someone who'd lived with a Poodle, had enjoyed the breed's lively and intelligent temperament, and hadn't wanted another one.

In the beginning, I used to leap to the breed's defense, but I rarely bother anymore. Faith's dignity and demeanor speak for themselves. And if she was big enough to ignore the occasional insult that came her way, I figured I might as well follow her sterling example.

Besides, I had yet to see a Poodle play the piano. If I did, I'd probably find it to be a pretty impressive accomplishment.

Movement over by the doorway caught my eye. Kelly had just entered the room. I glanced at her, then quickly looked again. Boss wasn't with her.

Then the Akita began to bark—a big, booming bass of a sound—and I realized that Steve was holding him off to one side. The excitement caused by Coach's performance, coupled with Kelly leaving him, had caused the big dog to become thoroughly agitated.

For the moment, Steve had control of the Akita, but he was struggling. The leather collar didn't offer the trainer nearly as much control as a choke chain would have. If the powerful dog decided to bound into the crowd, there wouldn't be much Steve could do to restrain him.

Kelly went straight to the pair. She put a hand on the Akita's muzzle—something I certainly wouldn't have wanted to do—and the dog immediately quieted. Steve leaned forward and whispered something in Kelly's ear. He looked tense and angry. She shook her head and snatched Boss's leash out of his hands.

Steve stared at her briefly. I wondered if he was assessing her control of the dog. Then, abruptly, he turned away and strode to the middle of the floor where Minnie and Coach had just ended their performance.

"Once again," he said, looking around at the assemblage of patients and nurses, "I want to thank the staff and the residents of Winston Pumpernill for allowing us to share their Sunday afternoons. We always enjoy our visits here, and today has been no exception. I hope you all have a wonderful week."

Before Steve had even finished speaking, Julie was already heading for the door. Mark and Stacey fell in behind her. Minnie was still busy talking to someone about Coach's tricks. I didn't see Paul; I assumed he'd gone to say good-bye to his great-aunt. When Kelly and Boss also started to leave, I decided to hang back a bit and give the pair a wide berth.

Steve went to get Minnie and hustle her along. She made a face at him, then hurried to catch up. She and I walked down the long hall together.

"So," she said, "wasn't that great? Did you have a good time? Are you coming back next week?"

"For Pete's sake, Minerva," said Steve. "Let Melanie catch her breath. We haven't even left the building yet. She may want to take a little time to digest the experience. Not only that, but she might have had more fun today if you hadn't decided to be such a show-off—"

Minnie's expression darkened. She turned back to frame a retort.

Then I heard the footsteps behind us and realized why Steve had stopped speaking. Paul was running after us down the corridor. Cora was at his side, her short legs pumping to keep up.

Paul's face was white; his features were drawn. He stopped beside us and thrust the Corgi's leash into the trainer's hands. "Take her, will you please? Something's happened. I can't leave right now."

"Of course," said Steve. "What's the matter? Is there anything we can do?"

"It's Aunt Mary." Paul choked on a sob. "I went to tell her I was leaving and I found her in her room. It just doesn't seem possible, but Aunt Mary is dead."

7

"Trouble just seems to follow you around, doesn't it?" Aunt Peg said.

A sad fact, and undeniably true. I wished, however, that my aunt didn't feel compelled to keep pointing it out.

We were sitting in her living room in Greenwich surrounded by a bevy of black Standard Poodles. After Paul's surprising announcement, I'd left Winston Pumpernill intending to drive home. Instead, with Aunt Peg's house only a short distance away, I'd found myself going there.

Talking to Aunt Peg is often helpful when I need to make sense of difficult situations. She's a good sounding board; plus, having lived a very full life, she's pretty much seen it all. Very few things shock Aunt Peg, and Mary Livingston's death was apparently no exception.

"We're talking about a woman who was how old?" she asked.

"In her early eighties, but she looked great. I was just talking to her half an hour earlier. There wasn't the slightest indication then that anything was wrong."

"In the sunroom," Aunt Peg said with a nod. I'd already described much of my visit to the nursing facility. "And yet shortly thereafter, she must have gone back to her room for some reason, even though the visit from your obedience club was still in progress. Was that normal for her—to leave in the middle like that?"

"I have no idea. This was the first time I'd ever been. People did seem to be coming and going all the time, however. Some stayed in the room for the entire visit and others didn't."

"But Mary Livingston had a family member present. A young man who was apparently responsible for the very fact that you were there. It seems unlikely she would have left unless she had a good reason. Perhaps she felt unwell and went back to her room to lie down."

That sounded like as good an explanation as any, especially in light of what had followed.

"Paul didn't say how his aunt died, although it was obviously sudden and unexpected. If he hadn't gone looking for her before we left, we would never even have known."

Aunt Peg pondered that. As always, there was a Poodle within easy reach. Her retired stud dog, Beau, was lying on the floor next to her chair. Peg rubbed her foot back and forth across the big dog's shoulders absently.

"You never really knew your grandparents, did you?" she said after a minute.

"No, they died when I was very young."

"You've probably never seen anyone you were close to grow old and have to deal with deteriorating health and the infirmities of advancing age. I know what happened today came as a shock to you, but to me it sounds almost like a blessing. To live to a fine old age and be in good health right up until the moment of one's death? I'd certainly rather go that way than in any number of other scenarios I can come up with."

"I know," I said with a sigh. "And it's selfish of me to think only of my own reaction. But I can't help it. I'd just met Mary and her friends. And I'd liked all of them. To have the visit end that way was unimaginable."

Aunt Peg settled back in her chair. Zeke, Eve's littermate, whom she had handled to his championship the previous year, got up and padded over. Faith was lying beside me on the couch, her neck and head snuggled along the length of my thigh. Zeke touched noses briefly with his dam, then stepped over Beau and laid his muzzle in Aunt Peg's lap.

Now she had two Poodles vying for her attention. Aunt Peg gave equal due to both and didn't miss a beat. She also had a question for me.

"From what I've heard so far, your group sounds a little different than the therapy dog programs I've heard about. Are they affiliated with any of the official associations?"

Aunt Peg is a wellspring of knowledge when it comes to anything having to do with dogs. Breeding and exhibiting in conformation are her first loves, but she also judges and does agility, not to mention serving on the boards of her local Poodle and all-breed clubs. With her vast array of experience in the dog world, I wasn't surprised that she knew all about therapy dogs. Not only that, but in anticipation of my visit to Winston Pumpernill, I'd been doing some reading up on the subject myself.

"For starters," I said, "we're not, at least in any way that I can see, a traditional therapy dog group. We're an obedience club that, at the suggestion of one of our members, happens to visit a nursing home on the side. I've been told this is an informal arrangement; one that Winston Pumpernill, luckily enough, is happy to accommodate.

"All the dogs have basic obedience training. They're all outgoing and well behaved." I paused, then amended that. "Well, all but one are, anyway. But as far as I know, none are certified as therapy dogs. We're really just a bunch of volunteers."

"I believe the same could be said of most people who work with therapy dogs," Aunt Peg said. "And I think it's admirable that your group has undertaken such a worthwhile endeavor. I'd imagine some of the dogs in your class have passed the C.G.C. test?"

C.G.C. stood for Canine Good Citizen. Dogs that wanted to earn the degree needed to be sociable, well socialized, and have some obedience training. Ten different exercises, mimicking those they might encounter in everyday life, were performed, and the dogs had to remain calm and friendly throughout. It wasn't unusual for dog shows to offer C.G.C. certification. Faith had passed when she was younger, and so had Eve.

"I haven't talked to any of the other handlers about it," I said. "But I wouldn't be at all surprised. There's only one dog in the group that looks as though it would have a problem. Or maybe he just looks as though he could *be* a problem. He's an Akita named Boss."

Aunt Peg lifted a brow. The gesture spoke volumes.

"I know," I admitted. "Bad sign."

"Indeed. Akitas are strong dogs. And they're strong willed. They need a determined owner who knows what he or she is doing."

"From what I've seen, I wouldn't exactly call Kelly Marx determined. And she does seem to have some difficulty controlling the dog. But at least she had the good sense to sign up for an obedience class so she could get some help."

"I presume your instructor stays on top of things?"

I nodded. "Steve Barton. I've only seen him in action twice so far, but he's very good with the dogs. He's also good at handling the owners. Except perhaps for Minnie Lloyd.

"Standard Schnauzer," I added automatically, before Aunt Peg could ask. Minnie's age, height, or the color of her hair would be immaterial to Peg. But the woman's preference in dogs would interest her enormously.

"Why do you suppose she would take a class from someone she didn't like?" she mused aloud. "There are obedience clubs all over Fairfield County. It shouldn't be that hard to find another one."

"I don't know. But I'm betting there's some history there. Most of the people who are in the advanced class have been training with Steve for a while. Aside from me, the only newcomers to the session are Kelly, with Boss, and Paul.

"It's really too bad you never got a chance to meet his Aunt Mary. She was a real dog lover. It was because of her that the visits came about in the first place. From what I was able to tell, the two of you would have gotten along famously."

"She does sound like someone whose company I would have enjoyed. Why don't you follow up with Paul, and I'll do some asking around of my own. Perhaps one of the local dog clubs would like to make a contribution in his aunt's name to her favorite charity."

"I'll do that."

I was just standing up to leave when the doorbell rang. Immediately, all seven Poodles that had been scattered on the floor around us leaped to their feet and ran from the room barking. They think of themselves as Aunt Peg's guardians, and they take their job seriously. They hate it when someone manages to get all the way up the driveway without being announced.

"Are you expecting someone?" I asked.

"Of course," Aunt Peg replied. The Poodles abruptly quieted, and we heard the sound of the front door closing. "Not everyone simply drops by whenever the mood strikes them. Most people call ahead and give me some warning of their intentions."

"At least I don't take the liberty of letting myself in," I said. I heard a low voice crooning in the hallway and greeting each of the Poodles by name.

"You would if you had this much junk to carry around," said my sister-in-law, Bertie. She appeared in the arched doorway, surrounded by the fawning pack of Poodles. Both her hands were full and a big bag was slung over her shoulder. I wondered how she'd managed to get through the door in the first place.

"Part of what you're so rudely referring to as junk is my new niece," I said with a grin. "Hand her over."

"With pleasure." Bertie crossed the room and plunked the sleeping baby into my arms. "In fact, if you'd like to hold her for the next three or four hours, I wouldn't mind having a nap."

"Fine by me." Since it didn't look as though I'd be leaving anytime soon, I sank back down on the couch.

Frank and Bertie's baby daughter had been christened Emma Margaret and had spent the first week of her life being called Emma. The name hadn't stuck, however. Frank kept tripping over it, and Bertie insisted that her daughter didn't have near the amount of dignity that a name like Emma required. They'd tried calling her Margaret, which had been quickly shortened to Maggie. Mostly, Bertie seemed to call the baby pretty much anything that popped into her head.

"Mags fell asleep in the car," she said. "Don't you just love it? The one time that I can't nap with her, she finally decides to take a snooze."

At four months of age, Maggie had yet to sleep through the night. Both Bertie and my brother were beginning to look a little worn around the edges. For my sister-in-law, that meant being downgraded from absolutely stunning to merely beautiful. Despite her complaining, however, Bertie glowed with a newfound happiness that was undimmed by her lack of sleep.

"Look at all this stuff." She shrugged out of her jacket and dumped the supplies she'd been carrying onto a chair. "Diaper bag, baby seat, change of clothing. I can barely leave the house without loading myself down like a pack mule. How come nobody warns you ahead of time that having a baby changes your whole life?"

"We did," I said.

"Well then," Bertie grumbled, "how come you didn't make me listen?"

"Because in some ways you're just like Melanie," Aunt Peg said briskly. "You take other people's opinions under advisement, but in the end you do exactly what you meant to do all along."

"Gee," I said, looking at Peg. "I guess some traits run in the family."

As one, the three of us gazed at baby Maggie, who was sleeping blissfully in my arms. Right at that moment, she scarcely looked capable of causing any trouble at all.

"Oh, yeah," Bertie muttered. "Like she's going to be easy."

"No possibility there." I unwound the warm outer blanket Maggie had been wrapped in and set it aside. "But think of all the fun you're going to have."

"Don't listen to a single rotten word I say. I'm having a blast already." Bertie sat down next to me on the couch and held out her arms.

"No way." I angled Maggie away. "I just got her. Wait your turn."

"While you two fight over the baby," said Peg, "I'm going to go see if there's any cake left in the kitchen."

"You can feel free to supersize my piece," Bertie said. Post-baby, she'd returned to her normally svelte figure in no time at all. "One of the best perks of motherhood is this breast-feeding thing. I may not be sleeping, but I can eat like a horse and not gain an ounce."

"Plus you get boobs," I pointed out.

"I always *had* boobs. You're the one who's a little sparse in that department."

"Maybe I *should* give you your child back. Separation anxiety is making you mean."

"Ha!" Bertie retorted. "I've always been mean. It just took you a while to notice."

"That's because we were so relieved to find

someone who would even think of taking Frank off our hands, we didn't dare say much for fear you might change your mind."

"Too late for that now." Bertie settled back. "I guess I'm in it for the long haul. You look pretty good holding that baby."

"Hard not to," I said, dipping my head down to kiss Maggie's tiny pink nose. "I can't believe she got your red hair."

"Frank loves it." Bertie sighed happily. "Shows what he knows. But since we're on the subject of babies . . ."

I lifted my eyes. What else could we be talking about with Maggie in the room? Well, dogs, I supposed. With Bertie being a professional handler, that subject usually got a lot of play, too. But Bertie looked so serious all of a sudden that I decided to place the sleeping infant back in her arms and see what was on her mind.

"You know I have to ask," she said.

"What?"

"Everyone wants to know."

"Me, too," Peg called from the kitchen. She has ears like a bat. "So wait until I get back."

"Know what?"

Bertie stared at me as though I were being inordinately slow. "When you and Sam are going to start trying to have a baby?"

"Oh, that."

"Yes, that!"

"We're newlyweds, Bertie. We try all the time."

"Of course you do. But is it *working*?"

I laughed out loud. "What kind of question is that?"

"The kind we all want to know the answer to," said Aunt Peg. She reappeared with a tray holding three pieces of cake, two glasses of milk, and a cup of tea.

"Milk?" I stared at the tray in horror. "You're already giving me *milk*?" The tea, I knew, had to be for Aunt Peg. And she'd been forcing milk on Bertie for months now. This was the first time, however, that she'd served it to me. "Don't you think that's a little premature?"

"I don't know," Peg said blithely as she handed the plates around. "Is it? And by the way, I hope you're taking folic acid, too."

I looked at my plate. Predictably, the piece of cake Aunt Peg had served me was big enough for two people.

"Has it occurred to you," I asked, "that maybe you should mind your own business?"

"Oh, pish," Peg replied. "If this isn't our business, whose is it? It took us three years just to get the two of you married off. Now we're ready for the next step. Some of us aren't getting any younger, you know."

"And some of us would like our children to have little cousins to play with," Bertie mentioned.

"Now you two are ganging up on me?"

"You got it, babe." Bertie stuffed an enormous piece of cake in her mouth and smiled blissfully. "So hurry things up, okay?"

I guessed I had my orders.

Like that hadn't happened before.

8

Monday morning found me at work, as usual.
For the last two and a half years, I've been
employed as a special needs tutor at an upscale
private school in Greenwich. Howard Academy of-
fers classes for kindergarten through eighth
grade. Upon graduation, most of our students go
on to their parents' alma maters, schools like
Choate, Taft, and Ethel Walker.

I love my job, and for the most part, I adore the
kids I work with. They're lively, sophisticated, and
intelligent. Some of them are sweet, many are
spoiled; and it always surprises me how many are
being raised almost entirely by nannies and au
pairs. One thing the majority of them have in common is that when there's a problem with school-
work, their parents don't want to deal with it. In
fact, according to Russell Hanover II, the school's
headmaster, they don't even want to hear about it.

It's Mr. Hanover's job to deliver only good news
to those people who pay the bills for our hefty tuition, it's my job to see that the good news is justi-

fied. Children who fall behind academically come to me during the course of the school day for additional tutoring, and we work closely together on the subjects with which they need help.

Mostly, I'm supposed to teach, but more importantly, I'm supposed to get results. Consequently, depending on what's needed, I might be called upon to assume the role of guidance counselor, mentor, best friend, or, occasionally, drill sergeant. At least my job is never dull.

One of the best things about Howard Academy is that it is a dog-friendly environment. From the time Faith and Eve were puppies, they've accompanied me to school, spending their days lounging on a big cedar dog bed I keep in the corner of my classroom. Over time, the Poodles have become unofficial school mascots. It's not unusual for kids to greet them before speaking to me upon entering the room.

Their absentee parents might not approve of such manners, but I don't mind a bit.

Brittany Baxter was my first student Monday morning. A seventh grader, she was twelve going on twenty. Other girls in her class wore braces, had pimples, or were coping with awkward growth stages. Not Brittany. All blond hair and creamy skin, she glided into the room like a queen, effortlessly pulling off the difficult feat of looking sexy in the school uniform: a plaid wool skirt, white button-down shirt, and knee socks.

"Hey, Ms. T," she chirped. "What's up?"

"Not your grades, apparently. I just got the results of your latest test from Mr. Weinstein." Ed Weinstein taught upper-school English, a subject with which, based on the test I'd seen, Brittany had only a nodding acquaintance. "He's under the impression that you haven't been keeping up with your reading."

"I can't imagine why."

Brittany batted her long eyelashes in my direction. The child was like a heat-seeking missile casting around in search of a target. Day by day her arsenal of sexy affectations—most probably gleaned from watching MTV—grew exponentially. If Brittany didn't fully understand her own power yet, she certainly would soon.

"Besides," she said when I didn't react to lash-fluttering, "Mr. Weinstein is way too strict."

"He's only hard on you because he wants you to get good grades."

"Yeah, I know. And work to my full potential, right?"

It was hard not to smile, but I managed it. Obviously, this kid had already heard the lecture.

"Besides," she said, "I do plenty of reading."

Teen fashion magazines, no doubt.

"Yes, but do you read the books that are assigned for class?"

"Sometimes."

Brittany dumped her things on a round table and crossed the room to hunker down in front of the two Poodles. Both lifted their heads. Their tails flopped up and down against the cushion.

Brittany stroked the top of Faith's head and rubbed under her ears. Eve was still "in hair" for the show ring. After glancing back over her shoulder to see if I was watching, Brittany scratched carefully beneath the bitch's chin, leaving her long mane coat undisturbed.

"I'm going to be a dog handler like you when I

grow up," she said. "Dog breeders don't have to read Shakespeare and poetry and stuff like that. So what's the point?"

"The point is that at your age, you need a well-rounded education. If you haven't been exposed to all the interesting things the world has to offer, how will you know what you want to be when you grow up?"

Prudently, I refrained from mentioning that a month earlier she'd wanted to be a supermodel, and before that, a rock star's girlfriend. Compared with those two choices, at least she'd raised her sights a little. Or more likely, she was just humoring me, fishing around to see whether currying favor with my dogs would earn her any extra points.

"My mom says the same thing," Brittany pulled out a chair and plopped down onto the seat.

"Your mom knows what she's talking about."

"Sometimes," she smirked. "And sometimes I think she's just making it up as she goes along."

Perceptive child, I thought. Her description of her mother probably applied to me as well. One thing about adulthood, sometimes it just seems like smoke and mirrors.

I pulled out a chair, joined her at the table, and we got to work.

During lunch break, I took the Poodles for an extended walk outside around the school grounds. Late April in Connecticut is undeniably beautiful. Tulips were in bloom; trees were just beginning to bud. After three long, dreary winter months, it was a pleasure just to be outside again. Faith and Eve raced and played. I unzipped my jacket, unwound my scarf, and turned my face up into the warm sun. With nothing pressing, we took our time, circling both hockey and soccer fields before finally ending our excursion at the tennis courts. The Poodles were panting happily by the time we got back to the classroom.

I opened the windows to let in some air and put fresh water in the dogs' bowl. Then I retrieved my purse from a desk drawer and fished around in it until I found the phone number Paul Lennox had given me after last week's class.

I didn't know Paul well, and I certainly didn't want to intrude on his grief. But his aunt's death had had an unexpectedly profound effect on me, touching me in a way I wouldn't have thought possible considering how briefly I'd known her. I wanted to extend my condolences and also to convey Aunt Peg's offer of a donation in Mary Livingston's name.

Paul picked up right away, and I identified myself. There was a pause, as if he was trying to remember who I was.

"Yes, of course, Melanie," he said after a moment. "With Faith. Sorry, I've been making so many calls and dealing with so many relatives, I'm not even sure I'd recognize my own mother's voice right now."

"I'm so sorry about your aunt. Even though we'd just met, I could see what a special lady she was."

"Aunt Mary was one of a kind." Paul spoke slowly; his words were heavy with sadness. "She had so many wonderful friends, and everyone who knew her felt the same way you did. That's what makes this whole thing so hard to understand . . ."

"I'm sure the fact that it happened so unexpectedly didn't help," I said gently. "Was it a heart attack?"

"No, although that's what everyone thought at first. It was a natural assumption. Aunt Mary had some medical issues related to her age, but she wasn't mortally ill. Yesterday morning, I had every expectation that she might live for another decade.

"But after . . ." He cleared his throat, then continued, "The director at Winston Pumpernill called the medical examiner. I gather that's standard when things like this happen. I thought it was just a formality. But when I called a few minutes ago to make arrangements for the funeral home to come and pick her up, I was told that the body wasn't being released. Apparently, there's a suspicion of foul play."

I gasped softly and couldn't think of a single thing to say. In silence, I waited for Paul to continue.

After what seemed like a long time, he did. "I guess I might as well just come right out and say it. The paper will probably be running a story in a day or two. The tests they do are so sophisticated now . . . it's more than a suspicion. The M.E. knows how Aunt Mary died. She didn't have a heart attack. She was murdered."

"Murdered?" I repeated. My voice sounded hollow. I was truly shocked by the news.

Let's be clear on this, okay? It's not as though I haven't had the misfortune to run across the occasional murder victim. In fact, it's happened often enough that you might think I'd almost be used to it by now. But somehow that hasn't happened. Actually, the reverse is true. Each one seems to hit me harder than the time before.

Not only that, but none of the victims I'd known in the past had seemed as unlikely a candidate for murder as Paul's Aunt Mary. And I could hardly come up with a more surprising setting than the Winston Pumpernill facility. No wonder Paul's grief was overlaid with shock and dismay.

"Do they know what happened?" I asked.

"She suffocated. It seems likely that she was smothered with her pillow. My aunt was quite sturdy for her age, but she wasn't a large woman. I suppose it wouldn't have been difficult for someone to overpower her. . . ." His voice broke, then trailed away.

"I'm so very sorry," I said again. The words felt totally inadequate. "If there's anything at all I can do, please don't hesitate to let me know."

"Thank you, I appreciate that. I guess I'd better get back to making my other calls. I have to break the news to the rest of the family before they get a chance to read about it in the newspaper."

I clicked off the phone and sat at my desk, staring off into space. After a minute, a cold, wet nose pressed itself into my hand. A paw came up and laid gently across my knee. Faith pressed her body close to mine, offering what warmth and comfort she could.

I'm not a particularly mystical person, but at times it's hard not to wonder how much dogs understand. Faith had met Mary the day before, too. Did she know what had happened? Or had she merely sensed my melancholy mood and responded to it?

I wasn't sure it mattered. I gathered the big Poodle up into my arms, buried my face in her hair, and felt enormously grateful for the solace she had to offer.

* * *

"I'm beginning to think," I said, "that cats are the bane of my existence."

It was six hours later, and I was sitting in my backyard enjoying a fine April evening. At least I would have been if fluffy Felix and his sleek black friend hadn't been so determined to breach the five-foot cedar fence that surrounded my small plot of land.

The fence had been intended to keep my Poodles in. It was a barrier meant to simplify my life. Winter mornings, I could race downstairs barefoot and open the back door without fear of my dogs escaping. Late at night, I didn't have to go outside and take them for a walk. The fence had been in place for three years, ever since Faith was a puppy, and the system had always worked beautifully.

Mostly, I was now realizing, because nobody had ever tried to break in before.

Every time the cats from next door showed their furry little faces over the top of the fence, the Poodles began to leap and bark, sounding their version of an intruder alert. Each time, I had to get up and quiet them down. No sooner would I get the pack settled then the cats would reappear.

I'd tried reasoning with the Poodles, but it wasn't working. The clear consensus among my canine population was that their property should be declared a cat-free zone.

What was it about *my* yard, I wondered, that so fascinated the new neighbor's cats? They had, after all, a yard of their own. Not to mention all the freedom they wanted otherwise. Unfettered in any way, they could have been out roaming the entire neighborhood. Or even the whole town of

Stamford. So why would they choose to come to the one place where five bouncing, barking Poodles had made it abundantly clear they weren't welcome?

Sheer and outright perversity, I thought. Those cats knew exactly what they were doing.

"Come on," Sam said with a laugh. "It's not that bad."

He walked down the steps, his fingers curled handily around two long-necked beers, and pulled a chair up next to my chaise longue. Davey was inside doing homework. A chicken was cooking in the oven; dinner would be ready in half an hour. I took the beer Sam held out to me and tipped it up to my lips.

"Maybe it's not the cats," I said, eyes narrowing speculatively. "Maybe it's Amber."

"Our new neighbor is perfectly pleasant."

"She needs more clothes."

"She was fully dressed when I saw her earlier." Sam was still laughing. "Socks, mittens, ear muffs, the works."

"You're not taking me seriously," I said.

Sam took a long swallow from his beer. "You're not good with change, are you?"

"Not particularly," I admitted. "I liked Edna Silano. She was a nice neighbor."

"Edna Silano used to spy on you."

"Yes, but at least she was honest about it. And it was kind of like having my own personal neighborhood watch. Besides, it was only because she didn't have much else to do."

"Once she threatened to put a curse on me if I didn't do the right thing and marry you."

Beer, swallowed the wrong way, made me cough and sputter as I sat up abruptly. "She *did*?"

"Yup. I tried to tell her it wasn't my fault, that you were the one who believed in long engagements, but she didn't buy it."

"Oh." I considered that. Maybe Edna hadn't been the paragon of virtue I'd made her out to be. "She actually *cursed* you?"

"I don't know. I didn't stick around to find out."

"Well," I grumbled, "then I guess I can see how you might think Amber was an improvement. And one cat I could probably handle. Maybe even two. Does she have to have seven?"

"Glass houses," said Sam. "Think about it."

Right.

"I don't let my dogs play in her yard." Need I mention, I've always been stubborn?

"She doesn't necessarily let her cats come here. Isn't that the whole point of cats? They pretty much do whatever they want."

"I don't care what they do, if they would just find someplace else to do it."

"Maybe after a couple of weeks they'll get tired of teasing the Poodles," Sam said. He didn't sound too convinced.

"Or maybe one of the Poodles will teach them a lesson," I said hopefully.

Sam's gaze flickered upward. The black cat had climbed a tree next door, then dropped down gracefully onto the top of the fence. Even now, he was balancing on the edge, peering down at the dogs sleeping peacefully beneath him in the grass.

"I wouldn't hold my breath," Sam said.

Me either, I thought with a sigh.

9

The mood at Thursday's obedience class was subdued.

As I'd done the previous week, I arrived a few minutes early. Though the parking lot at the Y was full, none of the class members was standing outside talking. Nobody was exercising their dogs or greeting new arrivals. I unloaded Faith, and we headed directly inside.

Nearly everyone was already gathered in the big room. Steve was finishing laying the mats, while the others were clustered in small groups speaking in hushed tones. I didn't see Paul and Cora or Kelly and Boss. Neither absence surprised me. I imagined Paul probably had family obligations to attend to, and Kelly seemed to make a habit of being late.

I took off my jacket and set it down on a metal folding chair with my purse and the thermos of water I'd remembered to bring. As I straightened and turned to face the room, I felt the tug of Faith's leash. She'd left my side to touch noses with Mark's Cairn, Reggie, who was straining at the end of his leash to reach her.

Mark reeled the little terrier in and beckoned me over. He was standing with Stacey, Julie, and Minnie. Their circle opened up to accommodate us.

Jack, the Doberman, lying complacently at Julie's heel, didn't even stir. Coach, the Schnauzer, cocked his head at Faith and wagged his stumpy tail. Bubbles, Stacey's Papillon, danced excitedly in place until given permission to come over and say a proper hello. Everyone waited until the dogs had settled again, then conversation resumed.

"We were talking about Paul's Aunt Mary," Stacey said. "What a horrible tragedy. I spoke with Paul yesterday. There's going to be a memorial service on Saturday at Saint Michael's in Greenwich. He wanted the class, especially those of us who'd visited Winston Pumpernill, to know that anyone who wanted to attend was welcome. Steve will probably make a general announcement, but I just wanted to make sure that the information got passed along to those of us who were there last week."

"Thank you," I said. "I appreciate your letting me know."

"Paul is taking Cora," Stacey added. "To a memorial service. Can you believe it?"

"I can," Minnie replied. "Why wouldn't he? His aunt loved that Corgi. In fact, she loved all our dogs. That's probably why so many of us feel like we bonded with Mary, even though we hardly knew her. Maybe we should go as a group and take all the dogs with us. You know, like a show of support for Paul and Cora."

"No way," Julie said firmly. "All these dogs in a

church? That wouldn't be a show of support, it would be a side show. Paul would be mortified."

"Sorry, Minnie," Mark weighed in. "I'm with Julie on this one. I know Coach goes everywhere with you, but the last thing we'd want to do is to intrude on the dignity of the service."

Minnie looked annoyed. "Speak for yourself. Coach and I are perfectly dignified."

"Goodness," Stacey said with a giggle. "Over-identify much? You make him sound like your date, not your dog."

Minnie's expression turned thunderous. She snapped Coach's leash with her left hand and the Schnauzer abruptly stood up. Minnie spun on her heel and the two of them left.

Frowning, Mark watched them go. "That was cruel."

"That was honest," Stacey replied. "Besides, sometimes cruel is the only thing Minnie understands."

The first time I'd met these people, I'd pegged Stacey as the most innocuous member of the group. Now I found myself reevaluating my initial impression. Stacey might have looked harmless, but she clearly was capable of giving as good as she got.

In the uncomfortable silence that followed, we all heard a clatter outside in the hallway, signaling the arrival of Kelly and Boss. The pair came skidding around the corner into the room. The Akita was leading the way and dragging his hapless owner along behind.

"Lord, I wish she'd get that dog properly leash broken," Julie muttered. "It's really not such a difficult concept."

"Maybe you should offer to give her lessons," said Mark.

Julie rounded back on him; she'd heard the same snide edge to his tone that I had. But Mark merely raised his eyebrows and shrugged innocently as if he couldn't understand why his words might have caused any offense. Julie's lips thinned into a hard line, but she didn't say a word.

"Look!" Kelly announced, heading toward us across the mats. She held up her arm and showed us her watch. "I'm not late! Class doesn't even start for another whole minute."

As she drew near, our group broke apart, all of us giving her plenty of room. None of us wanted to let our dogs stand in close proximity to the Akita. We were too concerned to be subtle about it; Kelly had to have noticed our withdrawal.

She stopped just outside the circle, snatched up Boss's leash, and said in a surprisingly authoritative tone, "Sit!"

To everyone's relief, the big brindle dog sat. Kelly beamed at him happily, then looked up at us. "We've been practicing."

"It shows," said Stacey. "Good job."

I wasn't going to be the one to mention that consistency was the key to a well-behaved dog. And that any dog who was still capable of dragging its owner around still had a long way to go where training was concerned.

"What'd I miss?" Kelly asked, including all of us in her smile. "You all were talking about Paul, weren't you?"

Her handling skills might have been lacking, but Kelly was cute and perky. It was hard not to want to like her. Mark immediately angled himself in her direction, but Julie spoke up first.

"Yes, we were," she said. "There's a memorial service for his aunt on Saturday."

"I know. I read about it in the paper."

So far, the *Greenwich Time* had gotten several days' worth of front page stories out of the murder. Greenwich was no longer a small town, but, thankfully, violent crime was still rare. The police were investigating Mary Livingston's death. According to the paper, they had yet to come up with any leads.

"Several of us are thinking about going," said Mark. "We'd like to offer a show of support for Paul."

"How very nice of you," Kelly said.

She did not, I noted, offer to join us.

Stacey shook her head sadly. "I only wish there was more we could do."

"About what?" asked Steve, walking up to stand beside Kelly.

She greeted him with a small smile, then turned back to the group. Boss, I was interested to see, didn't react to Steve's intrusion upon their space. Akitas tend to be very protective of their people. Boss's failure to challenge the situation led me to think he was probably accustomed to seeing Kelly and Steve together.

"Paul," Julie was saying. "We all feel terrible about what happened. Even more so, I suppose, because we were there at the time."

"That's what's so hard for me to understand," said Mark. "It was the middle of a Sunday afternoon in a semiprivate facility. We certainly weren't the only visitors; there were plenty of people around. Nurses, administrators, you name it. People were all over that building. How could someone have been murdered without anyone noticing?"

I'd been wondering the same thing myself. Under the circumstances—with all of us being so close to the situation—it was hard not to contemplate what might have been done differently.

"It had to have been a crime of opportunity," I said. "Paul's aunt must have been taken by surprise. Mark is right, the place was full of people. If she'd struggled or cried out, surely someone would have heard."

"Who says someone didn't notice?" asked Julie.

"That's a gruesome thought." Kelly let a hand drift down to rest on her dog's broad head. "And no one's come forward with any information. Don't you think someone would have if they knew something?"

"Not if they were afraid," said Julie.

We all turned and looked at her.

"Afraid of what?" asked Steve.

"You know, like those reports you see on the news about abuse of the elderly that takes place in nursing homes. What if something like that is going on and the murder happened as a cover-up?"

An interesting possibility, I thought. Stacey disagreed.

"I don't buy it," she said. "We've all been inside Winston Pumpernill any number of times, and it seems like an exemplary facility. Besides, most of those stories are about neglect as much as abuse. Older people who are alone in the world and don't have relatives to check up on them and serve as their advocates. Mary wasn't alone, and she certainly wasn't helpless. Paul would have done anything for her. All she would have had to do was ask."

"She may not have asked for help," said Mark, "but she obviously needed it. Otherwise, she wouldn't be dead now. What a shame for Paul that it had to happen during our visit. I think it would have been easier on him, and less shocking certainly, if he hadn't been on the premises at the time."

"I've been thinking about that," I said. "And it wouldn't surprise me if the reason the murder happened was precisely *because* we were there."

Now it was my turn to draw stares from the rest of the group. Steve and Stacey looked surprised, but Julie stiffened visibly. Even Jack felt her sudden anger. He pushed himself up off the floor and stood by her side. Automatically, her hand dropped to the middle of the Doberman's back, soothing him with a touch.

"Are you accusing one of *us* of being involved in Mary Livingston's murder?" she asked.

"Not necessarily." Not being a big believer in coincidence, however, it wasn't as though the thought hadn't crossed my mind.

Kelly crossed her slender arms over her chest. "Then what exactly are you saying?"

"The same thing I mentioned a minute ago. That this was most likely a crime of opportunity. And that our being there was what gave the murderer his chance to act."

Several years earlier at a dog show, I'd confronted a killer in the handlers' tent, a place where exhibitors prepare their dogs to be shown, and one that is normally teeming with activity. I'd had the bad luck, however, to encounter the murderer while Best in Show was being judged. There had been several hundred people on the dog show grounds, many within shouting distance. But their attention had all been focused elsewhere, and I'd nearly lost my life as a result. It was obvious to me that there were certain similarities between my misadventure and the event that had taken Mary's life.

"Think about it," I said. "Not only were many of the residents and much of the Sunday staff in the sunroom because of our scheduled visit, but once Minnie and Coach began to perform, even more people came into the room to watch. Areas of the building that would normally have had staff on duty, like the residential hallway where Mary's room was located, were probably pretty empty. Certainly emptier than usual. Our presence gave the killer the opening he was looking for."

"I hadn't thought about it that way," Minnie said. She and her Schnauzer were standing behind me and off to the right; I hadn't realized she'd drifted back to join the group. "I guess that makes me feel better *and* worse."

"I can understand the worse part," said Stacey. "But how on earth can anything make you feel better about our role in what happened?"

Minnie gazed around the circle of faces. "Coach and I were the ones out in the middle of the room putting on a show. Everyone was watching us. If that isn't an ironclad alibi, I don't know what is."

Kelly gasped softly. Maybe it hadn't occurred to her until right that moment that any of us might need an alibi. Actually, I found myself wondering why Minnie had been so quick to think of it herself.

"Hold on, Minerva," said Steve. "Before you start thinking you're off the hook, you might want to wait to see what the police come up with as a time of death. A few minutes earlier or a few minutes later and you could be as likely a suspect as any of us." He paused to send her a meaningful stare. "Or, perhaps, even more so, if you think about it."

Minnie's lips stretched into a smile, but behind

them her teeth were gritted. For a moment, tension zinged between the two of them like a wire drawn tight. Then Mark cleared his throat loudly and stepped into the breach.

"You seem to have given things quite a bit of thought," he said to me. "You're not in law enforcement by any chance, are you?"

"No." I laughed self-consciously. "I'm a private-school teacher."

"One who solves mysteries on the side," said Steve. "Isn't that right?"

I stared at him in surprise. Where had that come from?

Steve looked rather pleased with himself. "We have a small class here. In fact, most of us have been together so long, it almost feels like an extension of family. So I imagine I can be forgiven for checking out the backgrounds of the people who want to join us."

"You did a background check on me?" I asked, incredulous.

"Oh, nothing so formal as that. I got on the Internet and ran a Google search. I was surprised to see how many times your name had appeared in the local papers."

Well, yes, I thought glumly. There was that.

"So you're some sort of amateur detective?" Julie didn't sound impressed.

"Only by default," I admitted. "It's more like I seem to have a knack for being in the wrong place at the wrong time."

"I guess that explains it," said Mark.

"What?"

"We've been visiting Winston Pumpernill for months now, and nothing terrible has ever happened before."

Stacey nodded. "You said we were responsible for Mary's death. And it looks like we were, since we're the ones who took you there with us."

"Hey, people," Steve said sternly. "I don't like the direction this conversation is heading."

That made two of us, I thought. And things wouldn't have gone that way at all if he hadn't brought the topic up in the first place.

"Rather than believing the worst of Melanie, I think we ought to be grateful that she's here."

Grateful? That couldn't be a good sign.

"Who better to get on the case," Steve continued triumphantly, "than a member of our very own class?"

"The police," I answered quickly before anyone else had a chance to chime in. "They're exactly the right people for a situation like this."

"They are when they can get the job done," said Kelly. "But it doesn't always happen. Look at the Martha Moxley case. It took the Greenwich police more than twenty-five years to solve that one."

"That's right," Julie agreed, but at least she seemed to be teasing. "I doubt Paul will want to wait that long."

"For what?" asked Paul.

We'd all been so wrapped up in our conversation that none of us had noticed him and Cora entering the room. Even the dogs seemed surprised.

"It turns out that Melanie's a detective," Minnie announced. "She's going to solve your aunt's murder. Isn't that great?"

Paul shot me a startled look, for which I could hardly blame him.

I shrugged helplessly.

Great indeed, I thought.

10

"It's not like you didn't deserve that," Sam said. "A blind man could have seen it coming."

It was Friday evening, and Sam and I had invited Aunt Peg over for dinner. Davey was spending the night with his father; he'd taken Faith with him for company. That reduced the number of Poodles in the house to four, which meant they still outnumbered the humans. Par for the course around here.

We'd had salmon and asparagus, a meal healthy enough that none of us had really minded that Peg showed up carrying a torte from the St. Moritz Bakery. Sam and I were having coffee with our dessert; Aunt Peg drank her usual tea.

She was also currently enjoying a good laugh at my expense. Sam's comment had come in response to my admission that the members of the South Avenue Obedience Club seemed to believe that I was going to be solving Mary Livingston's murder.

"I think it's your karma," Aunt Peg said.

"Don't you start, too," I warned her. "You're the one who got me involved in solving mysteries to begin with."

"Just once," she said—a bald-faced lie if ever I'd heard one. "I needed your help. Who knew you'd keep it up?"

"It's not like I've had a choice."

"Sure you have," said Sam. Part of the reason it had taken us so long to get married was because he disapproved of my propensity to get involved in things that weren't any of my business. "All you have to do is say no."

"I *do* say no. But nobody ever believes me."

"That's because you're not firm enough," Aunt Peg said. This was obviously not a character trait she herself had ever been accused of possessing. "But listen to this. Something interesting occurred to me after the last time we spoke. I might have been acquainted with Mary Livingston's family when I was younger. Tell me a little about her. Had she lived in Greenwich her whole life? Did she grow up on Clapboard Ridge Road?"

"I don't know. I only met her the one time, and we didn't talk about her background. Mostly we talked about dogs."

"Perfectly understandable." Peg nodded, helping herself to another slice of torte. "Mary would have been a good bit older than me, of course, but I believe I went to school with several of her nieces. Where's today's paper? There must be a notice about the memorial service. That would tell me what I need to know."

Sam stepped over the Poodles sleeping at our feet and left the room. He returned several minutes later with the Greenwich paper; pages folded back to the information Aunt Peg wanted. She put on her reading glasses and skimmed quickly through the listing.

"Just as I thought," she said with satisfaction. "Paul's mother and I went to primary school together. First through eighth, right here in town."

"What are the chances of that?" I wondered aloud.

"It's not as unexpected as you might think. Back in those days, Greenwich really was a small town. Everyone went to the same schools and belonged to the same clubs. It wasn't unusual for families' lives to be intertwined. I remember Sylvia Livingston quite well. Of course, she'd be Sylvia Lennox now. I wonder if she would remember me as well."

"No doubt," Sam said. "You're pretty unforgettable."

Aunt Peg narrowed a glance in his direction. "I'll take that as a compliment. And if that wasn't the way you were heading, you'd do better not to admit it."

Sam merely grinned and admitted nothing. He could get away with things that would land me in all sorts of trouble.

"Now that I realize there's a connection," Peg said to me, "I expect I had better accompany you to the memorial service."

"Who said I was going?"

"Of course you're going. Where else do you intend to begin asking questions?"

"I'm not sure I do."

I glanced over at Sam. He seemed to be paying an inordinate amount of attention to the crumbs on his plate, all that remained of the large piece of pastry he'd been served earlier.

"Do I?" I prompted after a moment of silence.

Sam lifted his eyes. "Don't look at me," he said.

As if there *was* anywhere else to look.

"You're my husband," I said. "That entitles you to an opinion. Do you want me to say no?"

"I want you to do whatever makes you happy."

"That's not an answer."

Aunt Peg pushed back her chair and stood. "Maybe the two of you should discuss this in private."

"No," Sam and I said together. I was happy to see we could agree on something.

Peg sat back down. Just as I'd suspected, she was only bluffing. Trust me, it would take a steam shovel to remove her from a room where two people she cared about were arguing.

"I think you should go to the memorial service," she said. "It would be a nice gesture on your part. We can go together. After that, you can decide what you want to do next."

"Fine," I said. "If nobody wants to object."

Aunt Peg and I both looked at Sam. His expression was carefully neutral. I couldn't tell whether he was happy about the way things had turned out.

Then his gaze lifted, and he looked past me into the kitchen. Though all the Poodles were inside the house, I'd left the outdoor lights on. When I turned in my seat to see what he was looking at, I saw Amber from next door waving at us through the window.

Before I could react, Sam was already up out of his seat and heading her way. It fell to me to shush the Poodles when he opened the back door. Hearing that, they naturally assumed that something exciting was about to happen. All four jumped up to see what that might be.

As I tried to convince the pack not to make a

fuss, Sam invited Amber inside. To the Poodles' way of thinking, that confirmed what they'd suspected all along. Something exciting *was* happening: they had a visitor.

The four big black dogs scooted past me and burst through the doorway into the kitchen. Quickly, I followed behind, arriving just in time to see Amber scream, leap up in the air, and try to hide behind Sam. Her slender arms circled his neck in a stranglehold as she attempted to wedge herself between him and the counter. She looked like she might be seriously contemplating climbing up on his back.

Sam, who appeared to be thoroughly amused by the situation, was no help.

Luckily, Aunt Peg had gone out to the kitchen with him. Now she tried to run interference. "They're only trying to be friendly," she said. "They won't hurt you."

"My God, they're enormous!" Amber's voice was shrill. Her feet hopped up and down in place as the Poodles, mostly blocked by Sam and Peg, eddied around her legs. "They look like a pack of wolves!"

The Poodles seem to understand most things, but thankfully, they didn't understand that. I'm sure they would have been highly insulted if they had.

"And what on earth," Amber said, pointing at Tar and Eve, "is the matter with those two?"

"They're show dogs," Aunt Peg replied, beating Sam and me to it. Anyone who has ever owned— and shown—a Poodle is well accustomed to explaining why their dogs look the way they do. "The trim they're wearing is called a continental. Maybe you've watched the Westminster Dog Show on TV and seen the Poodles in the Non-Sporting and Toy groups?"

"No," Amber said flatly.

"It's a traditional German hunting clip," I said. "In the show ring, most of that long hair you see is loose. But at home, the topknot and ear fringes would get in the dog's way. That's why we have it wrapped and rubber banded like that."

I didn't think my explanation had been inordinately long, but Amber was already looking bored. Now that the Poodles had calmed down, and she'd stopped fearing for her life, she had lost all interest in them.

She was, however, still pressed pretty up tightly against my husband.

My thoughts must have been easy to read, because Sam caught my look and grinned. Reaching up, he unwound Amber's arms from his neck and stepped forward out of her embrace.

"We're having coffee," he said. "Would you like to join us?"

"Thank you, but no. I only stopped by to see if either one of you had seen Felix recently. He seems to have disappeared."

"Felix is your dog?" Aunt Peg was instantly sympathetic.

"My cat. Big, bushy, orange . . ." Amber's hands sketched an approximate size in the air. "Loud."

"Oh." Aunt Peg shrugged, looking deflated. She's a dog person through and through and makes no apologies for her allegiance. "Why would you think you might find him here?"

"Because he's been here every day this week," I said. "Felix likes to think of our yard as his second home."

Aunt Peg glanced around at the collection of Poodles, now scattered around us on the floor. "He must not be very bright."

"Shame on you!" Amber cried. "Felix is a very smart cat."

Aunt Peg folded her arms over her chest complacently. "Then why is he lost?"

"I didn't say he was lost, I just said he wasn't at home. All my cats like to go out exploring during the day. But they always show up at night when it's supper time. We're having tuna tonight; it's Felix's favorite. And it's not like him to miss a meal."

"Does he wear a collar with a tag?" Aunt Peg asked.

Amber shook her head.

"Is he microchipped?"

"No, but . . ." She sighed and plucked at her sleeve.

"But what?"

"He's a cat," Amber said, as if that explained everything. "Cats enjoy having their freedom."

"Well, then, there you go." Aunt Peg is a big proponent of responsible pet ownership. And heaven help the person who neglects to fulfill his or her duties. "I would expect that Felix is still out somewhere enjoying himself."

"But it's dark out!"

"Cats can see in the dark," I mentioned. "Probably better than we can."

I jumped slightly. Either one of the Poodles had bitten me in the ankle, or Sam had kicked me. Since the Poodles have better manners than that, I had to conclude that the culprit was probably my new husband. Maybe he was trying to kick some sympathy into me. It would have been better, I thought, if he'd tried to kick some sense into

Amber. If she was going to persist in letting her cats run around the neighborhood without supervision, something like this was bound to happen.

"Would you like me to go out and help you look for him?" asked Sam.

"That would be super," Amber said.

"Me, too," I offered without much enthusiasm. "Aunt Peg?"

"Not I. I have my own dogs to attend to, and I'll be running along. I'll see you tomorrow, however."

"Tomorrow?"

"The memorial service?"

Oh, right. I'd forgotten.

Aunt Peg headed for the front door and the rest of us, Poodles included, followed along behind. Presumably, Amber had already looked around our backyard. We might as well start in the other direction.

"What about James?" I asked Amber as we reached the front hall. "Is he out looking for Felix, too?"

"James is traveling," she said with a sigh. "As usual."

Our search didn't take long. As Aunt Peg drew open the front door, there Felix was. Her minivan was parked in our driveway. The big orange cat had climbed up onto the hood, probably when the engine was still warm, and had fallen asleep. Curled up tight, with his tail wrapped around his body and over his nose, Felix didn't even stir when I turned on the lights.

"Oh, bad kitty!" Amber hurried past me and down the steps. "Didn't you hear Mommy calling you?"

She reached over and gathered the sleeping cat into her arms. He was as limp and pliant as a feather pillow. His long tail hung down beneath her hands, swinging back and forth like a pendulum. I resisted the urge to walk over and check the minivan's paint for scratches.

"Crisis averted," Aunt Peg said cheerfully.

"Until next time," I muttered.

Amber hurried home to feed Felix. Aunt Peg left to drive home to her Poodles. As Sam closed the front door and locked it, I pressed my body against his from behind, winding my arms around his neck and pulling him close.

"Oooh," I whispered, lips close to his ear. "I'm so helpless, and you're so big and strong. Save me from the wolves . . ."

"That," Sam said, laughing, "is a terrible imitation." He turned in my arms and cradled my hips with his hands. "Cut Amber some slack. It's not easy to meet four big dogs at once if you're not used to them."

I lifted a brow. "You didn't see her climbing on me or Peg, did you?"

Sam lowered his head, lips grazing mine.

"And what . . ." I managed with effort, "is up with her husband? How come he's never home?"

He paused midkiss and pulled fractionally away. "Would you like me to go ask her?"

Silly man. I dropped one hand, threaded my fingers around his belt buckle, and pulled him closer.

"That's what I thought," he said.

11

The next afternoon, I picked up Aunt Peg at her house, and we drove down North Street to Saint Michael's Church together. Aunt Peg was in high spirits. She hadn't known the deceased, after all; she merely had a tenuous connection to the family. Plus the prospect of getting to do some snooping around appealed tremendously to her inner sleuth.

"Big crowd," she said as we drove up the driveway. "Mary Livingston must have been a popular woman."

"I'm not surprised." Only a few empty parking spaces remained. I found one and pulled the Volvo into it. "I really enjoyed our one meeting. I only wish I'd had a chance to get to know her better."

Aside from the assembled cars, two dark green vans were parked along the edge of the lot. The words *Winston Pumpernill, Skilled Nursing Facility* were written in gold on the side doors. I was glad to see that the other residents of the home had been given the opportunity to come and pay their respects.

"Let's split up," Aunt Peg suggested as we walked inside. The service wasn't scheduled to start for fifteen minutes or so, and friends and family were mingling in the foyer. "That way, we'll be able to cover more ground."

"This is a memorial service," I whispered, "not a fact-finding mission. Covering ground shouldn't be an issue. It's not as though we're going to subject people who've come here to mourn to questioning."

"Speak for yourself." Aunt Peg gazed around the room. "I'm pretty sure that woman by the window is Sylvia Lennox. I believe I'll go over and pay my condolences."

She melted into the crowd. I looked around myself, seeking familiar faces. About half the members of the obedience club were in attendance. I also saw a number of older men and women, some of whom I remembered meeting at Winston Pumpernill. Many of them were attended by nurses and had already taken seats in the chapel.

I heard a snuffling sound, then something brushed past my ankle. Startled, I looked down and saw Cora gazing up at me. I wondered if she'd been looking for a familiar face, too.

"Hello, girl." I squatted down to give the Corgi a pat. She wiggled her body happily in reply. "You'd better watch out. You could get trampled in this crowd."

"Don't worry," said Paul. "I'm keeping a pretty close eye on her."

I stood up and said hello. Though the majority

of the people around us were making small talk or
sharing reminiscences of Mary, Paul got right
down to business.

"Are you really a detective?" he asked. Class had
started shortly after he arrived on Thursday evening.
There hadn't been time then for us to talk.

"No," I answered quickly. And firmly. "As it happens, I've solved a couple of mysteries. I guess . . ."
I stopped and thought for a minute. "I guess I like
figuring out puzzles. And asking questions. And
maybe finding clues in unlikely places and trying
to figure out how all the pieces fit together."

Abruptly, I stopped speaking. Paul was looking
at me curiously.

I'd said more than I'd intended to say. In fact,
I'd said more than I was in the habit of admitting
to anyone, including myself. For years, I'd been
blaming Aunt Peg for getting me mixed up in one
murder after another. And now it turned out that
all this time, my involvement had been nobody's
fault but my own.

"So you're like an amateur detective," he said.

"It looks like it." I reached out and placed a
hand on his arm. "I really liked your Aunt Mary.
She seemed like a wonderful woman."

"Yes, she was. As it happens, I'd only come to appreciate her myself relatively recently. You know
what it's like when you're young. You're careless
about relationships; it never occurs to you that
people you love won't live forever. When Aunt
Mary was on her own, living in an apartment in
town, I don't even think I saw her twice a year. I
was so wrapped up in my own life, I thought I didn't
have the time to spare.

"Having her move to Winston Pumpernill the
year before last was a wake-up call for me. That's

when I realized that she wouldn't always be here, and that I should make the most of the time we had. The irony is that my mother moved Aunt Mary to Winston Pumpernill because she thought Mary would be safer there than she was living alone. Until last week, I'd have thought the same thing."

A perfectly understandable assumption. Too bad it had turned out to be wrong.

"Do the police have any idea what happened?" I asked.

Paul lowered his voice. In the close crowds, he didn't want to be overheard discussing the details of Mary's death. "All they know so far is that she died of suffocation. The evidence suggests that it happened right in her own bed."

"How awful," I said under my breath. "I guess she must have gone to her room to lie down. When was the last time you saw her?"

"Shortly after you and Faith moved on to talk to someone else. Aunt Mary was in her eighties, and she didn't have the strongest heart. Sometimes the excitement of a big visit like that would get to be too much for her. She loved meeting everybody and seeing all the dogs, but she tired easily. When that happened, she'd excuse herself and go to her room to rest."

"So then it wasn't unusual for her to leave, even though the therapy dogs and handlers were still there?"

"Not at all. Why?"

"Because maybe the killer knew that. Maybe he was counting on it. He knew our visit would provide a distraction, and he hoped that Mary would leave in the middle. He could have waited and watched and followed her when she went."

"Possibly," Paul agreed. "But how does that

help? Since no one was paying any attention at the time, we don't know who left the room around the same time she did. In fact, unless Winston Pumpernill kept some sort of a head count, we don't even know who was there to begin with."

"*We* don't," I said. "But surely the police would. That's just the sort of question they should have asked."

"I know they've spoken to Catherine Stone, Lynn Stephanopolus, and several of the other administrators. They've also questioned most of the staff who were there that day. So far, the facility hasn't let them talk to any of the residents. They're patients, really, and the administration is trying to protect them. Plus, of course, nobody wants to plant the suspicion in their minds that where they're living might not be the safest place for them."

Much as that made sense, I doubted that the facility could shield the residents forever. Unless the police got a lead that pointed them in another direction, they'd undoubtedly be back at Winston Pumpernill shortly.

"The police have talked to you as well."

It was more a statement than a question, but Paul nodded anyway. "Being family and being the one who found her, I was right at the top of the list. But I imagine they'll be in touch with you too pretty soon. The detective told me they were going to talk to everyone who was there, including all the members of the obedience club."

"Do you mind if I ask you a really nosy question?"

Paul cocked his head to one side and stared at me for a minute. He took his time before answering. "I really loved my aunt," he said finally. "And I want to see her murderer found. Since we're both being honest with one another, I'll tell you the truth. Consulting with an amateur detective seems to me to be about as useful as calling in a psychic to solve the case. But so what? I don't see how your involvement can hurt. And if it took hiring a psychic to figure out who killed my aunt, I'd be willing to try that, too.

"Honestly? I don't have a whole lot of faith in your ability to accomplish any more than the police can. But as long as you don't impede their investigation in any way, feel free. Have at it. Ask your nosy questions and I'll answer them."

He stopped abruptly and smiled. "Or if I think they're *too* intrusive, I guess I'll just tell you to go jump in a lake."

Well, that cleared the air.

Good for him, I thought. And good for me, too. Now we both knew where we stood.

"Winston Pumpernill isn't an inexpensive facility," I said.

Paul nodded. "You want to know if my aunt had money."

"Yes."

"And probably who stood to inherit."

"That, too."

"I understand where you're coming from, but nobody in the family did this to Aunt Mary."

"How can you be so sure?"

"Because you're right, she did have pots of money. But for the most part, so do the rest of us. Nobody needed hers. At least not badly enough to kill for it."

Too bad, I thought. That would have made things much easier.

"I know this will probably seem like an odd question, but did your aunt have any enemies?"

"You met her," said Paul. "How could a harmless old lady like that have enemies?"

"Maybe she wasn't always harmless."

"You think something like an old grudge might have gotten her killed?" Paul didn't look convinced. He was probably wishing I had psychic ability instead. "At this point, it all seems so unreal, I guess anything's possible."

Then his gaze moved past me to a couple who had just entered the room. "You'll have to excuse me," he said. "I see some people I should say hello to."

He and Cora had barely left when Mary's friends, Madeline and Borden, came walking by. Madeline stopped and squinted hard in my direction. "I know you," she said.

"I'm Melanie. We met last week. I have a black Standard Poodle named Faith."

"Met last week, did we?" asked Borden. He looked at me without recognition. "I'm glad to hear that. I'm always pleased to meet a pretty lady."

"Pay no attention to him," Madeline advised me. "He's nothing but an old flirt."

"That's not a problem," I said. "I like old flirts. Young ones, too, for that matter."

Her voice dropped as she added, "And he probably won't remember you from one day to the next."

"I heard that!" Borden announced. "My memory may be a bit faulty, but there's nothing wrong with my ears. Besides, Maddy dear, you're a fine one to talk. Who was it this morning who couldn't remember where she put her ruby ring last time she wore it? Held up the bus for ten minutes looking for it."

Madeline's gaze dropped to her ringless fingers. "Mary always loved that ring. It seemed only fitting that I wear it in her honor."

"Big as a grape, that ruby was. Don't know how you could misplace something like that."

"I don't either," Madeline replied. "But I'm sure it will show up in a day or two. Most things do, you know."

"Maybe it's in a safe?" I guessed. "Or a lockbox in your room?"

Looking at Madeline's other jewelry, it was easy to believe that the woman had a ring with a ruby the size of a grape. But surely she wouldn't leave something like that out lying around?

She waved a hand dismissively. The light from above glinted off the diamonds on her watch. "There's a safe in the office. We're supposed to use it, but mostly nobody bothers. What's the point of owning pretty things if you can't look at them, or put them on when the mood strikes you?

"Stuff goes missing all the time. Heather Winkleman can *never* find her glasses, and she wears them on a string around her neck. Mostly we just get a good laugh out of it, and everything seems to show up again sooner or later. At our age, we've learned the value of patience. Everything happens in God's own time."

"Not everything, Maddy," Borden said darkly. "Don't forget why we're here."

"I'm so sorry about what happened to Mary," I said. "I know you and she were very good friends."

"The best," Madeline agreed. "Mary was like a sister to me. You better believe that if I knew who was responsible, I might be tempted to knock somebody off myself."

"Now, Maddy, you know it doesn't do any good

to let yourself get all riled up." Borden looked at me and sighed. "It wasn't just the fact that Mary passed on that's so upsetting. It's the way it came about. By the time you get to be our age, well . . . you've lost a lot of friends. It's never easy, but at least you can learn to be accepting about it. But this . . ."

"It didn't need to happen!" Madeline snapped. "At least that's the rumor going around. Catherine, Lynn, the other directors, they're not saying much at all. Treating us like we're all senile, and thinking what we don't know won't hurt us. I guess it never occurred to them that what our imaginations conjure up might be worse than the reality."

I looked at them, incredulous. "You mean you don't know what actually happened?"

Borden and Madeline shook their heads. "Not for a fact. Even the newspapers have been missing from the morning room for the last couple of days. All we know is that Mary died last Sunday and there was something suspicious about it. Regina Mayhew, did you meet her?"

"I don't think so."

"She has a room right out front. She's seen several police cars come and go, but none of those nice young men in uniform come in and talk to us."

"Would you like them to?" I asked.

"Hell, yes!" Borden snorted.

Madeline lifted a brow but didn't admonish him. "Worst thing about growing old," she said, "is that people begin to treat you like a child. They think they're protecting you, but what they're really doing is preventing you from thinking for yourself. Like you're no longer capable of forming a decent opinion. And all this happens in the name of doing what's best for you. Mary was our friend, and Winston Pumpernill is our home. We have a right to know what's going on."

It was probably one of those moments when I should have stopped and thought. But I didn't. I went with my gut.

"Mary Livingston was murdered," I said. "Last Sunday afternoon, shortly after you saw her in the sunroom, she was smothered in her bed."

"I knew it," Borden muttered.

"Right in her own bed," Madeline said. She looked worried, and I felt a pang.

"Who did it?" Borden demanded.

"The police don't know yet. They're investigating."

"Wait 'til I tell Sandy," he said with satisfaction.

"Sandy?"

"One of his cronies," Madeline said. "Men say women gossip, but all the women I've ever known have nothing on Sandy Sandstrum. That man loves to talk. The only thing he likes better is smoking his cigars. That's probably why you didn't meet him. He waits until there's a function going on, then sneaks outside and has a smoke. Of course he isn't even supposed to have cigars, but he pays one of the orderlies to smuggle them in for him. This is a red-letter day for Borden. He almost never gets the scoop on Sandy."

"Just wait until we get back." Borden rubbed his hands in anticipation. "I'll have plenty to tell Sandy today."

"As long as you remember it," I mentioned.

"Don't worry about that," said Madeline. "When something's important to Borden, it sticks in his mind just fine."

"Ha!" said Borden. "I wish. When I was young, I

had a memory like an elephant. Nothing got past me. Now half the time it's in one ear and out the other. I've got a system, though." He opened his coat and pulled out a small pad of paper and a pen. "I make notes, see? I jot stuff down when nobody's looking. That way I can't forget."

"As long as you don't forget where you put your pad."

"Right here." Borden patted his pocket. "I keep it right next to my heart."

The doors to the chapel were opening. People were beginning to move inside and find seats. It was time for the service to begin.

A nurse came and collected Borden and Madeline. I looked around for Aunt Peg. The room had nearly emptied before I found her.

"Let's get some seats near the back," I said.

"Better yet," Aunt Peg whispered, "let's find a place where we can talk."

"But the service is about to start."

"Forget the service," said Peg. "Wait until you hear what I found out."

12

"What?" I said.

When everyone headed into the chapel, we'd gone the other way and slipped outside. Aside from a trio of smokers who were enjoying a few last puffs before the service started, we had the area to ourselves.

Aunt Peg slipped an arm through mine and pulled me close. "Mary Livingston had a lot of money," she said under her breath.

"I know that."

She leaned back and frowned. "Just because this is Greenwich doesn't mean everyone who lives here is rich."

Actually, for the most part, it did. Not that we needed to debate that at the moment.

"I was just talking to Paul inside. He told me the same thing. He also said that money wouldn't have been a motive. The whole family has plenty."

"I'm guessing he didn't mention his cousin, Michael."

"No. Should he have?"

"Michael is Mary's son, her only child. He's also apparently the black sheep of the family. He turned his back on them years ago."

"So why is he important now?"

"Because he showed up last month, eager to get back into his mother's good graces. He rented a little place in Byram, and according to Sylvia, he's been parading around town like he's the prodigal son."

"Not to put too fine a point on it," I said, "but it sounds as though he *is* the prodigal son. How did Mary feel about his return?"

"Just as you might expect, she was thrilled. The same can't be said for Sylvia and the rest of the family, though."

I didn't answer right away. Instead, I gazed out over the lush green lawns that wrapped around the neighboring parochial school. Spring doesn't arrive early in Connecticut, but when it comes, it's a feast for all the senses. Daffodils were in bloom; trees were beginning to bud. The sun felt warm on my face and shoulders. It seemed almost obscene that on such a beautiful day, everyone had gathered to mourn the passing of a vibrant woman who shouldn't have died yet.

I turned back to Aunt Peg. "I can't believe Sylvia Lennox told you all this when you hadn't seen the woman in decades."

"I might have had to do some reading between the lines," Peg admitted. "But the subtext was entirely clear. Besides, Michael is here today. And nobody in there is happy about it. So, of course, he was on her mind; everybody was talking about him."

"Paul wasn't," I said. I wondered why that was. "Which one was Michael?"

"Tall, dark hair, mid-forties. Wearing a rather ill-fitting suit."

I thought for a minute, then shook my head. I hadn't noticed him in the crush inside. "So why hasn't the family welcomed him back?"

"I gather the majority of the relatives are of the impression that he only returned because he needs money."

It figured.

"And now that Mary's dead, does her estate go to him?"

"Not all of it," said Aunt Peg. "There's a family trust. But probably enough to make a difference."

Enough to give Michael a motive, she meant. Under the circumstances, it seemed odd that Paul hadn't said anything to me about his cousin. He'd professed to want his great-aunt's murderer found, then neglected to mention the obvious suspect.

Family dynamics, the eternal mystery.

The last of the smokers stubbed out her cigarette on the walkway and hurried inside. When she glanced our way and held the door for us, Aunt Peg and I took our cue and followed.

I called Sam on my way home and he told me that I had a visitor waiting for me. Detective Edward O'Malley had stopped by to talk to me about Mary Livingston's murder and ended up being entertained by my eight-year-old son instead. When I arrived, Davey was holding a badge and a pair of handcuffs and looking very pleased with himself.

"Detective O'Malley read me my rights," he said.

"I hope that doesn't mean you're in trouble."

"I don't know," said Davey. "I'm supposed to consult an attorney. The police are going to give me one."

Davey is at the stage where he's capable of sounding very grown-up. He doesn't always entirely understand what he's saying, however. Or necessarily what he's heard.

"I don't think Detective O'Malley was entirely serious about that. How was your night with your dad?"

"Terrific. He told me to tell you hi. He and Sam were talking, but when the policeman showed up, he decided he'd better leave."

Bob would, I thought. He'd been enough of a bad boy earlier in life to harbor an innate distrust of men with badges. Faith, meanwhile, was hopping up and down in place and generally making it clear how happy she was to see me again.

I leaned down and gave her a hug. If I'd had a tail, it would have been wagging like crazy, too. Despite my shortcomings, in Faith's eyes, I'm always perfect. Dog ownership, what a deal.

Sam had performed the introductions when I walked in. Now, over Davey's protests, he left me and the detective in the living room and took my son outside to throw a ball around. The Poodles divided themselves between us. Faith and Eve remained with me. Sam's three got up and left.

O'Malley watched the reshuffling with some amusement. "I guess the two of you like big black dogs," he said, as Eve climbed up beside him on the couch and made herself at home. "You've got a pretty full house here."

"Too full," I agreed. "It's just temporary. We're shopping for something more suitable."

Over the past several years, I'd had occasion to meet police detectives from several of the local jurisdictions, Greenwich included. O'Malley and I hadn't crossed paths before, though, which was probably just as well. I liked the idea of having a clean slate—no preconceived opinions; no reason why we couldn't get along famously.

Then he gestured toward Eve, and said, "I'm looking at all these dogs and I don't see any collars, which means they're not wearing any tags. If I was to go downtown and check, would I find out these dogs all had licenses?"

"Yes," I replied mildly. "As I said, at the moment we're in transition. Three are licensed in Redding, where they lived until several weeks ago. These two have licenses from Stamford. They don't wear collars because they're Poodles, and collars would ruin the hair. Would you like to see their tags?"

"Not particularly."

That wasn't surprising. Stamford wasn't O'Malley's jurisdiction; neither was animal control. He'd just felt like flexing his muscles in the hope that I might be intimidated by the show. Another petty bureaucrat who enjoyed exercising his little bit of power. So much for thinking we might get along.

Come to think of it, Bob had been right to run. And maybe Davey did need a lawyer.

"Did you come here today to talk about my dogs?" I asked.

"No. They just took me by surprise, that's all. Being so big and so many of them. I'm more of a cat person myself."

Like I couldn't have guessed that.

"In that case, you should talk to my neighbor, Amber Fine. She loves cats."

He opened a small notebook, consulted something he'd written on the front page, and frowned slightly. "I don't have her name. Was she at the Winston Pumpernill nursing facility with your group last Sunday?"

"No. She simply likes cats."

I shifted in my chair and felt like an idiot. Or maybe like I was talking to one. Things were going well, don't you think?

"Lots of people like cats." O'Malley looked at me suspiciously, as if he was afraid I might be making fun of him. "But you went to Winston Pumpernill with a group of dog people?"

"That's right. The South Avenue Obedience Club."

"What was the purpose of the visit?"

I knew I wasn't the first person with whom he'd spoken. I was equally sure that he already knew the answer to that question. But since he'd bothered to ask, volunteering to waste both his and my time, I figured he deserved a complete response.

"How much do you know about therapy dogs?" I asked.

O'Malley shrugged. Noncommittal. Like everybody with a television set hadn't seen that tactic played out on *Law & Order. I say nothing, and you'll be tempted to spill your guts.*

Right. And in this case, I didn't even have any guts to spill.

"Therapy dogs are pets belonging to volunteers who make visits to nursing and care facilities, hoping to make a difference in the patients' quality of life. Not only is it fun for the residents to have the opportunity to see and interact with dogs, but it's been clinically proven that being able to touch and talk to animals, lowers stress and relieves depression."

"I thought you people were supposed to be obedience competitors."

"For the most part, we are. This is just something the class does on the side, as I discovered when I joined two weeks ago. The visits to Winston Pumpernill had originally been initiated because Paul Lennox's great-aunt was a resident there."

"And that's how you met Mr. Lennox, through the class?"

"Right."

These questions seemed simplistic to me, but then I didn't work for the government. For all I knew, O'Malley might be planning to drag this interview out for the rest of the afternoon, thereby totally destroying any plans I might have had to join Sam and Davey in their game of catch. I wondered, since it was Saturday, if he was getting paid overtime.

"And when did you meet Mary Livingston?"

"Last Sunday."

"The day she died?"

"Yes."

"You'd never had any previous contact with her?"

I frowned in annoyance. "Is there any reason you think I might have?"

"I'm just covering all the bases, Ms. Travis, that's all. So when you went to Winston Pumpernill last week, how long had you known Paul Lennox?"

"Three days."

O'Malley's brow rose. "And yet you accompanied him on a visit to see an elderly relative?"

"I didn't go with Paul, exactly. The entire class

took their dogs and went as a group. It was something they'd prearranged. Something the obedience club had been doing for months."

"But you hadn't been doing it for months?"

I sighed and prayed for patience.

"Would you like me to draw you a diagram?" I asked. "Maybe something with a timeline?"

"No. I'd like you simply to answer the questions."

Even the ones he'd asked two or three times, apparently.

"No, that was my first visit."

"Your first visit with the group, or the first time you'd been to Winston Pumpernill?"

"Both."

I saw what he was getting at. Any idiot would have. Mary Livingston had been fine until I'd gone to the nursing home, and now she was dead. However, considering there'd been no prior connection between me and Mary or any other members of her family, I was hard pressed to see how O'Malley could make that out to be anything more than a coincidence.

"I have absolutely no motive," I said, hoping that might hurry things along a bit.

Unfortunately, all I succeeded in doing was making O'Malley look suspicious again. "Is there a particular reason you think I might need to know that?" he asked.

I tried the shrug-and-be-noncommittal thing. That left both of us sitting in silence. I used the time to pull Faith up into my lap and comb my fingers through her ear hair. O'Malley just sat and stared at me.

After a minute, I couldn't stand it anymore. It

wasn't the tension that got to me, more like the boredom. Good thing I didn't really have something to hide.

"I have an alibi," I said. "When Mary Livingston was killed, Faith and I were in the sunroom with a whole lot of other people."

O'Malley glanced down and pretended to consult his notes. "As I understand it, people were coming and going from that room all afternoon. So unless there's someone in particular who might have noticed your whereabouts . . ."

"I talked to lots of different people. They might not remember me specifically, but they'd probably remember Faith. She's pretty memorable."

I gestured in her direction. The Poodle heard her name and lifted her head. She looked back and forth between O'Malley and me as if waiting to see which one of us was going to ask the next question.

You'd think that even a man who liked cats would have been impressed by her perception. No go. In fact, I got the distinct feeling that the detective wasn't much impressed by anything I had to say.

"Let's approach this from a different direction," he said. "How long were you and your group at Winston Pumpernill that afternoon?"

I thought back. "More than an hour, and probably less than two."

"You saw Mary Livingston, alive and well, at the beginning of your visit?"

"Yes."

"And when you left—again as a group—she was already dead."

"That's what we were told, yes. Paul came running out to the door as we were leaving and handed Cora to Steve. He said that something had happened to his aunt."

O'Malley looked up. "Cora?"

"His Welsh Corgi."

The detective wanted to roll his eyes. I could just tell. That was hardly my fault. Ask a dog person questions, I thought, and you're going to get dog details.

"Did you see anything you would consider unusual or suspicious during the time you were there?"

"No."

"Nobody needs a fast answer," said O'Malley. "Feel free to stop and think about that."

"I have thought about it. I mean, wouldn't you? We were *right there*, and none of us had the slightest inkling what was going on. It makes you think back and wonder what you should have done differently." Lips pursed in annoyance, I shook my head. "I haven't come up with a damn thing."

Something came and went briefly in O'Malley's eyes. Empathy perhaps. Maybe he didn't have a damn thing to go on either.

"Bear in mind, though," I said, "as I mentioned earlier, that was my first visit to Winston Pumpernill. So although everything seemed normal to me, I wouldn't exactly know what normal is."

"No disturbances? Nobody behaving in a way you wouldn't expect them to?"

I shrugged. "Mostly I was paying attention to our group. Everyone seemed fine, but again, I don't really know any of them well enough to know what to expect. You'd be better off talking to the rest of the obedience club members about that."

"We intend to." O'Malley flipped his notebook shut.

"You've spoken to Mary Livingston's family?"

"We have."

"Did anyone mention Mary's son? She has a son named Michael who's been out of touch with the family until recently."

"So I heard." He edged away from Eve, then braced a hand on the arm of the sofa and rose. "Considering that you claim not to know any of these people, I'm wondering how you happen to know that."

So much for trying to be helpful. I supposed I should have seen that coming.

"I went to the memorial service yesterday," I said.

"And he was there?"

I nodded and let O'Malley think what he would. That seemed like a better idea than admitting that Aunt Peg and I had been poking around asking questions.

He pulled a business card out of his pocket. "You think of anything I need to know, you'll give me a call, right?"

"Of course."

The Poodles and I walked him to the door. O'Malley's car was parked along the curb. Watching through the window, I saw him open the driver's door, then pause to stare back at the house for a minute before sliding into the seat.

Part of me wondered what he was thinking.

And another part was pretty sure I didn't want to know.

13

Sunday morning we got up and went house hunting, yet again.

When I'd thought of Sam, Davey, and me living together, I'd harbored rosy fantasies of the three of us spending our weekends doing things as a family, such as going on outings to places like the Nature Center or Binney Park. In the time since Sam and I had gotten married, however, our lives had been so hectic, that virtually the only activity we managed to do as a threesome was look for another place to live. I was pretty sure that said something about the state of the modern American family, and equally sure that it wasn't something good.

"I've combed through the Stamford listings up, down, and sideways," Marilyn said. She handed Sam and me a sheaf of pages as we all climbed into her car. "There are some possibilities in other towns, but I've only got one new house to show you here, and I can tell you right now you won't like it."

Marilyn was the best kind of real estate agent,

the kind who actually listened to what her clients had to say. She didn't try to convince us that we wanted something in a higher price range or a fancier town. Instead, she accepted our parameters and worked diligently within them.

"What's wrong with it?" Sam asked.

"Nothing." Marilyn glanced back over her shoulder to check for traffic—usually nonexistent on our small street—then pulled away from the curb. "It just isn't what you told me you're looking for. For one thing, it's new construction."

"I don't mind that," I said, picturing Palladian windows, walk-in closets, and granite countertops.

Our current house had been built half a century earlier, one of a whole neighborhood just like it that had been thrown together quickly to provide affordable housing for returning World War II veterans. Although it was cozy and well built, it lacked all but the most basic amenities. The idea of a modern kitchen and updated bathrooms sounded like heaven to me.

"It has eight thousand square feet of living space," said Marilyn.

I took the beautiful house I'd just envisioned and doubled it in size. All right, so it was more room than we needed. Well, actually *a lot* more room than we needed . . .

"On a half-acre lot."

Oh.

My shoulders slumped. "It's a McMansion, isn't it?"

"Pretty much," Marilyn admitted.

That pejorative term was being applied to much of the new housing in Fairfield County. As far as developers were concerned, any lot with a building permit was fair game. Older houses, even those in good condition, were sold as tear-downs; and hundreds of homogenized mansions were being erected in their stead.

"Do you want to look?" asked Marilyn. "Or should I just cross it off the list?"

Sam and I exchanged a glance. Half an acre wasn't nearly enough land for a house that size and our five Poodles. Plus, with that many dogs, we'd need more of a buffer between ourselves and the neighbors.

"I want to see a McMansion," Davey chimed in from the backseat. It was the first house he'd sounded enthusiastic about.

"Then let's go have a look," I said.

By lunchtime we'd seen five houses, all unsuitable for one reason or another. It wasn't as though we were being extraordinarily picky; just that the right house for us simply wasn't on the market at the moment. Judging by what we'd seen so far, it was beginning to look like I might spend the rest of my married life squished into six small rooms.

Then I glanced over at Sam. He caught my eye and smiled. We reached toward each other, laced our fingers together, and both squeezed.

Maybe making do wasn't such a bad thing after all.

To my surprise, neither Steve nor the administrators had canceled our visit to Winston Pumpernill that afternoon.

"We're on the calendar," Steve had said when he'd called the night before. "Catherine hates to cancel a scheduled activity. She says the residents thrive on consistency and knowing what to expect. And they're expecting us to appear tomorrow at two. Paul, of course, won't be able to make it, and maybe one or two others. So I really hope you and Faith will be able to fill in."

It didn't take much to convince me.

Let's see, I thought. What were my options? Driving around in a car to look at houses I didn't want? Or going to Winston Pumpernill, where I might find out more about Mary's murder? The latter definitely had more appeal. At the very least, I knew Faith and I would enjoy spending time with the elderly residents.

So while Sam and Davey opted to keep house hunting, I picked up Faith and headed down to Greenwich. I was running a little late; the group had already gone inside by the time I arrived. I rang the bell beside the front door, and Lynn Stephanopolus came out to meet me.

As she'd done the first time we'd visited, Lynn immediately put a hand down to greet Faith. The Poodle responded by sitting and offering the woman her paw. I'd never taught my dogs any tricks before; but after having seen how much the patients had enjoyed Coach's performance the previous week, I'd decided to add a few enhancements to Faith's education. She had always enjoyed learning new things and had quickly picked up a small repertoire of stunts.

Lynn laughed, took the offered paw, and shook it gently.

"Catherine's already taken the others back to the sunroom," she said. "Usually she's too busy to take such a personal interest, but after what happened, we're keeping an extra close eye on things. Come on, I'll walk you back to join them."

"I hate to bother you. Faith and I can find our own way, if you like."

"It's no trouble at all. I was ready for a break." Lynn was already striding down the long hallway. "Besides . . ."

"You don't want anyone wandering around unescorted," I finished for her as Faith and I caught up, then fell into step beside her.

"Pretty much. I hope you're not offended by that."

"Not at all, I can see your point. I imagine this must be the first time you've had to cope with something like this."

"Thank goodness," Lynn said fervently. "Just about everything around here has been in turmoil ever since. I hope the police figure out what happened soon, so we can move on and try to get things back to normal. God knows we're all ready to do that."

I wondered if the "all" she referred to meant the residents or the administration. Although I could see how the latter would want to put such an occurrence behind them, I couldn't imagine that those who had known Mary would get over her loss that quickly. Granted, I didn't know much about the inner workings of the facility, but Mary Livingston had seemed like an integral and well-liked member of the population.

"I imagine the other residents must miss Mary a great deal," I said.

"Of course they do."

Abruptly, Lynn stopped walking. I shot right past her, with Faith trotting obediently at my side. We spun around and doubled back. Lynn looked worried, like she was concerned she wasn't getting her point across.

"Caring for the elderly can be hard," she said

after a minute. "You tend to get emotionally attached, whether you want to or not. But you have to be realistic, too. And the reality is, sometimes we have to cope with illness and death. Many of the patients here have already outlived most of their friends and family. It's always difficult for them, as well as the staff and administrators, when someone passes on. But it's the nature of what we do. That doesn't mean that we're not affected by it, however. Everybody here loved Mary, and we all miss her."

Lynn sighed. "But in this case, things are especially difficult. Until last week, none of us had any idea that such a thing as murder was even possible here. It's not something we gave any thought to. Or, to be honest, had initiated any precautions against. It never occurred to us that we needed to."

"You felt you were safe here," I said.

"Exactly. And now we've lost that sense of security. Or that innocence, if you will. Of course, we've always done thorough background checks on the staff, and we keep our medicines securely locked up, but we want the residents to think of this facility as their home, a place where they don't have to worry about anything going wrong. What happened here last Sunday has ruined that. Not just for the patients, but for all of us."

I understood how she felt. Perhaps even better than Lynn might have imagined. I'd been the victim of an act of violence myself, and I knew how such an occurrence changed everything.

A week earlier, the staff at Winston Pumpernill had thought they were doing a good job, that they had everything under control. Now they knew there were certain things that were simply beyond the scope of their management. It might have seemed like a small change, but its ramifications were monumental.

"It makes sense that you would want the police to find the murderer and remove him from your midst as quickly as possible."

"Actually." Lynn shot me a wary look out of the corner of her eye. "We're hoping that the person who was capable of doing such a terrible thing isn't part of our family at all."

"You'd rather it was a visitor."

She nodded.

"Like maybe someone from the obedience club?"

"No offense," Lynn said quickly, "but I have to hope that, don't I? The alternative is that somehow in the time I've been here at Winston Pumpernill, I've been living with a monster. I've been working side by side with someone who was capable of committing such a heinous act, and I didn't even realize it."

Annoyance got her moving again. She started to walk, and Faith, always quick on the uptake, caught up before I did.

"How long have you worked here?"

"Three years in June," Lynn said. "And for the most part, I've loved every minute of it. The administration is top-notch, and the majority of the patients are wonderful. The kind of people who— if you had met them in a different context—you would have felt privileged to call your friends. I've never understood why American society treats the elderly like a disposable commodity. It's inhuman, not to mention incredibly shortsighted. These seniors' knowledge and experience should be revered as one of our greatest resources. . . ."

She paused and smiled self-consciously. "I'm lecturing, aren't I?"

"Go ahead, I don't mind. And for the record, I totally agree with you. I have an aunt in her mid-sixties who can outthink and outdance most people half her age. And to our chagrin, she does so regularly."

"You see?" said Lynn. "That's exactly what I'm talking about. Why should physical age be allowed to limit our expectations? It's crazy. It's backward—"

"It's human nature," I said.

"Well, screw human nature—it's just plain wrong." As if hearing her own words for the first time, Lynn suddenly looked horrified.

I grinned and was glad to see her shoulders relax.

"Sorry," she said. "I guess this whole mess has gotten me more upset than I realized. Just the thought of someone as good and as kind as Mary being overpowered just because she wasn't physically capable of defending herself makes me absolutely sick."

"Me, too," I agreed. "I imagine you wouldn't have any idea why someone would have wanted to murder one of your residents?"

"I wish I *could* answer that question," Lynn said. "In my spare time, I love reading mystery novels. I'm one of those compulsive types. I drive myself crazy trying to decipher the clues and figure out the ending ahead of time. So don't think it hasn't occurred to me that this is a real-life mystery right in front of me. And now, when it counts, I find I haven't the slightest idea what went wrong."

"Have you met Mary's son?" I asked.

"Michael? No. I've heard about him, though."

"From Mary?"

"From my boss, Catherine. Apparently he hadn't been a presence in Mary's life for quite some time."

"Until recently," I said.

"Right. I gather he showed up unexpectedly. When he did, Mary's family issued very specific instructions that he wasn't to be admitted to see her."

"Do you know why?"

"They said they didn't want him to upset her. That she was too fragile to handle a visit from someone who was sure to be a disruptive presence. Frankly, it sounded like a lot of baloney to me. He was her son, for Pete's sake. It should have been left up to Mary to decide whether she wanted to see him."

"You mean she didn't even know that he'd returned to Greenwich?"

"Not at first. We were supposed to be keeping that information from her, too. But somehow she found out he was around."

"Maybe he called her?" I suggested.

"No." Lynn shook her head. "All our calls go through the switchboard. Because of the instructions from the family, a call like that wouldn't have been put through."

"Interesting," I mused aloud. "So your security has been breached twice recently."

Lynn didn't look happy. "At least the first time, it was for a good cause. Because once Mary found out Michael had returned, she very much wanted to see him."

"And did she?"

"Unfortunately, no. Once again, the family stepped in and took control of the situation. Just

one more instance of an elderly person being rele-
gated to minor status even where her own personal affairs were concerned. Eventually Mary was
able to sway a couple of family members over to
her side, though. They'd finally set up a meeting.
Mary was supposed to see Michael last week."

"And did she?"

We'd reached the door to the sunroom. Faith
paused in the doorway, and when she saw the
other dogs inside the room, woofed softly under
her breath. I reached down and stroked her neck
to steady her. I wasn't moving until I heard what
the administrator had to say.

"No," said Lynn, "it never happened."

"Why not?"

"Because Michael was supposed to be here Monday morning. And by Sunday afternoon, Mary was
dead."

14

Lynn left us just outside the sunroom. Or, rather, she passed us along to our next escort. In contrast to our last visit, this time the entrance to the room was being watched. An orderly, whose name tag identified him as Jay, stepped aside when we approached and held the door open for us.

Jay was big, with broad shoulders and taut, sinewy arms. He had smooth skin the color of dark chocolate, and his wiry black hair was cropped close around his skull. "Pleased to meet you," he said in a surprising soft voice as his large hand swallowed my much smaller one.

Then he squatted down so that he was eye level with Faith. "Hey, big Poodle."

Seeing her cue, Faith sat down and offered him a paw.

"Her name's Faith," I said as Jay shook the paw and returned it gently to the floor.

"We had a Poodle when I was little," he said, rising to his feet. "Name of Frenchie, on account of, you know . . . French Poodle?"

The Poodle breed actually originated in Germany, and the stylized trim worn in the show ring is a remnant of a traditional German hunting clip, but Jay's designation was a common mistake.

"I'll bet he was the best dog you ever owned," I said with a smile.

"You got that right." He nodded toward Faith. "I saw her last week, but I didn't have time to come over and say hello. She's a big one, isn't she? I didn't know they made Poodles that big."

"Faith is a Standard Poodle. It's the largest of the three varieties. You probably had a Mini?"

"I guess so." Jay held up his hands about fifteen inches apart. "Like this size."

"That would have been a Mini. Toys are the really little ones."

"The yappy ones."

"Sometimes," I said. "And sometimes not. As with any dog, it's all in how well they've been trained by their owners. Lots of toy dogs are very well behaved."

"Your Poodle looks like she's had a lot of training. Is she a show dog or something?"

"She used to be." I reached down and ruffled my hand through Faith's topknot. "She's retired now."

Jay laughed out loud. "A dog that's retired. That's a good one. I never met a dog that had a job before."

He glanced over his shoulder at the rest of the room. "If she's retired, then she's in the right place, considering this is like a retirement home. Most of the people here are retired from something or other."

As we spoke, I'd been looking around as well. During our previous visit, the sunroom had been filled with patients, obedience club members, and the occasional attendant. It wasn't until Minnie and Coach had begun their performance that nurses and staff members had appeared from other parts of the building. Today, however, there were at least as many staff members in the room as there were visitors. They were trying to remain unobtrusive, and most were staying in the background, but their presence was unmistakable.

I was looking at heightened security. The precautions were probably unavoidable; still, I was sorry to see them. It was just one more thing that would make Winston Pumpernill feel a little less like home to the people who lived there.

"Some of these people, you know . . ." Jay paused, then chose his words with care. "They were pretty impressive in real life. They had nice houses, good jobs. They had some power. It's kind of sad to see them here now."

"But they're happy here," I said. "Aren't they?"

"I guess they seem to be."

Jay looked to be in his mid-twenties; he still had everything ahead of him. The concept of wanting to slow down probably wasn't even on his radar screen.

"It just isn't what you want for yourself," I guessed.

"Hell, no. Me? I'm going out with a bang."

The eternal optimism of youth. "Not anytime soon, I hope?"

"Nah." Jay cupped an arm around my back and ushered me into the room. "Not anytime soon. Don't you worry about that. Now look here, I shouldn't be monopolizing your time. Mr. Beamish over there is staring at us like he thinks I'm talking too much. Probably right, too. That man, he's just sitting there waiting for a visit from a pretty lady and a big Poodle. You'd better get going now."

"I will," I said. "But thanks. It was nice meeting you."

"You, too," Jay replied.

Mr. Beamish was indeed eager for a visit from a big Poodle. Seated in a wheelchair in the sun with a lap robe thrown across his legs, the old man reached out his hand as soon as he saw Faith head in his direction. His face creased in a broad smile.

"I knew if I waited long enough, someone would make their way over here and find me," he said.

"No complaining now," said the nurse standing behind his chair. A name tag affixed to her track-suit revealed her name to be Molly. "You haven't even been in here but five minutes."

The old man's eyes twinkled. "Maybe so, but at my age, every five minutes counts. Come on over here, girl. What a pretty doggie you are."

Faith preened from side to side, as charmed by the older man as I was. She sniffed his fingers, then pressed her body up against his legs, so he could run a gnarled hand down her back.

"Her name is Faith," I said. "And I'm Melanie."

"Pleased to meet you, miss. Sit down and stay a spell. I think I've met most of the other dog handlers, but I've never seen you before. Why is that?"

I dragged over a chair and had a seat. Molly, seeing that everything was under control, faded back to give us some space. At a nearby card table, a spirited game of bridge was in progress. The nurse strolled over to kibitz.

"This is only my second visit," I said. "Faith and I

just joined the obedience class, and we came here last Sunday for the first time."

"Not a great start for you, was it? I guess you know what happened to poor Mary Livingston."

"Yes." I'd only spoken to Borden and Madeline the day before, but word had evidently gotten around.

"Hell of a shame, pardon my French."

"Yes, it was."

"Hard to imagine what this world is coming to when something like that is even possible."

"We . . . all of us . . ." I gestured toward the rest of the obedience club members, who were scattered around the room. ". . . are really sorry about what happened. And we're sorry it happened while we were here."

"Can't say it had anything to do with you and your dogs. Leastwise, I wouldn't think so." Mr. Beamish frowned, peering at me closely. "Would you?"

"Um, no."

"Me neither. So that's enough of that. Why talk about something depressing when you don't have to? Aren't you supposed to be cheering me up?"

"I think so." When he smiled at me and lifted his brow, I couldn't help but smile back. "But I'm new at this, so you tell me. All I know for sure is that I'm supposed to be letting you play with my dog. You know, since you're not allowed to have pets here, and maybe you miss having them around."

While we were speaking, Faith had climbed quietly up the side of his chair and placed her front legs across his lap. Her head was resting against his chest. His fingers were curled through her thick coat. The two of them were breathing in unison.

"Never had a pet before in my life," he said cheerfully. "Can't miss what you never knew."

"Didn't you just tell me that you knew all the other handlers? I thought you were a regular for the dog club visits."

"Of course I'm a regular. Look around, wouldn't you be?"

I did. The room didn't look any different than the last time I'd scanned it a few minutes earlier.

"All those nice young women want to come and pay an old man a visit, you think I'd be crazy enough to stay in my room?" He shook his head, looking very pleased with himself. "Nope, not a chance."

Young, I thought, was a relative term. The ages in our group ranged from Kelly in her late twenties to Stacey's early forties. Compared with Mr. Beamish, however, I supposed we were a group of youngsters.

"Everybody doing okay over here?"

Molly materialized beside us. She stared hard for a moment at Faith, and belatedly I wondered whether dogs were allowed to climb up on the patients. Then the nurse's gaze lifted, and she smiled.

"Looks like you're making friends, all right. I have to run out for a minute, but I'll be right back. Our bridge group is breaking up, and two of the players have decided they'd like to try another game, but that nice leather backgammon set seems to be missing from the cabinet. Everybody knows the games aren't supposed to leave this room, but somehow that doesn't stop them from walking all over the building. Let me just go see if I can hunt up another set."

While Molly was gone, the bridge players got up from their table and wandered over to say hello. I already knew Borden Grey and, luckily, he seemed to remember who I was. He introduced me to his partner, Sandy Sandstrum. It was no wonder the foursome had broken up; these two were still bickering over the outcome of the rubber they'd just finished.

"When I open with one heart, you aren't supposed to come back and say three hearts when you're only holding two of them in your hand," Sandy said to Borden. He looked over at me, "Isn't that right?"

"Umm . . . I don't know. I've never played bridge."

"Well, then, you can take my word on it, it's just plain wrong." His hand reached down absently to stroke Faith's hindquarter. She wagged her tail in reply. "I'll tell you this," he said to Borden. "We would do much better as partners if you could remember some of the rules of the game."

"It's not my memory that was at fault, it was your playing," Borden replied. "I had fourteen points and two aces. That's an opening hand right there. Anyone would have jumped in my position."

"Jumped maybe, but not in hearts. Why didn't you bid your own suit?"

"Because I didn't have a suit, so I figured we ought to go with yours. It was perfectly clear to me."

"Clear as mud," Sandy muttered. He pulled over a chair and sat down. "I went to game when we didn't even have the majority of the cards in our own suit, and we went down in flames. Thanks, partner."

"Anytime," Borden said with a grin. "Don't you mind, Sandy," he told me. "He takes his games a little too seriously."

"If you're going to play," Sandy grumbled, "play to win. No point in doing it any other way."

"Here, here." Mr. Beamish thumped a fist on the

arm of his wheelchair. Startled, Faith lifted her head. Bracing her feet gently on either side of him, she hopped back down to the ground.

"I heard about you," Sandy said to me as Faith came back to my side. "Borden said you were the one that gave him the news."

"I guess I was." I hoped that was a good thing.

"Thank you for that, then. There's nothing worse than being coddled like we're a bunch of old fogies who wouldn't know how to handle the truth. At least now we know what we're up against. This way we can be on the lookout."

"For what?"

"You know, a killer." Sandy's voice dropped to a confidential tone. "A murderer among us, so to speak."

I must have gone slightly pale, because Borden clapped a hand heartily onto my shoulder. "Now, Melanie, don't you pay any attention to old Sandy there. He's always had a flair for the dramatic. None of us has any intention of hunting down any murderers."

"Good," I said faintly.

"Speak for yourself, you big chicken," Sandy snapped, and Mr. Beamish began to laugh.

"Now, Harry." Borden looked wounded. "You wouldn't be laughing at me, would you?"

"I'm laughing at the whole lot of you," said Harry Beamish. "It looks to me like the only one around here with any sense is that big black Poodle." He glanced at me and added, "No offense, miss."

"None taken. But since we're already on the subject, do the three of you mind if I ask a question?"

"About Mary, you mean?"

"What else would she mean?" Sandy inquired

tartly. "That's what we've been talking about, isn't it?"

"We don't mind," said Harry. "You go ahead and ask."

I paused for a moment and glanced around. The majority of the residents and staff in the room were occupied with other members of the obedience club. Molly hadn't returned yet, and nobody seemed to be paying any attention to us.

"I guess the three of you probably knew Mary pretty well," I said.

"Some better than others." Sandy offered a broad wink.

Borden reached over and slapped him on the knee. "Cut that out! The lady is trying to ask a simple question here. No sense in your clouding things up with all sorts of gossip and innuendo."

Actually, gossip was exactly what I was looking for. That and a little insight into how things really worked at Winston Pumpernill. According to Madeline, Sandy was the man who regularly had his forbidden cigars smuggled into the nursing home. I wondered how much he'd be willing to admit about the route his contraband supplies traveled.

"Did any of you ever hear Mary talk about her son, Michael?" I asked.

The three of them shared a glance.

"Only recently," Sandy said after a pause. "And then not very much. Why?"

"I know he'd just arrived back in Greenwich after a long absence. I heard he was anxious to see his mother, and that she was equally anxious to see him."

Borden hung his head; he looked down at the hands that he'd clasped in his lap. "Her family was against it," he said quietly. "Didn't even want her to know he was here. We didn't think that was right."

"I can see why you wouldn't," I agreed. "I only met Mary once, but she seemed quite capable of making her own decisions."

"That's what we thought," Harry piped up. "When she got word that he was around and nobody had let her know, she was pretty upset. And let me tell you, she had every right to be."

"That's what I wanted to ask you about," I said. "I know the family tried to keep the news from her. So how did Mary find out that Michael was here?"

"That part's easy," Sandy said with a sly grin. "You know the old expression, "Money talks"? Well, that's just as true here as it is everywhere else. When you want access to something badly enough, a means can be found to obtain it."

"Like your cigars," I said.

Sandy frowned at Borden. "Tattletale."

"Right," Borden snorted. "As if you can keep a secret."

Sandy leaned toward me and said in a low voice, "Only reason Borden doesn't blurt out everything he knows is because he forgets most of it the minute after he learns it."

"I heard that!" said Borden. "Why do people keep saying things right in front of me like they think I'm not even here?"

"Because they know how bad your memory is," Harry chortled. "Even if you get mad, you wind up forgiving us because you always forget what you were mad about in the first place."

"I guess that's true," Borden admitted.

"Back to the cigars," I said firmly. Monitoring this crew was like trying to herd cats.

"What was the question again?" Sandy asked.

"How did Mary find out that her son was back in town?"

"Somebody passed her a note," said Harry. "That's where the news came from."

"Who?"

Sandy glanced toward the orderly who was still standing by the door. "We figure Jay must have given it to her. You want something brought in under the table, he's the one to see."

Harry nodded in agreement. "It was a note from her son, Michael, all right. And it made her mad as blazes."

"I remember that," Borden said. "I'd never seen Mary lose her temper like that. She was such a gentle person. Hard to imagine that something could set her off that way."

"Do you know what the note said?" I asked.

The three men looked at each other. "I never saw it," said Sandy. "You guys?" The other two shook their heads.

"So you don't actually know whether she was angry about Michael's presence being kept from her, or whether it was something he'd written that upset her?"

"I guess not," Harry admitted.

"She was planning to see him, though," said Sandy. "Said there were some things that needed to be set straight between them."

"What things?" I asked, but nobody answered.

For once, not one of them had anything to say.

15

An hour later, as Faith and I were leaving Winston Pumpernill, Minnie and Coach caught up to us on the front steps.

"I saw what you were doing in there," she said.

I stopped and turned to face her. Faith, who'd bounded a couple of steps ahead of me, hit the end of the leash, spun a quick circle on her hindquarter, and came trotting back. She hates it when I do something she hasn't anticipated.

"What are you talking about?" I asked. The other members of the obedience group filed around us and continued on to their cars. There was something in Minnie's tone that I hadn't liked at all. "I was doing the same thing you were."

"You were asking questions."

The administrators of the facility had a right to an opinion about my behavior. And perhaps Steve and Paul, too, since I was there under their aegis. But what I did or didn't do was none of Minnie's business.

Keeping my voice purposely mild, I stared her down, "So?"

"So I guess that means you really are a detective, like Steve said at class."

"Not a detective," I corrected, "more like an interested bystander. Someone who would really like to see Mary Livingston's murderer found and brought to justice."

"Geez, are you for real? I thought we were just fooling around the other night. You mean you actually investigate things?"

"Sometimes."

"And you, like, solve crimes?"

"Occasionally."

"And you're going to solve this one?"

With each question, Minnie's tone had grown more incredulous. Now she was staring at me like I had suddenly grown a pair of spiked horns. Being the object of that much scrutiny was somewhat unnerving.

"I don't know," I said with a shrug. "We'll see."

I glanced down at Faith. Having been caught flatfooted a minute earlier, she was at my side, nose tipped upward, watching to see what I was going to do next. What a good dog.

I cued her with my hand and hopped down the last step. The Volvo was parked at the near end of the row. All that stood between me and the opportunity to escape was one very annoyed-looking woman. And a large Standard Schnauzer.

"But you're working on it," Minnie persisted, not allowing herself to be left behind.

"Yes, I suppose I am. Does that bother you?"

"Should it?"

I stopped again, exasperated. My key was out and in my hand. I'd already beeped the locks.

"I have no idea," I said. "Is there something you'd like to talk about?"

"Oh, like what? Like you think I should confess to you?"

"That depends." This conversation was growing stranger by the moment. "Do you have something you want to confess?"

I had a cell phone. And although I didn't happen to know the number of the Greenwich police station, I could press nine-one-one. If Minnie wanted to confess to Mary Livingston's murder, she could do so directly. I wouldn't even have to be involved.

Except that Minnie didn't answer my question.

So much for the possibility of an easy solution, I thought.

I opened the car door and loaded Faith into the backseat. The Volvo had been sitting in the sun, and the interior was warm. I rolled down both windows on the passenger side.

"Look," Minnie said finally, "it's not what you're thinking."

"Until you followed me out here," I told her, "I wasn't thinking anything."

"Don't try to play dumb. I know you heard what Steve said the other night."

I thought back. Had Steve said something incriminating? My mind was a blank. "Steve said lots of things. I'm not sure I know—"

"Can we go somewhere and talk?"

"Sure," I agreed. The way things were going, she probably would have followed me home if I hadn't.

The manicured grounds of the nursing home spread out around us like a verdant blanket. At various places around the lawn, hardwood benches had been placed beneath trees that were not yet in bloom. It was still early enough in the year, however, that feeling the sun on our backs was preferable to the shade that would come later.

"How about out there?" I said, gesturing. "We could take the dogs and go sit on a bench."

"Fine by me."

I retrieved Faith from the car, and the four of us walked across the lawn. I wondered whether we were being watched from inside the building. Considering the extra security precautions that were now in place, it seemed likely. Good reason, I decided, not to unhook Faith's leash and let her run free.

Minnie must have felt the same way, because when we sat, she gave Coach the "down" command. The Schnauzer lay at her feet and cradled his head between his paws.

"Everybody has things in their past they're not proud of," Minnie said before Faith and I had even gotten settled. "I guess I'm no exception."

"Let me stop you right there. There's no reason you have to tell me anything you don't want to. I'm not an official detective. I don't work with the police. Maybe this is none of my business."

That sounded pretty good, right? Still, I'd be the first to admit I was hoping like crazy that she wouldn't take me up on it. So what if what she was about to confess had nothing to do with me? By now she had me curious as hell. In fact, if Minnie changed her mind and walked away, I'd probably have to go digging around in her past and find out this stuff for myself.

"Steve and I had an affair," Minnie blurted out.

I waited, hoping she would add something more. She didn't.

That was it? I thought. *That* was the big secret?

Based on the way they behaved around one another, I'd suspected as much already. I also couldn't
see why the news made any difference.

"People have affairs all the time," I said.

"Steve's an idiot."

That surprised a laugh out of me. "You wouldn't
be the first woman to say that after the fact."

"Yes, well, it took me a while to figure it out. And
before I did, we were pretty close."

"How long were you together?"

"Fifteen months. At one point, I even thought
we might be heading toward getting married."

"Did Steve think so, too?"

"Apparently not," Minnie said with a frown. "We
had a bit of a blowup over the subject. That was
the beginning of the end."

The slats of the bench felt warm against my
back. I leaned back and rested my arm along the
top. Faith and Coach were lying nose to nose at
our feet, both of them snoozing in the sun. There
were worse ways to spend a sunny spring afternoon.

"So how come you still train with him?"

"Why not?" asked Minnie. "He's good; the best in
Fairfield County, anyway. Why should I give that up
just because we're not sleeping together anymore?"

"Maybe because it's obvious that the two of you
don't get along very well?"

"If we don't get along, that's Steve's problem,
not mine."

I sat in silence and enjoyed the view.

"Besides," she added after a minute, "maybe I
enjoy needling him a bit every now and then."

Yes, I thought, remembering back to the first
class Faith and I had attended. She did.

On the other hand, if an educated guess on my part would have told me that Steve and Minnie had a past, a second conjecture might have brought me to the conclusion that Steve and Kelly Marx were sharing a present. Right under Minnie's nose.

"And maybe he enjoys needling you, too," I said.

"You mean Kelly?"

I nodded.

"I told you he was an idiot."

That was a cheap shot.

"I don't know," I said. "Kelly seems nice enough."

"I imagine she *is* nice enough," Minnie said in a dismissive tone. "Why wouldn't she be? It's that dog of hers that's ridiculous. Steve would never put up with behavior like that from one of his own dogs. Or from Coach, for that matter. That's how I know he isn't serious about her. He's just biding his time with Kelly, waiting for something better to come along."

"And do you think she's biding her time with him?"

Minnie shrugged. "How should I know? Why should I even care?"

Good question. If I knew the answer to that, I might even have known why the two of us were sitting on a bench in the sun discussing the topic in the first place. Since Minnie didn't seem inclined to enlighten me, I decided to prod her along.

"What does all this have to do with Mary Livingston?"

"I'm getting to that," Minnie said. "I just wanted to give you some background first. You know, so you'll understand the context."

I nodded in what I hoped was an encouraging

way. Minnie folded and unfolded her hands in her lap.

"When I was with Steve," she said, "I told him some things about my past. Things that I assumed he'd keep in confidence. But now we're obviously not together anymore, and it's beginning to look like my secrets are fair game."

"So we're back to what he said the other night?" In the interim, I'd been replaying the scene in my mind. "Steve was talking about how any one of us could be a suspect. And he implied that the police might want to take a closer look at some of us than others."

Minnie nodded. "That was his not-so-subtle way of taking a jab at me. The main thing you need to know about Steve is that he's a control freak. He has to have everything exactly his own way or he gets all bent out of shape. That's probably why he and Kelly get along. She doesn't seem like the kind of woman who's capable of much independent thought."

That was cheap shot number two, in case you're keeping track. And as it happened, I was. For a woman who was supposedly over her past love, Minnie sure enjoyed slipping in a few jabs of her own.

"And you refused to let Steve control you," I guessed.

"You have to understand, he starts out like this really nice guy. The whole 'I'm in charge' thing doesn't happen overnight. But little by little things happen that eat away at you. In the beginning, I didn't even realize what was going on. When I did, of course, I stood up to him. I had to stand up to him. . . ."

When her voice trailed away, I turned to look at

her. Minnie wouldn't meet my gaze. Her lower lip was trembling, as though she might be on the verge of tears. Deliberately, I looked away again, giving her time to collect herself and her thoughts.

"I was involved in an abusive relationship once before," Minnie said when she was ready. "I knew the signs, damn it. I was stupid enough to ignore them the first time, but I certainly wasn't about to let it happen again."

"Was Steve physically abusive to you?" I asked gently.

"No." She gave her head a firm shake. "Never. And seeing the way he handles the dogs, I doubt that he ever would have been. In fact, that was one of the things that attracted me to him in the first place, his gentleness. With Steve, it's more of a mind game. He likes to believe he can outthink people, outplay them, if you will. That's what he's trying to do now, manipulate me with the threat of revealing something I told him about my past."

"About the other relationship you were involved in before him?"

Minnie gazed out over the lawn. "I was married when I was very young."

"And now you're divorced?"

"Widowed."

That was a surprise. I'd assumed Minnie was only a couple of years older than me. She was young to have lost a husband.

When I didn't comment right away, she drew in a deep breath and slowly let it out. Then, for the first time since we'd sat down, Minnie shifted around to look me straight in the eye.

"I killed him," she said.

I guess I'm not very good at hiding my emotions. Because not only did I start in my seat, I also managed to inadvertently kick Faith. The Poodle leaped up in response. For some reason, that made Minnie laugh.

"Don't rush off," she said. "Despite some evidence to the contrary, I'm not actually dangerous."

"Sorry," I mumbled, settling Faith back down at my feet. "I didn't think you were. You just surprised me, that's all."

"Shocked is more like it." Minnie looked satisfied by the reaction her words had produced.

Since she didn't mind discussing the event, there didn't seem to be any need for reticence on my part. "How did your husband die?"

"I shot him. The bastard deserved it."

"The earlier, abusive relationship?"

Minnie nodded. "Except with Dan, when the time came that I realized I needed to get out, he refused to let me go. Like it was his choice, instead of mine. I packed my bags and filed for divorce. That's when he started stalking me. I reported him to the police; I took out a restraining order. None of it did a damn bit of good. The authorities didn't do a thing to help."

"So you took matters into your own hands."

"Damn straight. And trust me, in my shoes you would have done the same thing. I went out and bought a gun for protection. I took some lessons and learned how to use it. The next time Dan came after me, I was ready. It was time he learned how it felt to be on the receiving end for a change."

Ready for revenge, I thought. And holding a loaded gun.

While I would like to think that I would never let a man walk all over me, I wasn't at all sure that in her position I would have reacted the same way. "You shot him in self-defense."

"Exactly. There was only one problem."

I lifted a brow.

"As it happened, I shot him in the back."

Oh.

"I was arrested," said Minnie, "but never arraigned. I had a good lawyer, the gun was legal, and there was plenty of supporting evidence that Dan had been harassing me. My lawyer made it clear that if the police wanted to pursue a case against me, we would feel obliged to go to the press and make it known how little they'd done to protect me, when they'd been aware for months that I was in danger. Eventually, they decided to simply drop the investigation and move on."

"And you moved on as well."

"To Steve. How's that for history repeating itself?"

"Not your best choice," I admitted.

"It could be worse," Minnie said matter-of-factly. "At least he's not stalking me. In fact, up until last week, I thought we were managing pretty well."

In a thoroughly dysfunctional way. Then again, considering some of the things my family had been up to, who was I to throw stones?

"And now?" I asked.

"My lawyer got the arrest record expunged. That's supposed to mean that it doesn't exist anymore. It's off the books. But of course some enterprising police detective could probably still find it, if he was tipped off where to look. That's what Steve's been threatening me with, revealing something that I told him in confidence that could potentially get me in a whole lot of trouble."

"But you were never charged," I said.

"Like that would matter. I was arrested for manslaughter. Judging by what I read in the newspaper, the police don't have any idea who killed Mary Livingston. You don't think they'd love to have a suspect hand delivered to them? Someone who'd admitted to committing an earlier murder, and who was on the grounds at the time? They'd be all over me in a minute.

"You were right about what you said earlier, I *have* moved on. I have a good job, a new circle of friends. None of them know anything about my past. None of them need to. Bringing it all back out in the open now would ruin my life. And for what possible purpose? I didn't kill Mary. I don't have any idea who did. All I want is to be left alone to live my life in peace."

Abruptly, Minnie stood up. She nudged Coach with her toe and the Schnauzer rose, too. She hesitated before walking away, though. She seemed to be thinking about something.

"I'm not the only one in that obedience class with skeletons in her closet," she said finally.

"Who else?" I asked. If Minnie wanted to supply me with leads, I didn't see any reason why I shouldn't take them.

"Talk to Julie." Minnie cued Coach into position by her side. "That's all I'm saying, all right? Just talk to Julie."

16

"I've been thinking," Sam said later that night. "We should invite Amber and James to dinner. You know, to welcome them to the neighborhood. We could ask the Brickmans to come, too."

Alice and Joe Brickman lived down the street. Their son, Joey, was Davey's best friend, and Alice and I had been pals since we bonded over baby playdates eight years earlier.

"Great idea," I said. "But we'll have to figure out a time when James is actually here. What do you suppose is really going on with him?"

"What do you mean?"

"For starters, where is he?"

"On the road somewhere, apparently."

"Even on weekends?"

Sam shrugged. "I'm just glad I don't have his job."

"Whatever it is," I muttered.

Sam shot me a look.

"Import/export," I said. "Could Amber have

been any more vague? Actually, she didn't sound as though she even *knows* what he does for a living. He's probably into money laundering, or he's an illegal bookie—"

"I doubt it," Sam said with a laugh. "James probably has a normal, perfectly boring job, and you're letting your imagination run away with you."

"Like that would be something new. You've had years," I said. "Haven't you ever noticed that trait before?"

"Before was different." Sam reached out and pulled me closer. "Before you weren't my wife."

I leaned into him, perfectly happy to snuggle closer. "And now?"

"Now I want to know everything there is to know about you."

"I hate to have to tell you this, but I'm no great mystery. I think you've pretty much figured me out already."

Sam chuckled again. I could feel his chest rumble beneath my cheek. "Trust me, Mel, there isn't a man in the world who would believe that."

I tipped my head back and tried out an innocent look. "I can't imagine why not."

Sam started to reply, but I missed what he wanted to say. Abruptly, I drew back and sneezed. Once, twice, then again. By the third sneeze, Sam was looking at me with concern. My eyes had begun to water.

"Are you okay?" he asked.

"I think so." My nose was still tingling. "I can't imagine what brought that on."

"Look, Mom," Davey said from the doorway.

I turned to see what he was up to. Then froze. Davey was holding Felix, the big, fluffy orange cat from next door, in his arms. The feline was nestled against my son's chest, eyes half closed, purring loudly. Felix looked utterly content. As his hooded eyes fastened briefly on mine, the cat also looked thoroughly smug.

I pushed away from Sam and stood up. "Davey, what's that cat doing in here?"

"I had a great idea."

It was not very likely, I thought, that any idea involving cats inside my house was going to sound great to me. Davey, however, was looking very pleased with himself. I figured I might as well hear him out.

"What was it?" I asked.

"You know how Mrs. Fine's cats were bothering you?"

"Yes."

"I figured it probably wasn't the cats that were the problem. It was that they kept coming over here and making the Poodles bark and run around. That's what was making you nuts."

Aside from the nuts part—which was a vast overstatement of the facts—my son was very astute for an eight-year-old. Then the full implication of his words hit me.

"Hey, wait a minute," I said, looking around the living room.

Four of our five Poodles were lying on the floor around the couch. Only Tar was missing; I could hear him drinking water out in the kitchen. Several of the dogs had lifted their heads when Davey entered the room, but none had bothered to get up. Though they had to have noticed Felix, they hadn't reacted at all.

"How come nobody's barking?" I asked.

"That was my idea," Davey said importantly. "I brought the cats in the house and introduced them to the Poodles. You know, so the dogs would understand that the cats were their friends and it was okay."

"You brought the cats inside . . . ?" I repeated faintly.

Davey nodded. Felix had begun to squirm in his arms. The big cat wanted down.

"How many cats?"

"Six. I was going to bring all seven, but I couldn't find Bunny."

"Bunny." I was beginning to sound like an echo. Probably because, at that moment, I was incapable of thinking of anything else to say.

"Bunny's the calico," Davey informed me. "She has big ears. Mrs. Fine said she was probably out catching mice. She's a very good mouser."

"How nice for her." The last word ended on a sneeze. It was followed by another. Beneath my shirt, my arms were beginning to itch.

Sam looked back and forth between my son and me. Tears were now running down my cheeks. "Davey, let's take Felix outside, okay?"

"Okay," Davey agreed. "But I just wanted Mom to know that she doesn't have to worry anymore. The Poodles met the cats and now they're all friends. So it won't matter if they live next door and they come and visit, because everything is just—"

Growing increasingly impatient with confinement, Felix tried the same trick on Davey that he had with me. He braced both back paws against my son's chest and pushed off hard. The cat went rocketing out of Davey's arms and landed on the hardwood floor in the hall.

Unfortunately, Tar had chosen that moment to finish what he was doing in the kitchen and come looking for the rest of his family. He was trotting down the hallway from the other direction, minding his own business, when the fluffy orange cat came flying out of nowhere and landed right in front of him.

Tar wasn't the brightest Poodle, and thinking fast wasn't his forte. Another Poodle might have processed the information; Tar merely reacted. He slid to a stop, his head jerking up in the air. His eyes opened wide. His startled bark shook the walls.

Felix responded by humping his back, waving his bushy tail over his body, and hissing loudly.

"No!" I cried, leaping toward them.

Felix had his claws out and ready. One well-aimed swat across the nose from those sharp talons and Tar would be out of the show ring for a month.

My sudden move didn't help matters any. Not only did the other four Poodles jump up to see what was going on, but Felix apparently decided he was under attack from the rear. He spun around and dashed between my legs.

Standing face to face with Felix, Tar had been frozen in indecision. But once the cat ran, instinct kicked in, and the big Poodle chased after him.

Under normal circumstances, the hallway would have been wide enough for him to go past me. But Tar was so focused on his quarry, that he barely even noticed I was there. As he scrambled by, his shoulder caught my leg and sent me sprawling onto Davey. The two of us went down in a heap.

Felix, meanwhile, dashed into the living room— a strategy that launched him out of the frying pan and into the fire. It didn't take him long to figure that out. Especially since all five dogs were now milling around barking.

The cat's first bound took him onto the coffee table; his second, up onto the back of the couch. Before Sam could grab him, the big cat jumped again; this time he scaled a pair of nearby drapes like a mountain climber flying up the sheer face of a cliff.

Reaching the top, Felix swung up onto the curtain rod and balanced there, a feline high wire act. Yet again, I thought, my house had turned into a circus.

I could have gotten up off the floor, but really, what was the point? It was just as easy to lie where I was and survey the chaos from down below.

Five big Poodles pretty much filled up the living room. Especially when they were chasing around in utter confusion, bouncing on and off the furniture, and threatening—if I'd read their canine language correctly—to disembowel the feline interloper who'd awakened them so unexpectedly from their nap.

Felix, mostly safe and crouched just below the ceiling, was still hissing. Every so often, he reached down and gave a low swipe with one of his paws. Those meager attempts at a defense passed at least several feet above the head of his nearest attacker, but they seemed to make him feel better.

Davey was yelling, I wasn't entirely sure why. He's eight, after all. Maybe he simply liked the idea of adding to the noise.

Sam, bless his heart, was laughing—doubled over, body shaking, totally beyond redemption, laughing.

I might have been tempted to laugh with him, but, unfortunately, I was too busy sneezing.

"That cat," I sputtered when I finally managed to catch my breath, "has got to go."

"Consider it done." Sam was eyeing the distance between Felix and the floor. And possibly debating whether he'd need a ladder to make the rescue. "Davey, take the dogs and put them out back."

My son complied, whistling to the Poodles, who followed him through the dining room, into the kitchen, and out the back door. As soon as the dogs disappeared, Felix relaxed visibly. His tail stopped swishing back and forth like a pendulum. He crouched low on the curtain rod and gazed around, appearing to consider his options.

"Good cat," Sam crooned. "Come back down the way you went up."

I levered myself up off the floor. "I don't think cats are very good at taking orders."

"No, but they're great at looking out for their own self-interest. After he thinks about it for a minute, I bet Felix will realize he's much better off down here than up there."

Sam was right. And it didn't even take a minute. Within thirty seconds, the big orange cat was nestled in Sam's arms. The drapes, unfortunately, were looking somewhat the worse for wear. And I was still sneezing, damn it.

"You know," I said, "I've never been around cats before. I think I must be allergic."

"You can get shots for that."

Sam was striding toward the front door. He opened it, leaned down, and deposited Felix on the step. Slowly, disdainfully, the cat sauntered off into the night.

"Or I could stop being around cats."

"Yeah." Sam grinned. "You could try."

He shut the door, and I turned the dead bolt for good measure. Like that was going to do any good. My gaze slid up the stairs. I hoped Davey didn't have any other surprises tucked away in his bedroom.

"How come my Poodles have to be confined or on leashes and her cats can go wherever they want?"

"They're cats," Sam said with a shrug. "It's the way of the world."

It was as good an answer as any.

The next day at school, I called Aunt Peg during my lunch hour.

"I have a job for you," I said.

"*You* have a job for *me*?" I could just picture her brows rising up into her forehead. "That's different."

It certainly was. Aunt Peg loves to delegate. And, unfortunately, the person most likely to be delegated to was me.

"I want you to call your old friend, Sylvia Lennox, and find out where Mary's son, Michael, is staying. Maybe get a phone number where I can reach him."

"Oh, good," said Peg.

"Oh, good . . . what?"

Call me suspicious. Or maybe just pragmatic. But Aunt Peg sounding smug was not necessarily a good thing.

"It's about time you asked."

"I only learned of the man's existence on Saturday."

"Two whole days." She made it sound like an

eternity. "I all but handed you a prime suspect, and it's taken you forty-eight hours to show any interest in him."

"Maybe *you* should have gone and talked to him," I said mildly.

"Me? I'm not the one who signed up for an obedience class in New Canaan when there was a perfectly good agility group meeting in Greenwich."

"And of course murders only happen around people who do obedience, never agility."

I was being facetious, but Aunt Peg took me seriously. "So far, so good," she said.

"Will you help me?" I asked.

"I already have. I've got Michael's phone number right here. He's probably expecting your call."

"Why would he be doing that?"

"Because I told Sylvia all about you, of course. She was only too happy to give me his contact information. I gather the family wouldn't mind a bit if he was subjected to a little harassment."

"That's what you told her I was?" I asked, incredulous. "A source of harassment?"

"Now, Melanie, I got you the phone number, didn't I?"

"Yes, but—"

"Here it is. Are you ready?"

I sighed and picked up a pen. "Ready."

Aunt Peg read off the information, then asked what else I'd been up to.

I told her about my visit to Winston Pumpernill the day before. I related the conversation I'd had with Harry Beamish and Sandy Sandstrum. And, saving the best for last, I repeated everything I could remember about what Minnie Lloyd had told me about her past.

Much as I complain about Aunt Peg's interference, she listens well and often comes up with good ideas. It's not unheard of for her to pull apart what I've said and ferret out some small piece of crucial information that I might have overlooked. Something I knew but hadn't processed in the same way she did. Aunt Peg might make my life difficult at times, but I never discount what she has to say.

"That's some group you've gotten yourself involved with," she said when I was done. "I might have to come to class with you sometime just to meet them. Imagine already having a murderer in your midst. That's quite impressive."

"Don't forget the control freak," I said. "Not to mention the mysterious Julie."

"What's her breed?" Aunt Peg asked.

"Doberman. His name is Jack."

"Black or red?"

"Black," I said. "Why?"

"No particular reason. I'm just trying to form a picture."

Dog people. It's to be expected.

"You can often tell quite a lot about a person by his choice of dog," Aunt Peg continued. "People who have Dobermans tend to be smart, low maintenance, punctual."

That sounded like what I knew of Julie, at least so far. Or maybe it was just coincidence. I doubted that Aunt Peg's hypothesis was grounded in scientific fact. Or even based on empirical evidence.

"I wonder if Michael has a dog?" she mused.

"The way my luck's been running, he probably has a cat."

"Now, now, don't be such a pessimist."

Moi? I thought. Perish the thought.

"A pessimist might think he had five cats. Or maybe ten."

Aunt Peg sighed. "I don't know what it is with you these days. You seem to have cats on the brain."

Life, I thought. That's what it was.

17

Wonder of wonders, Michael Livingston actually was expecting my call. Not only that, but he wanted to talk to me.

I'd barely even started to explain who I was when he broke in and said, "Let's meet somewhere. Where are you now?"

"At work," I replied, evidence to the contrary notwithstanding. "I can be done by four." These days, with Sam in residence, I didn't have to run straight home to meet Davey's bus.

"Are you in Greenwich or somewhere else?"

"Greenwich," I said. "Just north of downtown. And you're in Byram?"

Michael mumbled an assent. Byram wasn't the best address in the area, but rents were cheaper there, and spur-of-the-moment lodging was easier to come by. It was a bit of a come-down, though, for someone who had grown up on Clapboard Ridge.

"We can meet in the middle," he said, naming a

little bar on the Post Road. "Do you know where that is?"

I'd driven past the small, dark building but never ventured inside. I always thought it looked like the kind of place one might meet for an illicit assignation. Or maybe to buy drugs.

"Sure. I can find it."

"Four o'clock then," he said and hung up.

I snapped my own phone shut as Brittany Baxter sauntered into the room. She walked over to greet the Poodles, casting a sidelong glance at me out of the corner of her eye. Wanting to make sure I noticed, no doubt.

"I might as well just stay right here on the floor and play with your dogs," the seventh grader said when I looked up. "Because we don't have any work to do. I'm all caught up on my reading. Even Ed says I'm doing great."

"*Ed?*"

"You know. Mr. Weinstein."

"Yes, I know Mr. Weinstein." I got up and came out from behind my desk. Faith and Eve were lying on their big cedar bed in the corner. I walked over to stand beside Brittany, who was crouching down in front of them. "I just wasn't aware that his students had started calling him Ed."

"Not all the students." Brittany's lashes fluttered. A becoming pink blush rose on her cheeks.

"Just you?"

"Just me." She smiled. I felt the pit of my stomach go hollow.

"And you've caught up on all your reading?"

"Yeah, sure. Ed scheduled a couple of special catch-up sessions for me, and we went over the stuff together. Now I'm not behind anymore."

I sat down on the floor next to her. "I thought that was my job."

"Is that why you're looking so grim?" Brittany giggled, and for a moment, she looked every bit like the twelve-year-old child she was. Close up, I could see the dark liner she'd smudged around her eyes and the stain she'd applied to her lips. "Are you afraid I won't need you anymore?"

I resisted the impulse to reach out and smooth back the bangs that brushed low over her forehead. Beneath that wispy fringe, her eyes were a startling shade of blue. When I was twelve, I'd still been playing with dolls. Brittany, I suspected, was playing with fire.

"No," I said softly, "that's not what scares me at all."

Promptly at four o'clock, I was standing outside a squat, dark brown box of a building. The bar had been plopped between two strip malls on Route One and was surrounded on all four sides by asphalt. Neon advertisements for various beers filled the small front windows. The sign over the door read Bubble Bubble. I wondered if that was a Shakespearean reference and, if so, whether those who had named the bar realized that the line after that was "toil and trouble."

From the looks of the place, I suspected they might have.

Cars zipped by on the four-lane road behind me. Having come straight from school, I had the Poodles in the Volvo. Being April, it wasn't really hot yet; but still the day was warm enough that I didn't want to leave them parked in the sun.

Finally, I found an area around the side that was shaded by the building itself. I cracked all four windows, locked the doors, and left Faith and Eve with explicit instructions not to talk to any strangers.

It looked like that kind of neighborhood.

I walked into the bar and stood for a moment in the doorway, letting my eyes adjust to the darkness within. When they did, I saw that the place was mostly empty. The lunch crowd had departed; the after-work drinkers had yet to arrive. Two pool tables took up half the room; a row of booths lined a side wall. A big TV, bracketed to the ceiling, was tuned to ESPN. On a weekday afternoon, there didn't seem to be much sports action going on.

Nevertheless, the bartender was reclining back, his elbows propped against the lip of the bar, and his eyes fastened on the brightly lit screen as if it were the most fascinating thing he'd ever seen. After a minute, he reluctantly straightened. His gaze shifted my way. "Help you?"

I didn't particularly want a beer, and this didn't look like the kind of place where you'd want to ask for a glass of water. "Coke, please," I said.

As I spoke, a man slid out of one of the booths. He was tall, broad shouldered, and not particularly handsome. The hair at his temples had begun to go gray, and his eyes looked tired. His pullover sweater was cashmere, but his jeans and loafers looked old and worn.

As he came toward me, he was already extending a hand. "Are you Melanie?"

"I am."

"Thanks for taking the time to see me. Booth okay?"

I hadn't even had time to nod before he walked

over to the bar, picked up my drink, slid the bartender a bill, and then carried the glass back to where he'd been sitting. Having little choice in the matter, I simply followed.

I had thought this was going to be my meeting. But since Michael seemed to think he was in charge, I opted instead to hang back and let him dictate the pace. It didn't take him long to find his stride.

"I imagine you've probably heard all sorts of terrible things about me," he said when I slid in across from him. Michael pushed my glass toward me. As I took it, our fingers brushed briefly; then we both retreated to our own sides of the table.

"Actually, no. I don't know much about you at all."

"Really? I'd have expected Sylvia to fill your head with lots of nonsense. It's the kind of thing she likes to do."

"I've only met your cousin once," I said. Aunt Peg had introduced us when the memorial service ended. "It was at the service on Saturday. Your name didn't come up."

Michael nodded. "I remember seeing you there. You were a friend of my mother's then?"

I hesitated for a moment before answering. I didn't want to admit that I'd only met his mother one time, too. "I liked your mother a great deal," I said finally. "She seemed like a wonderful woman. I was at Winston Pumpernill with a therapy dog group. That's how Mary and I became acquainted."

"Paul's group."

"Yes." I lifted my drink and took a sip. The soda was extra sweet, as though the syrup to seltzer ratio was off. It tasted great. "I gather you don't get along very well with most of the family."

"That would be an understatement. As you might imagine, that's why I left."

"How many years have you been away?"

"Too many." The answer came quickly and without thought, as though Michael had heard the charge leveled at himself so many times that he'd adopted the accusation as his own. "Twenty, I guess, maybe more. My father died shortly after I graduated from college. That seemed like a good time to leave and strike out on my own."

"Nothing unusual about that."

"You wouldn't think so, but that wasn't the way the family felt. Tight-knit bunch, the Livingstons."

"You didn't want to keep in touch?" I tried to keep my tone neutral. The last thing I wanted to do was sound accusatory and put Michael on the defensive. But lots of people went off and made their own way after college; few totally lost contact with their families as a result.

Michael shrugged and sipped his drink. Amber liquid in a highball glass. Scotch, I was guessing.

"Do you come from a big family?" he asked, after a minute.

"No. Although sometimes it feels as though there are more of them than there really are. I have a brother. There were just two of us when we were growing up. Our parents died about a decade ago. No grandparents still living, but I have a couple of aunts that I see frequently."

"In a big family like mine—a family that sees itself as an important entity—it's easy to get smothered by people's expectations. From the time I was a very young child, I knew I was being groomed to go into the family business. I was supposed to follow my father's career path and to be just as successful at it as he had been."

"And you weren't happy about that?"

"Not entirely." His words were clipped. "No."

"Lots of people just starting out wouldn't mind having that kind of opportunity handed to them."

"I might not have minded, either, if I'd ever had even the slightest choice in the matter. Suppose from the time you were a child you were told that when you grew up you were going to manufacture widgets?"

"Is that what your family does?" I smiled. "Makes widgets?"

"We're talking hypothetical here." He tried to sound stern, then gave up and smiled, too. The lines around his eyes softened. "Actually, I don't think it would matter to them what they did, as long as it pulled in a boatload of money."

"In your place," I admitted, "I guess I might have found the prospect of all that widget making a little restricting."

"Precisely. Just for the record, I never said that I wouldn't join the company. Only that I wanted to see a bit of the world on my own terms first. It shouldn't have been a big deal. And it wouldn't have been if my father had still been alive."

The bartender pulled his eyes away from the television set long enough to lean over the bar in our direction. "Need any refills?"

We both shook our heads, and he went back to his show. Customer service wasn't a priority at the Bubble Bubble.

"Problem was," said Michael, "when Dad died unexpectedly, it left a hole that needed to be filled. And the family looked to me to fill it. No matter that I wasn't ready, that I had no experience in the business, that I'd planned to work my way up. It was just presented to me as a fait accompli. Here's your office, here's your secretary, see you on Monday."

"So you bolted."

"I ran like the dickens." Michael shifted uncomfortably on the shiny vinyl cushion. "Sylvia and some of the others will tell you that I left like a thief in the night. That I never even stopped to explain or say good-bye, but that isn't true. I spoke with my mother. She knew I was doing what I felt I had to do. At the time, I was sure she understood, maybe even supported me."

"And later?"

Michael snorted derisively. "Later came along pretty damn quickly. The way I heard it, I hadn't even been gone twenty-four hours before the shit hit the fan. And since I wasn't there to protect her, my mother got the brunt of it. Recriminations from just about everyone else in the family about what a spoiled, ungrateful child she'd raised."

"Did you think about returning at that point?"

"I might have, but I'd already left the country. It didn't even occur to me that her own relatives would turn on her like that. While she was listening to their vitriol, I was on a plane to Paris, making plans to bum around Europe. I didn't have a clue what was going on back home."

"Mary never called and told you?"

"Don't forget, we're talking twenty years ago. No cell phones, no laptop computers. Everything wasn't easy access like it is now. When I left, I told my mother I'd get in touch after a while and let her know how I was doing. In the meantime, she wouldn't have had any way of finding me. I fired off a few postcards and went backpacking in Spain. Probably a month passed before I got around to calling home."

"After all that time your mother must have been worried about you," I commented.

Michael stared at me across the table. "Don't think I don't know what you're really thinking. That I took the coward's way out and left my mother to pick up the pieces."

"Well . . ."

"I was twenty-two, okay? Maybe I didn't make the best decision at the time. But I had no idea that everything was going to blow up in both our faces. By the time I called home, the relatives had already had plenty of opportunity to work on her. They'd managed to convince her that I was the selfish, disloyal jerk they all wanted to believe I was.

"One thing I have to say for the Livingstons, when you're a member of the family, they'll do anything for you. But they view the world strictly from their own perspective, and they're a pretty unforgiving bunch. Once they begin to see you as an outsider, you're done as far as they're concerned. They don't want anything more to do with you."

"So you only intended to be gone for a couple of months, but while you were away, the family ostracized you."

"That's about it." Michael frowned, whether at the memory or his near-empty glass, it was hard to tell. He tipped back his head and drained the last of the drink.

"Be right back," he said. He got up and carried his glass to the bar for a refill.

Before meeting him, I'd thought of Michael as the villain. His story portrayed him as the victim. Of course, I was only hearing one side. Too bad, I thought, that I'd never be able to find out how

Mary had felt about all this. She was the linchpin around whom the entire episode had revolved. And now, she was the one who was dead.

I tried to imagine a circumstance in which Davey might do something so unforgivable that I could be convinced to disown him. I couldn't make it happen. No matter what, he would always be my son. I'd find a way to bring him back, and if that wasn't possible, I'd go to him.

Michael slipped back into the seat opposite me. His glass was full, and he'd swiped a bowl of unshelled peanuts from the bar. "Protein," he said, pushing it toward me.

"And lots of fat." I scooped out a couple anyway.

"Live it up." He stopped and sighed. "That was one of my mother's favorite sayings. She was a big believer in getting the most out of every day, so that you wouldn't be left with any regrets later on. And now the irony is that I was so busy living my life that I'm left with the biggest regret of all. That I never got to see her again before she died."

He looked utterly swamped by remorse. And yet . . .

"Twenty years is a long time," I said.

"Livingstons tend to carry a grudge."

"You're a Livingston. Does that include you?"

"I guess so. They wouldn't forgive me, and I refused to forgive them. So we reached an impasse, and neither one of us tried hard enough to get across it."

"So what finally brought you back to Greenwich after all this time?"

Michael reached for the bowl and dragged it toward him. He pulled out a peanut and went to work. The shells on mine had popped right off. Michael made a production of his.

"I guess there was some guilt involved," he said finally.

"A sudden attack of conscience?"

"No. More like a sudden realization that nobody lives forever."

"Your mother had been in Winston Pumpernill for quite a while. Had her health recently taken a turn for the worse?"

"It wasn't my mother I was worried about," Michael said softly. "You met her. You know what she was like. I thought she would always be there."

"Then who . . ." I began, then abruptly stopped. The answer was staring me right in the face.

"Colon cancer," said Michael. "Caught early, prognosis good. But still it makes you stop and reevaluate."

Yes, I thought. It would.

"Did your mother know?"

"Of course not. I was going to tell her. But for obvious reasons I wanted to do it in person. That's partly why I came back, and also why I wanted so badly to see her."

"Your relatives think you came back for your mother's money."

Michael was holding a peanut between his fingers. He squeezed the shell so hard that the nut shot out and skittered away across the table. "My relatives have been wrong before."

"Now that your mother's gone, have you told your family about your illness?"

"I haven't told them a damn thing. Which is exactly what they deserve. You want to tell them, that's up to you. I guess maybe they ought to know. Though now, with the Livingstons being the only reason I didn't have the opportunity to see my mother before she died, I'm in no mood to extend any olive branches myself. That's why I figured I'd talk to you. You want to pass the news along, feel free. Maybe that will finally end this acrimony once and for all."

I swallowed heavily. No wonder Michael had thought this was his meeting. He'd been the one orchestrating the flow of information and dropping all the bombshells. I'd merely been along for the ride.

"They know where I'm staying. They have my phone number." Michael levered his arms on the table. He pushed himself up and out of the booth. "Anyone wants to get in touch with me, they know how to find me."

I was in my car driving home before it occurred to me that I'd forgotten to ask him about the note he'd had passed to Mary Livingston. I still didn't know what it had contained, or why it had upset her so much.

18

I didn't call any of the Livingstons to tell them what I'd learned from my conversation with Michael. For one thing, despite what he'd said, I didn't feel it was my place to convey news of that magnitude. For another, I had no desire to get involved in their internal family squabbles.

Perhaps it was my silence that caused Paul to waylay me outside class on Thursday evening. He and Cora walked up as I was unloading Faith from the car. It didn't appear to be a chance meeting. I got the impression they'd been waiting for our arrival.

"Let's walk a bit," he said.

I glanced at my watch. We had about five minutes to spare and several other people had yet to go inside. "Sure. Let me just hook up Faith's leash."

The Poodle danced in anticipation while I tried to snap the lead to the small choke collar loop that was buried in her thick neck hair. She loved going to class. It gave her time alone with me and a chance to perform in front of an audience; it also made her think. For a Poodle, a combination like that was pretty much nirvana.

Paul watched impatiently for a few seconds, then strolled away, leading Cora onto the grassy verge beside the parking lot. A small stone wall separated the Y property from the middle school playing fields next door. They climbed the wall, hopped down the other side, then kept walking. Finally catching the loop and securing the lead, Faith and I hurried to catch up.

"It's been a week," Paul said when I settled into stride beside him. "I want to know what you've found out."

His tone was curt, almost preemptive, as if he thought I owed him answers. That, plus the fact that I hadn't found out very much, was enough to get my hackles up. Paul hadn't asked me to look into Mary's murder; he'd merely acquiesced grudgingly. Not only that, but he'd likened my detecting skills to those of a hotline psychic. By my count, I didn't owe him much of anything.

"A week isn't very long," I said.

"It's long enough. Or at least it should be. I know you saw Michael."

"Really? How?"

"Your aunt got his phone number from my mother."

"That doesn't mean I called him."

Abruptly, Paul stopped walking. "Look, let's stop dancing around here. I know you had a drink with my cousin, okay? I'm sure he told you some sad story about how the family had treated him abominably and he only wanted what was best for his mother. Knowing Michael, he probably never mentioned a thing about his own failings."

"Michael told me he'd been out of touch with your family for more than twenty years."

"So?"

I'd stopped when Paul had. Now I resumed walking, and he was forced to follow if he wanted to hear what I had to say. "So you must have been a teenager when he left. I'm surprised you would think you know him or what he might be likely to do."

"Some people don't change."

"Maybe they're not given the opportunity."

Paul scowled. "I guess he really got to you, didn't he?"

"I have no idea what you mean by that. In fact, I'm not sure I even want to know. Frankly, I'm still wondering how you know that Michael and I met for a drink."

"You have no idea—"

"Who I'm dealing with?" My tone was snide. It matched my mood. "You make that sound ominous."

"That wasn't my intention." Paul moderated his voice. He reached out and laid a hand on my arm. Like we were friends, buddies even. "I just don't want you to get sucked into one of Michael's deceptions. First meeting, he comes off like a great guy. But once you get to know him better, you realize that you can't trust a word he says. It's nothing new; he's always been like that."

I slid a sidelong glance in Paul's direction. Either Michael had been lying to me on Monday, or Paul was lying to me now. I wondered which one it was.

"All he wanted was to come home and see his mother," I said. "I'm not sure I understand why your entire family had to be involved in that decision."

"For starters, Greenwich wasn't Michael's home anymore. He took care of that a long time ago. On top of that, Aunt Mary's health was fragile. That was why she was living at Winston Pumpernill, where she would have around-the-clock access to medical care. Everyone in my family loved Aunt Mary. Of course we would see it as our duty to protect her."

"From her own son?"

"If need be."

"Mary knew Michael was back," I said. "She wanted to see him."

"I'm sure my cousin would say that now, since there's no way to refute his claim."

"Michael isn't the only one who said so. Mary's friends at Winston Pumpernill told me the same thing."

Paul gazed at me speculatively. "I guess you have been busier than you let on. What else do you know?"

"I know that Mary was planning to meet with Michael the day after she was killed, and that your family would have done almost anything to prevent that meeting from taking place."

"Now you're the one who's beginning to sound ominous." A smile twitched at the corners of Paul's lips. "Surely you don't think anyone in my family had anything to do with her death."

"Last time we spoke, one thing you did mention was that your Aunt Mary had a great deal of money. Money your mother seems to think Michael needed and might have been trying to gain access to. And, oddly enough, when we talked at the memorial service, you neglected to mention your cousin at all."

"Maybe I didn't think he was important."

"Fair enough," I said. "Then why are we having this conversation?"

It was Paul's turn to look annoyed. "Maybe because I want to cover all the bases?"

"Consider them covered." I gave Faith's leash a gentle tug and turned around. Everyone else had already gone inside. "We should get back. We're going to miss the beginning of class."

"Steve never starts on time," Paul replied, but he and Cora circled back, too.

If I was ever going to tell him about Michael's illness, I thought, now was the time. Maybe the news would help smooth relations between Michael and his relatives. Except that now Paul had managed to plant just enough doubt in my mind to keep me from blurting out what I knew.

Had I been duped? Was Michael Livingston a liar? Unfortunately, I had no idea.

I hate it when that happens.

We came to the wall; Paul clambered over it first, then reached back a gentlemanly hand to help me balance on the rocks. Cora scrambled over, leaping from stone to stone, while Faith merely jumped the low obstacle with her customary grace.

"How are the police coming with their investigation?" I asked when we were all on the other side.

Paul shrugged noncommittally. "It's not as if they feel any compunction to keep us informed. Our attorneys have to keep checking in with them, and even then I suspect there's a whole lot they're not telling us. From what we understand, they're pursuing the possibility that drugs might have been involved."

I looked at him in surprise. "Why do they think that?"

"You know, since it was a medical facility, where all sorts of controlled substances might potentially have been available."

"Yes, but . . ." From my admittedly limited experience, when crimes were committed, the police often suspected there was some sort of drug connection. That was either a sad commentary on our current society or else on the narrow-mindedness of law enforcement. "Your aunt seems like an unlikely candidate to have been involved with drugs."

"I won't argue with you there. Truthfully, I think they're just baffled, and it's the only thing they can come up with. They may be spinning their wheels, but at least it makes them look like they're doing *something.*"

"Lynn Stephanopolus told me Winston Pumpernill does background checks on all their staff."

Paul nodded. "I'd imagine that must be standard these days."

"But I've also heard that one of the orderlies can be bribed to smuggle things in and out."

We'd reached the building. Paul pulled the door and held it open so Faith and I could precede him into the hallway. "Who told you that?"

"I gather it's common knowledge." My answer was purposely vague. No way was I going to rat out my sources. "Even Michael, after all, was able to find a way to contact his mother after you and your relatives tried to block him."

Before Paul could reply, Faith and I ducked through the doorway into the classroom. I threw my things down on the nearest chair and joined the group of dogs and handlers already lined up along the mat. Paul stared after me for a moment, then found a place for Cora and himself at the other end of the line.

"Well, Kelly," Steve said, flicking a glance in my direction, "I guess you're going to have to relinquish your title as the lateness queen."

"Sorry." I maneuvered Faith into heeling position at my side. "I got caught up in a conversation and forgot what time it was."

"Good excuse," Steve nodded, playing to the crowd. "That's why we all come to this class once a week, isn't it people? For the good conversation?"

The question produced a laugh, as it was meant to. But somehow that didn't ease the unexpected tension that seemed to be eddying between us. I wondered if Steve expected me to apologize again.

Instead, I lifted my chin and said, "I'm ready now."

He rolled his eyes theatrically. "Thank God for small favors. Everyone else?"

Handlers looked down and checked their dogs. Only a beginner made the mistake of assuming that his dog was where he'd been placed moments earlier without checking to make sure.

"Ready," several people called back. Others nodded their agreement.

"Forward," Steve said. We all gave our dogs the command to heel and the line began to move.

"Don't pay any attention to Steve," Julie said to me over her shoulder. She and Jack were directly in front of us. They were striding out; Faith and I had to really move to keep up. "He's got a bug up his butt for some reason this evening. Before you walked in, he was picking on Stacey. I'm sure she was thrilled to see you two show up late and take the heat off of her."

Rounding a corner, I glanced down and monitored Faith's position. Since she was on the inside, it would have been easy for her to forge ahead for a step or two, but she'd seen the turn coming and moderated her pace so that her shoulder remained even with my thigh.

"Do you know what he's upset about?"

"Not me." Julie gave her head a small shake. While I'd been checking on Faith, she'd been staring at Steve. The line was long enough to fill nearly half the matted floor, and he had his back to us as he watched the handlers on the other side. "I don't have the patience to deal with Steve's moods. When he starts getting pissy, I just try and stay out of his way."

"Good idea."

We heeled another circuit of the ring, going faster, then slower, then back to normal speed in response to Steve's commands. "About turn!" he announced after another round.

Now Julie was behind me, but I could still see her and Jack in the mirrors that lined one wall of the room. They were doing a great job. The Doberman was focused on his handler to the exclusion of everything else.

Faith and I were novices at the exercise, we were still using a leash. Julie had removed Jack's lead before the exercise began, but you never would have known it to look at them. The Doberman was glued to her side; the two of them were moving as one.

I'm not the only one with skeletons in my closet, Minnie had said. *Talk to Julie.* No time like the present, I decided.

Steve finally called the exercise to a halt, and we all fell out of formation. Many of the handlers were breathing hard. A few of the dogs were panting. Julie had barely broken a sweat, however, and

Jack looked as though he could have gone on all night. I let Faith relax, spooling out her leash as I sidled over closer to Julie.

"So what was Steve getting on Stacey's case about?"

"You know." She shrugged. "The usual."

"The usual?"

"Oh, that's right, I forgot. You're new. Steve hates it when Stacey talks baby talk to Bubbles and treats her as though she's a child rather than an animal. Actually, I think he hates the fact that he even has a dog named Bubbles in his class."

Julie and I shared a complicit grin.

"Papillons are smart little dogs, one of those 'big dog in a small package' breeds. But Stacey's always coddling Bubbles—slipping her treats, or picking her up and carrying her everywhere. She doesn't give her a chance to think for herself. And Bubbles is no fool. She's learned that if she acts whiny and helpless, Stacey will respond by giving her even more attention."

Not an unusual problem with little dogs. Toy Poodles were just as smart and capable as their bigger cousins, but it was amazing how many were spoiled by improper handling.

"Does it do any good when Steve yells at her?"

"Not much," Julie admitted. "Stacey's pretty set in her ways. Besides, she's not really a serious competitor. She signed up to take this class for fun. So if Bubbles never gets past her C.D., I don't think Stacey will be terribly disappointed."

"You seem to know a lot about most of the people here," I said.

"It happens. Most of us have been training together for a long time. Some people you become friends with, some you don't. But either way, you end up finding out all sorts of things about one another."

"Like what?"

Julie gave me a measuring look. "Why do I suspect that question isn't nearly as casual as it sounds?"

I laughed in spite of myself. "Maybe because at this time last week Steve was announcing that I was an amateur detective?"

"That must be it. Welcome to the South Avenue Obedience Club. Nobody has any secrets around here."

"That's not what I heard."

"May I ask who from?"

"You can ask," I said. "I'm not going to answer."

"So you're discreet. I suppose I should take that as a good sign. Isn't it about time for you to tell me that anything I say to you will be held in strictest confidence?"

"Not necessarily," I said. "It depends on what you tell me."

"And if I choose to say nothing at all?"

I looked at her and shrugged. What did she expect? That I'd pull out dental tools and rubber hoses?

"Then we're done," I said.

"You got that right," Julie replied. She flipped a curt hand signal to Jack and the two of them walked away.

19

We practiced the recall next, and Steve turned the exercise into a game. We began by lining up, side by side, on the mat that ran down the length of the room. Our dogs were seated beside us, facing forward. On Steve's command, we told our dogs to stay, and left them, walking straight across to stand facing them on the opposite mat.

There were twelve of us in the class. Steve divided the group down the middle into two teams of six and announced that the recall would be held as a relay race.

"When I give the signal," he said, "I want the two of you at the opposite ends to call your dogs. As soon as they've come and are sitting in front of you, the person next to you can call his or her dog. And so on, until we reach the middle of the room. Whichever team succeeds in bringing all their dogs to the other side of the room first is the winner."

Having been told only to prepare for the recall, most of us had lined up randomly. Now we all looked around to see who else was on our team.

Julie and Jack, probably the strongest pair, were at the other end of the room from Faith and me. On the other hand, that team would be slowed down by the inclusion of Kelly and Boss, who often had trouble keeping their minds on business.

Minnie and Coach were standing next to me, which was good. Like Julie and Jack, they'd be tough to beat. All in all, the two teams looked pretty even. I could only hope that Faith, easily the least seasoned of the participants, wouldn't get distracted and turn in a poor performance.

"Trust Steve to take something simple like a recall and use it to pit us against one another," Minnie muttered.

"I think it sounds like fun," Stacey said from her other side. "Bubbles may be small, but she's fast." She looked down the line and counted. Her Papillon would be crossing the room at the same time as Mark Terry's Reggie. "Faster than a Cairn, at any rate. We'll beat them easy."

"We shouldn't have to beat anybody," said Minnie. "The recall is an exercise in obedience, not a race. At a trial, it doesn't matter how quickly the dog comes in as long as he keeps coming."

"Comments, Minerva?" Steve placed his hands on his hips and stared. "Maybe something you'd like to share with the rest of the class?"

"Not in this lifetime," Minnie replied.

"Because you and Coach can feel free to sit this one out if you'd rather not participate."

"Of course," Paul pointed out, leaning forward to address the line, "that would leave us with an odd number, so someone else would have to sit out, too."

"We'll do our part," Minnie said shortly.

"See that you do," Steve replied. "You wouldn't want to let your team down. Everyone else, no cheating, no anticipating. Wait until the dog beside you has its fanny on the floor before calling your own. Make it a fair fight."

He looked around and lifted an arm in the air. "Everyone ready? Go!"

Faith and I were third in line to perform. When our turn came, the two teams were still evenly matched. Seeing the dog beside her leap up and run back to its owner, I'd been afraid Faith would break her stay and blow the whole thing. But although the Poodle sent me a searching look from across the room, she held her ground.

As soon as the Cocker belonging to the handler beside me sat down, I called Faith in. She jumped up with apparent relief and came galloping toward me. She was seated in front of me before Paul's Corgi on the opposing team was even halfway home.

"Good job," Minnie said under her breath. She whipped Coach to her with a strong hand signal. "We've got them on the run now."

As it turned out, we did. Our team didn't win by much, a length or two at most, but it was enough to secure bragging rights.

"What do we get for winning?" Stacey asked, as we cheered to celebrate the victory.

Steve grinned. "How about a break? Well done, everyone. Take ten minutes. Have a smoke, get your dogs something to drink, and then we'll start up again."

The group disbanded. Most of us walked to the chairs near the door where we'd left our things. After the excitement of the race, Faith was happy to lap up a bowl of ice water and flop down on the floor for a rest. I was about to sit down beside her when Mark and Reggie came walking over.

The little Cairn was wearing his leash and collar. He was also carrying a loop of the lead jauntily in his mouth. It didn't look as though the race had tired him out at all.

"So," Mark said, pressing up next to me. "How are things coming?"

"Just fine," I replied. "You?"

"No, I mean how . . . are . . . things . . . coming?"

Even with the added emphasis, the question didn't sound dramatically different to me than it had a moment earlier. I looked at him and shrugged.

"You know," he lowered his voice to a confidential tone, "with the investigation."

Oh. Those things.

"That seems to be the question of the evening," I said. Too bad I didn't have any really satisfactory answers.

"Have you found the murderer yet?"

"No. If I had, I'd have taken the information to the police, and you would have been able to read about it in the paper." I smiled to soften the impact of my words, but *come on*. Did he actually think I might have figured out who had killed Mary and was keeping the news to myself?

"Good," Mark said.

"Good?" I took a step back to give myself some space. "What's good about that?"

"Because I was thinking maybe I could help you." He stepped into the small space I'd put between us. If Mark were any closer, he would have been in my pocket.

"Help me how?"

"You know. Investigate. I think I'd be pretty good at it."

I tried taking another step back. Thankfully, this time when the space opened up, Reggie moved to stand between us. The Cairn and my Poodle touched noses.

"All I've been doing is asking a few people questions. I'm not part of the investigation; I don't have an official standing. There's nothing stopping you from doing the same thing. In fact, the more people who ask questions, the sooner someone might come up with some answers."

"So, like, you could take me on as your assistant?"

I sighed softly. Clearly, I wasn't getting my point across. "I don't need an assistant. And you certainly don't need me for a boss. What I'm doing isn't rocket science. It's just . . . well . . . looking around and gathering information."

"Precisely." Mark looked pleased. "That's what I was thinking I might help you with."

"Feel free. Have at it. Go to town."

"You mean on my own?"

As opposed to being attached to my hip? Definitely, yes, I thought.

"I have to tell you something," Mark whispered, leaning close to my ear as if we were coconspirators. "I already have."

It was one of those moments when I knew I should just walk away. Why even prolong a conversation that is undoubtedly heading places you have no desire to go? Whatever Mark was up to, I had no need to be a part of it. Good in theory, right?

But I had to admit, he'd made me curious.

"You've done *what* exactly?" I asked.

"Started investigating. It's really kind of cool, isn't it? Just like that stuff you see on TV."

Actually, no, I thought. My life didn't at all resemble the crime shows I'd seen on television, and if I was lucky, things would remain that way.

"Where did you start?"

It was such a simple question. Basic, even. But the response it produced was anything but. Mark grinned happily; his eyes lit up with enthusiasm. He shoved Reggie's leash into my hands.

"Hold this," he said. "I'll be right back."

He strode over to a jacket that was lying on one of the chairs and pulled a sheet of paper out of a pocket. He unfolded the paper and handed it to me. "I made a timeline. You know, a schedule of where everybody was that day at Winston Pumpernill."

"Good idea." It was more than I had done.

Mark looked warily around the room. He positioned his body in such a way as to block others from seeing what we were up to. Not that it mattered, nobody else showed even the slightest interest in what we were doing.

I scanned the page quickly. Mark had listed the names of all the class members who'd visited the nursing facility that afternoon. Beside each name he'd written a description of their whereabouts during our time there.

Faith's and my entry read:

arrived on time, inside with group. interacted with various patients, including ML. never left sunroom?

It was accurate up to a point, though I did wonder about the question mark at the end. Did Mark

know where Faith and I had been for a fact, or was
he just guessing?

I looked at another entry. This one was for
Minnie and Coach. Theirs read:

> one of the first to arrive. went inside briefly then
> came out to rejoin group. bathroom break? enter-
> tained the troops.

Again, there seemed to be some holes that
needed filling. Had Minnie and Coach remained
in the sunroom for the duration of the visit, or
hadn't they? The one unusual move Mark had reported, "went inside briefly then came out," had
taken place while Mary was still alive—indeed, before I'd even met her—so it was hard to judge its
significance.

"Pretty good, huh?" Mark was leaning down to
read over my shoulder.

"Um, sure. Although a little more detail might be
helpful."

He looked up. "Like what?"

"It would be better if you knew everyone's
whereabouts for the specific time period after
Mary Livingston left the sunroom and went to her
room to lie down."

"How do you expect me to know that?"

"I don't." I'd been there, too, and I hadn't been
keeping tabs on everyone's movements. Nobody
had; that was the problem. "I'm just saying it
would be useful to know, that's all."

"Okay," he said, enthusiasm undimmed, "how
about this one?" He pointed to the entry for Stacey
and Bubbles. "Read this and see what you think."

> entered home with group. went straight to ML
> and friends upon entering sunroom. suspicious?

chatted up others. stepped out of room at least
once while talking on cell phone. didn't see in
room during Coach-arama. not there or just
short? left with others.

"Interesting," I said. "Why do you think it's suspicious that Stacey spoke with Mary and her
friends first?"

Mark stared at me as if the answer were obvious.
"Because Mary's the one who ended up dead. So
doesn't that make you wonder why Stacey was so
anxious to speak with her?"

"Maybe she wasn't," I said. "Remember, Mary,
Borden, and Madeline were sitting very near the
front of the room. It made sense that the first person through the door would have gone to them,
especially as they'd all met during earlier visits,
and Mary was known to enjoy interacting with the
dogs."

"I guess," Mark admitted.

"Now this part"—I pointed at the page—"does
make me wonder. 'Didn't see in room during
Coach-arama . . .' By the way, Coach-arama?"

"You know." He flashed a guilty smile. "The performance by our resident diva. I suppose I could
have called it 'The Minerva Show,' but that might
have been cruel."

And the alternative wasn't?

"Were Stacey and Bubbles out of the room during that time, or do you think you just didn't happen to notice them?"

"Unfortunately, I'm not sure. Stacey had already
left the room once earlier. Maybe she stepped out
again, because I don't remember seeing her there.
But it's not like those two would stand out in a
crowd."

No, they wouldn't, I thought. Stacey was small and so was her dog. I could see how the two of them might have escaped notice even if they'd been standing right there.

"I'll tell you who wasn't in the room, though," Mark said.

"Who?"

"Steve."

I looked at him with interest. "How do you know that?"

"Because when Minnie started performing, I fully expected him to stop her. You know how the two of them act around one another."

I nodded.

"It's like he does his best to annoy her, and she reciprocates in kind. So considering how much Minnie likes to be the center of attention, I just assumed he'd step in and put a stop to the proceedings. When he didn't, I looked around to see why not."

"And he wasn't there?"

"Not anywhere. Because I checked."

I thought back, sorting through my memory of that afternoon. Kelly had been out of the room around that time as I recalled. When she'd returned, I'd noticed that Boss wasn't with her. Instead, he'd been standing by the back of the room with Steve.

"Did you look over by the windows?" I asked. "Because I saw him standing there with Boss."

"That was later," Mark said firmly. "By then, Minnie and Coach were just about finished. By the way, those may look like windows along that side of the room, but they're actually French doors. When the weather's nice, the staff leaves them open so a breeze can blow through."

Well that put an entirely new wrinkle on things, didn't it?

Until that moment, I hadn't realized that the room had another entrance and exit, much less one so readily accessible. Steve wouldn't have had to go in and out of the sunroom through the main door. He easily could have slipped out and slipped back a few minutes later undetected. And Steve wasn't the only one. Potentially, anyone else in the class could have done the same thing.

Mark watched the play of emotions across my face. "I came up with something important, didn't I?"

"Yes, you did."

"I knew it!" he exulted. After a moment, he added, "If you don't mind my asking, what was it?"

"Doors."

"What about them?"

"Access," I said, handing back the sheet of paper. "And who had it."

"Excellent. So do you know who did it now?"

"No."

"You're closer though?"

"Maybe." It wasn't exactly the truth, but he looked so hopeful I hated to disappoint him.

"See? What did I tell you? I *knew* I'd be good at this." Mark pumped a fist in the air and walked away. Reggie, forgotten on the floor, had to leap to his feet and scramble to catch up.

I hoped I hadn't created a monster.

20

Friday, while I was at school, Sam was busy at home inviting all my relatives to dinner. Since my entire family could sit side by side on a short couch, the undertaking didn't involve very many phone calls. Frank and Bertie begged off as Maggie had an ear infection, and my Aunt Rose and Uncle Peter had a previous engagement. That left Aunt Peg and my ex-husband, Bob, as the two lone acceptees.

What a way to liven up a Friday evening.

Sam's relatives are spread out all over the country, and he doesn't get to see them as often as he would like. So I'd been delighted when he'd adopted my family as his own. But he hadn't yet come to grips with the fact that certain personality combinations didn't work well together; and placing Aunt Peg and Bob in the same room topped the list.

To be sure, their relationship had grown much smoother of late. Now that Bob was living in Connecticut, playing a role in Davey's life, and

working as Frank's partner in their wildly successful coffeehouse, The Bean Counter, she'd begun
to see him as something more than just the man
who'd walked out on my son and me when Davey
was just a toddler.

Bob had good qualities—to my mind, they were
even more in evidence now than they had been
when we were living together a decade earlier—
and Aunt Peg was slowly beginning to appreciate
them. Which didn't mean she couldn't continue
to carry a grudge on my behalf. Family loyalty
meant a great deal to Aunt Peg, and heaven help
the person who hurt one of her own.

"Which one did you talk to first?" I asked Sam. I
was standing at the kitchen counter slicing fresh
mushrooms for the salad.

"Peg, of course." Sam was putting together a
pesto topping for the salmon he was planning to
grill. He glanced over at me and grinned. "You
know she would hate not being the first call."

All too true.

"So does she know it's just her and Bob, or are
you planning on springing that on her when she
arrives?"

"What kind of a masochist do you take me for? I
called her back and warned her after I'd spoken to
everyone else."

"And?"

Sam chuckled. "She said she'd bring dessert."

Typical.

"Maybe she's mellowing in her old age," I said
thoughtfully.

"Don't bet on it." Sam leaned close. His hand
skimmed up my bare arm. "And if I were you, I
wouldn't make any 'old age' comments, either."

"Don't worry. I already learned that lesson the

hard way." I gently pushed him away. "You do know that we have guests coming? Guests that *you* invited."

"Not for fifteen minutes." Sam nuzzled my neck.

"So I'm guessing foreplay is out."

"Out, hell," Sam murmured, "this is it."

"Marriage has ruined you," I said with a sigh. But I did put down the sharp knife.

When Sam turned me into his arms, I reached for him just as eagerly. Then heard the Poodles begin to bark at the front of the house.

Reluctantly, I drew back. "Someone's here."

"It'll take them five minutes to get inside." Sam slid his hand under my shirt. "More if we don't answer the door."

I heard a clatter on the stairs. Davey was coming down to see who had arrived.

"This is wishful thinking on your part," I mentioned.

"What can I say? I'm an incurable optimist."

Now his fingers were toying with my waistband. Two more minutes and I'd be naked. One more minute and I wouldn't care.

"Ahem." A throat cleared loudly in the doorway. I opened my eyes and looked over Sam's shoulder. Bob was standing there watching us.

"I guess I'm early," he said.

"Nah." Davey pushed past him and entered the kitchen. He didn't even glance in our direction. "They do that stuff all the time. You get used to it."

Bob laughed out loud as Sam dropped his hands and took a hasty step back. I pulled down the hem of my shirt and decided I looked presentable. Sam, who'd had higher hopes, was taking a little longer to recover.

"Good evening," I said to my ex-husband. "I see you brought wine."

Bob crossed the room, kissed my cheek lightly, and delivered the bottle of chardonnay into my hands. "Sorry to interrupt," he said under his breath. "Would you like me to take Davey for a walk around the block?"

"Not at all," Sam said quickly. He maneuvered himself between Davey and the cookie jar, placing a carrot stick in my son's hand instead. "We were just putting the finishing touches on dinner. Grab a beer out of the refrigerator and talk to us while we work."

"Carrots," said Davey. "Yuck." He glared at the offending vegetable.

I glanced over. "I thought you liked carrots."

"The other kids get cupcakes with their lunch. I get carrot sticks."

"And cookies," I mentioned.

"They get cookies, too."

"Cookie and cupcakes?"

"Wow, good deal!" said Bob. I glared at him. "You know," he amended hastily, "if you want to grow up overweight and unhealthy."

"Nobody will trade with me," Davey grumbled.

"That's a good thing," I said. "I pack you a great lunch. I'm happy to hear you're eating it."

"A little trading never hurt anybody," said Sam. "Maybe we could slip a little something extra into your lunch a couple of times a week."

"Cupcakes?" Davey asked.

"We'll see."

"Cool." He took his carrot and left the room.

"Geez, Mel, carrot sticks?" Bob said when Davey was out of earshot. "That's cruel. You might as well pack him Brussels sprouts."

"He likes carrot sticks. Or at least he did until he realized nobody else had them."

"Compromise," Sam said, like the diplomat he is, "is a good thing."

"So we've learned," Bob replied. He opened the fridge and pulled out a beer. "Which is why Melanie and I get along so well now."

"I thought it was because you'd finally come around to my way of thinking. You know, moving back to Connecticut and all."

"No." Bob popped the cap off the bottle and took a swallow. "That wasn't it. It was definitely compromise."

I thought about debating the issue—briefly— then said instead, "Would you like a glass?"

"Nope." He sat down at the table. "I figure I'll just chug this down before Peg gets here. You know, a little fortification before I have to face the dragon."

"Now, come on. You and she have been getting along much better lately."

Bob looked at me suspiciously. "Did she tell you that?"

"No, why?"

"I'm just trying to keep up, that's all. You know Peg. She likes to assign people roles. And if she's given me a new part to play, I'd hate to be the last to know."

"It's true," Sam said. "Even I've noticed. Peg is finally beginning to warm up to you."

"Whereas you," I said to Sam, "have been her fair-haired boy since the moment you two first met."

"What can I say? I just seem to have that effect on women."

I hooted loudly, and Bob started to laugh. "Older women, anyway," he pointed out.

"Don't you start." I turned away from the cutting board and pointed my knife at Bob. "How old was your last wife? Fourteen?"

After we'd separated, Bob had gotten involved in a brief and ill-advised marriage in Texas that had culminated in a quickie divorce in Mexico. I'd never met his second wife, but I'd seen her picture. She was blonde and cute in a chipper, cheerleader sort of way; and the thought of her acting as stepmother to Davey had made my blood heat. Thankfully, it had never come to that.

"Jennifer was twenty," Bob said, looking not nearly so smug as he had a moment before. "Maybe I'll have a second beer."

"I think I'll join you," said Sam.

I wondered if he was reconsidering the wisdom of this family gathering he'd engineered. And to think, the chief rabble rouser hadn't even arrived yet.

Nothing like having something to look forward to.

Bob sat down at the kitchen table and eyed the dinner preparations. He wasn't much of a cook, but for Davey's sake, he'd been trying to learn how to prepare a few meals.

"Are you going to bake that?" he asked, watching Sam spread the pesto sauce over the salmon.

"No, I brought my grill down from Redding the other day. I'm going to cook it outside."

For years, I'd been hassling with coals and lighter fluid. Sam had a gas grill. Push one button and voilà! *Man make fire.* And still they managed to be ridiculously proud of the achievement. It was enough to make you shake your head in wonder.

"It's a rite of spring, don't you think?" Sam asked. "The first barbecue of the year?"

Bob nodded. "That and the first lawn mowing. I

don't know what I was thinking buying a house on two acres of land. I'm a city boy. Look at these hands." He held them up for our inspection. "I don't think I was built for manual labor."

"You do have a riding mower," I pointed out.

"Yeah, but then there's seeding and pruning and fertilizing. Not to mention shoveling snow all winter and raking leaves in the fall. It's like *Green Acres* over there. With a yard that size, there's always something that has to be done."

"Sounds perfect to me," said Sam. "I enjoy working outdoors. It makes a great break from being on the computer all day."

"Any time you want to get your hands dirty, feel free to come on over. I'll find something for you to do."

"With luck, pretty soon we'll have a bigger place of our own," I said. "I imagine Davey's mentioned we've been house hunting. Something in your neighborhood would be perfect for us. I don't suppose you know of any neighbors that are getting transferred?"

"Or divorced?" Sam tried.

"Or have lost their jobs and need to downsize?"

"Or inherited a fortune and are moving to Greenwich?"

The two of us threw out questions, and Bob kept shaking his head. "Wow, you guys really are desperate, aren't you?"

"Believe it," I said. "Between the five Poodles and the three of us, we're packed in here like sardines. We need room to expand."

"Whereas I'm not using half the space I have."

Bob had been in his new house a year now. Originally purchased with an eye toward its investment value, the home was a four-bedroom colonial in a family neighborhood. Over the winter, he had finally finished furnishing the living room and bought a butcher block table for his kitchen, but the dining room and library still remained mostly empty. Davey could ride his scooter inside the house without fear of crashing into anything besides walls, and the front hall had a distinct echo.

"Sometimes it's like walking around a big, empty mausoleum," Bob said dolefully.

Meanwhile, both Sam and I seemed to have been struck dumb. I wondered if he was thinking the same thing I was.

"Maybe you'd be happier in something smaller," I ventured. "Something cozier."

"Something with charm and character," Sam added, "and a yard that's easy to take care of."

"Something with a gas grill," I said.

Sam shot me a dirty look.

What the hell? I thought. If we could make this idea work, we could buy another grill.

"What's going on?" Bob asked.

Maybe the second beer had dulled his wits. It wasn't as if we could have hinted any harder.

"We're offering you an option," I said. "A way out of all that hard work you've been doing."

"And a change of address to go along with it," Sam added helpfully.

"Huh?"

Bob was slow tonight, all right. Sam and I went back to cooking. Bob thought about things and nursed his beer. After a minute he looked up. The light bulb had finally begun to flicker.

"I get it," he said. "You guys want to trade houses."

Bingo.

"It wouldn't be a trade exactly," Sam corrected.

"Your place is obviously worth more than this one. We'd be looking at a trade plus cash to make up the difference. I'm sure we could come to an agreement that would offer you a decent return on your investment."

"I don't know." Bob obviously still needed some convincing. "It sounds kind of crazy. You actually think I should move in *here*?"

"Think about it," I said. "It would be perfect. This is a great house. Just the right size for one or two people. It's structurally sound and in good repair. And you already know what a nice neighborhood this is. Plus, it would be half the work of your current place."

"There is that . . ." Bob admitted.

"And you wouldn't have to buy any more furniture. The stuff you already have would fill the place up."

"That, too."

"And when Davey came to stay with you, he'd be right at home in his old room."

"Maybe it's not such a bad idea," Bob said slowly. He looked around the kitchen as though he'd never seen it before, appraising it with fresh eyes. "I am kind of lost in my current place."

"Don't forget," said Sam. "Everything in Fairfield County is appreciating in value—small houses, as well as big ones. You'd never have to worry about resale value."

"Or pruning and seeding," I said. "Or raking mountains of leaves."

"How many bedrooms do you have here?"

"Two," I replied, as if he didn't already know. Bob was interested, all right. Right before my eyes, he was morphing into a savvy shopper. "But both are a good size."

"Oil heat?"

I nodded. "And this place is economical, too. It hardly costs anything to heat. Probably a fraction of what you're paying now."

"Central air?"

Get real, I thought. "Built in the forties," I said out loud. It was as much of an answer as he needed.

"Basement and attic," Sam said. "Fenced backyard."

No point in mentioning the cats who were apt to be showing up from time to time, I decided. Though maybe I should tell him about the new neighbor whose husband was always out of town. The one who occasionally went walking around outside in her negligee. Maybe Bob would see that as a plus.

"You know," he said thoughtfully, "I think you two might be onto something."

"Onto what?" asked Davey, appearing in the doorway. "I came to tell you Aunt Peg is here. I just saw her car pull up."

"Your Mom and I are thinking about switching houses," Bob told him. "What would you think of that?"

Davey's eyes grew wide. "For real?"

"For real," I confirmed. "That way you could stay right in your same school and keep the same friends. And when you came to spend time with your dad, Joey would still be right down the road."

"Yippee!" cried Davey, twirling in place.

"I think that means he approves of the idea," Sam said with a grin.

The Poodles began to bark out front. Almost immediately they were shushed. Only Aunt Peg exerted that kind of authority over dogs that weren't even hers. My guess was confirmed a moment later when she loomed behind Davey in the doorway. My son was still spinning in giddy celebration.

"That's quite a greeting," Peg said. "To what do I owe the honor?"

"We're moving into Dad's house," Davey announced.

Aunt Peg didn't look amused.

"And he's moving here," I added.

Her expression brightened. "What a capital idea. Who came up with that?"

The three of us looked at each other.

"Joint effort," I said.

Aunt Peg walked across the room and patted Bob on the shoulder. The gesture was a benediction of sorts.

"There may be hope for you yet," she said with satisfaction.

21

Fortunately, that auspicious beginning set the tone for the rest of the evening.

Bob had never actually had Aunt Peg's approval before. Now, suddenly, he was her new favorite relative. He basked in the light of her esteem. It had to have been a heady feeling.

As for me, I had a sneaking suspicion that I knew what Peg was up to. Any thoughts Bob might have entertained about backing out of the plan we'd hatched so precipitously were being jettisoned by default. He wasn't even being given the opportunity to think about the deal he'd just made. Instead, he was being praised for a decision that had already begun to seem like a fait accompli. And just like that, what had sounded like a crazy idea only half an hour earlier was turning into fact.

Sometimes Aunt Peg's penchant for underhanded maneuvering wasn't necessarily a bad thing.

After dinner, Bob and Davey left early. Davey

was going to be spending the weekend with his father, and Bob had promised him that they could take in a new animated movie opening that evening. Davey kept some clothing and a spare set of toiletries at Bob's house, so he didn't even have to pack a bag. As soon as he had finished eating dessert, he jumped up, ran around the table to give me a quick hug, and declared himself ready to go.

"I guess I have my orders." Bob pushed back his chair and stood. "Thanks for dinner, Mel. As always, it was interesting."

Watching him walk out, I got the distinct impression that sometime later that night my ex-husband was going to wake up out of a deep sleep, sit bolt upright in bed, and mutter to himself, "Did I just agree to trade away my house, or was it all a bizarre dream?"

I was willing to bet money that he'd be calling me the next morning to check.

"Good," said Peg, when the front door had closed behind them. "Now let's get down to business."

I paused in the act of gathering up the dishes to take them out to the kitchen. "What business is that?"

"Mary Livingston's murder. I want to hear everything."

"I don't *know* everything."

"Then tell me what you do know, and it had better be good. Why else do you think I'm here? I gave up my bridge night for this."

Nothing like high expectations to live up to, I thought. Then stopped. "What bridge night? I didn't know you played bridge."

"Of course I play bridge. I went to Vassar, didn't

I? We had demitasse and cards every night after dinner. Wonderful game. I was a bit of a star, if I do say so myself."

That didn't come as a surprise.

"Several friends and I got together recently, formed a foursome, and set up a regular night. This is it."

"I hate to say it since you're already here, but your bridge game might have been more entertaining."

"I take it that means you don't have any idea who sneaked into Mary Livingston's room and smothered her."

"I have plenty of ideas. I just don't happen to know which is the right one."

"Perfect," said Aunt Peg, leaning back in her chair. "I love having a choice. Tell me all about them."

"I guess that's my cue to do the dishes," Sam said, rising. He gathered up an armload of plates and headed for the kitchen.

"That man," Peg said under her breath, "is a saint."

And also, I thought, remembering his pre-dinner antics, a bit of a sinner. Really quite a perfect combination. And, tonight, with Davey out of the house . . .

"Melanie?"

Peg's tone was sharp. My head snapped around. "Yes?"

"If it's not too much to ask, I'm trying to have a conversation here. Suspects?"

Right. Back to work.

"You may as well begin with Michael Livingston. I assume he's on your list."

I nodded. "For starters, he's not the ogre his family makes him out to be. He never turned his back on his mother, at least not intentionally. They were the ones who kicked him out when he balked at taking over his place in the family business."

"Twenty years is a lot of balking," Aunt Peg said.

"That was the Livingstons' idea, not his. Once he left, it was made perfectly clear that he wouldn't be welcomed back."

"And yet he had the audacity to return on the eve of his wealthy mother's demise. If nothing else, his timing has to be counted as suspicious."

"Michael told me he's sick," I said flatly. "He has colon cancer. He came back to deliver the news to his mother in person and because he was hoping they would finally be able to reconcile after all these years."

Aunt Peg sat back in her chair with a windy sigh. "Well, that changes things, doesn't it?" she observed. "Nothing like a look at your own mortality to slap some sense into people."

"He could have been lying to me," I felt compelled to admit. "Paul certainly implied as much. But I don't necessarily think he was. I just can't see that he had any reason to wish his mother harm."

"Unless he needed her money to pay his medical bills."

"From what I hear, Mary had plenty of money, probably a good deal more than was needed to maintain her lifestyle at Winston Pumpernill. I'm sure if her only child was in dire need of funds, all he would have had to do was ask for help."

"Does the family know?" Peg asked.

"About Michael's illness? No. He planned to tell his mother and let her do what she wanted with the information. Then, of course, he never got the chance. Surprisingly, he seemed to think I might want to break the news to them."

"But you didn't."

"Not yet, at any rate."

"Why not?"

"For one thing, I'm not sure I want to get involved in their family squabbles."

"Poppycock." Peg blithely disposed of that objection. "As soon as you agreed to look for Mary's murderer, you were involved in their feuding whether you meant to be or not."

"For another, Paul just rubs me the wrong way. The first time we talked about his aunt's murder, he compared my skills to those of a hotline psychic."

"No!"

"Yes."

"Funny, Sylvia doesn't have much of a sense of humor. Paul must have gotten his from his father."

"It wasn't meant as a joke," I said sourly.

"Even better then." Aunt Peg was relishing my annoyance. "Think how stupid Paul will feel when you show him up."

"*If* I show him up."

"Which you will, of course, succeed in doing," she replied firmly.

Aunt Peg is a great believer in motivating people to dance to her tune. She's never confronted an obstacle she couldn't surmount and has no idea why any of her relatives should either.

"Tell me about your other suspects," she said.

"Unfortunately, I have nearly a whole class full of them."

"I take it you're referring to your obedience club?"

"Right."

Aunt Peg considered that. "What makes you think that one of them would make a more likely murderer than someone, say, in Mary's own family?"

"To begin with, we were all there when it happened. Unless one of the other Livingstons happened to sneak in a back door during our visit, the only one who physically had the opportunity was Paul."

"I wouldn't rule them out simply because of that."

"I haven't," I admitted. "Especially since one of the administrators told me that up until the time of the incident, security hadn't been very tight. Apparently they hadn't seen the need."

Sam's older Poodle, Raven, came wandering into the dining room. Peg beckoned the bitch to her side. Given the choice, my aunt would always rather have her hands on a dog than not.

"I've been to Winston Pumpernill," she said. "The atmosphere there is very casual, as much like living in a private home as they can manage to make it. That's one of the facility's strongest selling points. I can see how a phalanx of guards roaming around would have been at odds with the image they want to promote."

"Not only that, but I just found out recently that aside from the front door, the building has a number of other exits and entrances, ones that don't lead into a reception area or straight past the administrative offices."

"So we haven't entirely eliminated the family, we've just set them aside for the moment." Peg was busy coaxing Raven's front legs up onto her lap. One of my Poodles would have acquiesced immediately. Sam's trio presumably had better manners. "Tell me about your esteemed classmates."

"Well, obviously there's Paul."

"Mary Livingston's great-nephew. The man who was responsible for taking your group to Winston Pumpernill to begin with."

"That's right—"

"The man who thinks you may be a charlatan." Aunt Peg allowed herself a small chuckle.

"Yes, but—"

"The one who told you that Michael is a liar, but the rest of the family is above reproach."

I stopped trying to get a word in and just sat and stared at her.

Peg lifted a brow and stared back.

"Am I telling this story, or are you?" I demanded.

"Sorry," she said, not sounding so in the slightest. "Please continue."

"So I guess we've covered Paul." I was ready to move on.

"Except for one thing."

"What's that?"

"You've never told me what kind of dog he has." Of course. How could I have forgotten that?

"Cora's a Welsh Corgi."

"Cardigan or Pembroke?"

"Cardigan."

"So Paul's a nonconformist. Good for him. Also, apparently, not one of those men who needs a big dog to cover for his own inadequacies. He doesn't mind a dog that needs some exercise, but probably doesn't care much for grooming. Cardis can be standoffish with strangers. Perhaps not terribly trusting of people they don't know."

"Sounds a little like Paul," I said.

Aunt Peg looked pleased. Pop psychology according to canine. She was a master at it.

"Who's next?" she asked.

"I've already told you about Minnie Lloyd."

"The lady with the Standard Schnauzer and the criminal record?"

"Yes."

Sam poked his head in the door, saw we were still busy, and withdrew. Seeing him, Raven hopped down from Peg's lap and followed.

Aunt Peg glanced over at the empty doorway, then back at me. "You have no idea how very lucky you are."

"Yes," I said softly. "I do."

"Marriage is a partnership. It takes work from both sides."

"I know that—"

"Don't blow it."

"Yes, ma'am."

Sometimes it's easier just to give her the response she's looking for.

"What about the lady with the Doberman?" Aunt Peg segued right back to our previous topic. It was enough to make my head spin.

"Julie Hyland."

"You thought she might have a secret or two."

"That's what Minnie told me. Or at least what she implied. But whatever her secrets are, she doesn't seem to have any intention of sharing them with me."

Aunt Peg gave me a look. The same one I aim at my students when they haven't satisfactorily completed their homework. "I suppose you'd better skip ahead to somebody else then."

"Stacey Rhoades," I said. "She has a Papillon named Bubbles, isn't terribly serious about learning obedience, and likes to talk baby talk to her dog."

"Paps are known for their intelligence. It sounds as though Bubbles might be smarter than her owner. If she isn't serious about obedience, what is she doing in your class?"

"Maybe she signed up for fun."

"Pish," said Peg. "Obedience is work. Agility is where you go when you want to have fun."

"Says you." I was almost tempted to stick out my tongue. Thankfully, the impulse passed.

"Might I point out that nobody connected with my agility class has ever been murdered? And what about that class of yours has been fun? So far, it sounds like one problem after another."

I thought for a minute. "We had a relay race the other night to practice our recalls. That was fun."

That sounded pretty lame, didn't it?

"Whoopee," said Peg.

I guessed that answered my question.

"So far everyone you've told me about except Paul has been a woman. Aren't there any men in that class? If I remember correctly, there should be one running it."

"Steve Barton. He seems like a nice enough guy, though several of the women think otherwise."

Aunt Peg looked interested. "And when he isn't being a nice guy, what does he do?"

"I've been told he's a control freak, and there have been inklings of that kind of behavior in class. He and Minnie had a relationship in the past, and he's still trying to control her by threatening to reveal things she told him in confidence."

"Which would make him not so nice, after all."

"Steve also had an opportunity to commit the crime. He was missing from the sunroom for at least ten or fifteen minutes after Mary had also left. He slipped in and out a back door."

"Motive?" Peg asked.

"None that I'm aware of."

"Pity."

"Indeed. By the way, Steve was holding Kelly Marx's Akita at the time. She was also missing for a while, and she might possibly have a motive."

"This would be the woman who had the temerity to name her dog Boss?"

I nodded.

"Go on."

"As you might imagine, Boss is a big, strong dog. Kelly's had some problems controlling him on previous visits, and Mary Livingston had made a complaint about their behavior. Kelly had been told that if anything else went wrong, she and Boss would be banned from visiting again."

"You're stretching if *that's* what you're calling a motive for murder," Peg said with a frown. "Why do I get the feeling you're grasping at straws?"

"Perhaps, because I am?" I said unhappily.

"Is that everyone who was in your group that day?"

"There was one other person, a man named Mark Terry. He has a Cairn named Reggie, and for some reason he's decided that I need an assistant. He's been drawing diagrams and making time-lines. He says he wants to help me investigate."

I half expected Aunt Peg to roll her eyes. Instead, she looked interested. "I certainly hope you didn't turn him away."

"I did my best," I admitted.

"Dear girl, don't be silly. Call the man and get him back! From where I sit, it looks as though you could use all the help you can get."

Trust Aunt Peg to point out the truth.

22

Life is never simple. What great philosopher said that? Whoever she was, she must have been a mother.

Thankfully, when I woke up Saturday morning, the child I was worried about wasn't my own, which didn't make my concerns any less daunting. Ever since my tutoring session with Brittany Baxter at the beginning of the week, I'd been trying to find a few minutes to corner her English teacher, Ed Weinstein. Somehow, given the demands of both our hectic schedules, it hadn't happened.

So I'd sent him a note on Thursday and told him to pick a time for us to meet to discuss one of his students. Improbably, he'd chosen Saturday morning at Hay Day, a country market in Greenwich that sold fresh fruit, sinfully delicious pastries, and great coffee.

I arrived first, purchased a cream cheese croissant and a cup of Colombian brew, then staked out a small table by the windows overlooking the parking lot. Ed drove a dark blue Buick, a sturdy, no-

nonsense car that suited his sense of propriety and would be easy to spot among the bevy of sleek imports already filling most of the spaces. I leaned back in my chair, sipped at my coffee, and waited for him to drive in. I was so busy looking out the window, I didn't hear him come walking up behind me.

"Good morning!" Ed sang out cheerfully, and I jumped in my seat.

He slid into the chair opposite me and set a mug of herbal tea and a protein bar down on the table. When I'd first met Ed two years earlier, he'd been sarcastic and argumentative, and he'd smoked like a chimney. To be fair, he was also semi-brilliant in his own pompous, professorial way.

Since then, he'd gotten divorced, shaved off an unflattering mustache, and started jogging. He looked five years younger, and his attitude toward life had improved markedly. Fortunately for his students, the edgy brilliance remained.

Ed was wearing nylon shorts, a black T-shirt, and a pair of serious-looking running shoes. His shirt was damp, and a bead of sweat trickled down the side of his face. No wonder I hadn't seen him drive in; he'd jogged over to Hay Day to meet me.

"I hope you haven't been waiting long," he said.

"No, I just got here."

"I apologize for my appearance. Saturdays I run five miles, and I hate to give it up. Especially after a long week at work, exercise really restores the soul."

Ed plucked at his wet, form-fitting T-shirt and pulled it away from his body. The move had a practiced look to it, and it achieved its purpose. I noticed how smoothly muscled he'd become.

"Divorce agrees with you," I said, breaking off a piece of my croissant.

He laughed, and I wondered if he'd gotten his teeth whitened, too. "Divorce agrees with everyone. Freedom regained. What's not to like?"

I wondered if his ex-wife felt the same way. Not that it was any of my business. The subject I'd come to discuss was touchy enough. No point in starting the conversation by getting his hackles up.

"You just got married, didn't you?"

News travels fast at Howard Academy; gossip travels even faster. I wasn't surprised that Ed was familiar with the details of my personal life. In a closed community like our private school, there were times when we all seemed to live in one another's pockets.

"Last month," I said.

"And are you blissfully happy?"

"So far, so good."

If someone else had asked the question, I might have provided a few details. But there was something about the deft smoothness of Ed's demeanor that made me wary of sharing confidences.

"But that's not what you asked me here to talk about."

"No." I picked at my pastry. The croissant was delicious. Too bad I was mostly just shredding it with my fingers. "Brittany Baxter."

"Fourth period English. What about her?"

"As you know, she's been seeing me for tutoring."

Ed nodded. His tea was green and it smelled vile. I'd have wrinkled my nose if I had to drink it, but he didn't seem to mind.

"She was getting behind in her reading. Maybe I jumped on her too hard, but I hate to let stuff like that get out of hand. Let a kid drop back some, and pretty soon they get it in their heads that they can't catch up. Fortunately, we seem to have gotten things sorted out. I'm sure the sessions she had with you were a big help."

"Plus, I hear you scheduled a couple of extra sessions with her yourself."

A look of surprise came and went briefly in Ed's eyes. He recovered quickly. "That, too."

"I was told she's started calling you Ed."

His shoulders rose and fell in a negligible shrug. The soft material of the black shirt pulled across his pecs. Ed busied himself getting the wrapper off his protein bar.

"Do all your students do that now?"

He glanced up, but his eyes looked past me. "A couple."

"The girls?"

"No." Ed's voice was suddenly curt. "Not just the girls. The ones that call me by my first name are the ones that need a little extra nudge in class. I've been a teacher for a long time. I've seen how it helps when I develop a real relationship with the kids. I want them to know that I'm not just some unapproachable authority figure. That I'm there for them if they need me to be."

His explanation sounded okay. But I wasn't sure I was buying it. Not yet anyway.

"Brittany's very pretty," I said.

Ed gave up toying with his plate. Now his eyes met mine, and his gaze was smoldering. "What are you suggesting?"

"She's also very young."

"I know exactly how old Brittany Baxter is." His tone was low, ominous. "She's twelve, for Christ's sake, a seventh grader. She's not even a teenager yet. And if you're trying to say you think I would have done anything even *remotely* inappropriate . . ."

Ed shook his head, ground his teeth. His features curled in a snarl. "We're done here. This meeting is over."

He shoved back his seat and stood. The chair wobbled for a moment, then tipped over backward. Diners at other tables looked in our direction.

"Ed," I said quietly, "sit down."

He stood there, thinking about it. At least he didn't leave. After a minute, Ed reached around behind him and righted his chair. Once it was upright, he stared at it hard, then finally sat back down.

"How dare you?" he demanded.

"You know the answer to that," I said. "I'm a teacher, I love my kids. I'd do anything to protect them. You're a teacher, too. You know what I'm talking about."

His nod was short, almost imperceptible.

"Brittany told me some things that made me nervous. I had to check them out. In my place, you'd have done the same thing."

"In your place, maybe I wouldn't have been so quick to rush to judgment. I wouldn't have started by making accusations."

"This isn't an accusation," I said. "All we're doing here is clearing the air. If I had wanted to accuse you of something, I'd have gone straight to Russell Hanover."

"I guess now I'm supposed to be grateful that you didn't?"

"No." I braced my elbows on the tabletop and leaned toward him. "What you're supposed to do is think long and hard about the perception that's created by the relationships you have with some of your students. I know perfectly well Brittany's at a difficult age—"

"It's not just Brittany," Ed said. "It's all of them. The boys are nearly as bad as the girls. Sometimes I look around my classroom and think I'm less of a teacher than I am a traffic cop at Hormone Central."

"They're testing you," I said. "And each other. Trying out their sexuality to see what works and what doesn't."

"It didn't used to be like this," Ed grumbled. "Ten, fifteen years ago, kids didn't grow up so fast. Third grade boys with pierced ears. Fourth grade girls wearing bras. It's like none of them want to be children anymore. They have no idea where they're going, but they're all in a huge hurry to get there. It confounds the heck out of me, and it makes me sad at the same time. It's not like the outside world is such a great place. Why don't their parents shelter them a little longer?"

"Because most of them are too busy," I replied. "That's why they're paying that enormous tuition. So we'll do the job of raising their children for them. If Brittany's parents were paying enough attention to their daughter, they'd be the ones sitting here across from you this morning instead of me."

"It's stupid," Ed muttered.

"I agree."

"Look, I gotta go." He drained the last of his tea and pushed away his plate. "Are we okay on this issue now? If Brittany thinks I'm giving her the wrong idea, I'm just as happy to keep my distance. She's still got her sessions with you. *You* keep her on the straight and narrow. I'll keep my nose out of it."

"Done," I said, and Ed turned and left.

He'd said all the right things, I thought. Now it remained to be seen whether his actions backed them up.

I'd be watching.

Back in my car, I gave Steve Barton a call.

It took me a while to get used to cell phones. In the beginning, I carried one for safety's sake, but never turned it on. The thought of actually making a call while I was driving was unthinkable. But, eventually, I got with the program and stopped thinking of my cell phone as a necessary evil. I wasn't in love with the gadget like some people, but I could appreciate the convenience it occasionally afforded me.

Steve was mowing his lawn when I reached him. I told him I was in the neighborhood—a lie, but what the heck, I was heading that way—and asked if he minded if I stopped by and asked him a few questions. Steve seemed somewhat surprised by the request, but was otherwise amenable to having his Saturday interrupted, so I hopped on the Merritt Parkway and drove up to New Canaan. By the time I found his house, a tidy ranch on a cul-de-sac two blocks from South Avenue, Steve had finished his chores.

The sweet aroma of freshly cut grass hung in the air as I climbed the front steps and rang the bell. Subconsciously, I braced against the barrage of sound that, in my experience, inevitably followed. Can I help it if nearly all my friends are dog owners? Most, in fact, shared their homes with more than one dog. Now that I thought about it, it seemed unusual that Steve, a man who taught an obedience class to other dog lovers, wouldn't have at least one dog himself. And yet, he'd never brought one to class.

Nor, I discovered now, did one accompany him to the door. Instead, Steve pulled the door open wide like someone who had no fear that a dog might slip out. He smiled, stepped back, and motioned me inside.

"Come on in," he said. "I'd been expecting your call."

"You were?"

"Of course. I know you've been talking to everyone else in class. I figured it was only a matter of time before you worked your way around to me."

As I followed him to the living room, I was still looking down, as if waiting for a dog, any dog, to magically appear. Apropos of nothing, I noted that Steve was barefoot and that his hardwood floors were blindingly clean. Much cleaner than mine, unfortunately. Maybe that was because I was living with a bevy of carousing canines and he wasn't.

"Looking for something?" Steve asked. A large recliner dominated one side of the room. He waved me toward a couch beneath the front window; then he walked over and sat down in the big chair.

"I'm just wondering why you don't have any dogs." The couch was much lower. Once I sank into its cushions, I found myself looking up at him. It wasn't the most comfortable feeling. "With your interest in obedience, it seemed likely that you might have one or two."

"I'm between dogs at the moment." Steve picked up a framed photograph from a side table, carried it over, and handed it to me. "This was my last dog, Stealth."

The picture was a close-up shot of an attractive German Shepherd. The dog was staring directly at the camera, and his dark eyes were piercingly intense. He was sitting down, but somehow didn't appear still at all. It was as if the lack of motion was only momentary as he waited for his next command.

"Very nice," I said.

"He was better than nice." Steve replaced the picture and sat down. "Stealth was a dog in a million. He already had his U.D.X. and C.G.C., and he was only four when he died."

An impressive array of titles, especially for a dog so young. "What happened?" I asked.

"Bloat." Steve grimaced. "You own a big dog like that, you know you're taking your chances. I knew there was a genetic predisposition in his family, but I thought I could manage his care well enough to keep things under control. Turns out I was wrong. So much for trying to play God."

"I'm sorry," I said, and really meant it. Bloat, or gastric torsion, was a horrible thing, and a horrifying way to watch one's pet die.

"Me, too. I'm looking for another dog to start over with, but I'm taking my time about it. I've always loved Shepherds, but I'm not sure I can deal with another one right now. Too many memories there. I've been thinking about looking at Poodles. Smart as they are, I bet they'd be a blast to work with. But they're susceptible to bloat, too, aren't they?"

I nodded. "Standards are. So far I've been lucky; there hasn't been any incidence of it in the line my girls come from. Plus, like you, I manage their care pretty carefully. If you ever decide you want one, let me know. I'll introduce you to my aunt. She's

Faith's breeder, and she knows just about everything there is to know about Standard Poodles."

"I'll do that. In the meantime, I suspect you didn't come here today just to talk to me about dogs?"

"No, not entirely," I admitted. "I suppose you can already guess that a couple of your students had some rather interesting things to say about you."

A smile played around the corners of his mouth. "And yet they continue to come to class."

A point that hadn't been lost on me either.

"Minerva and I had a bit of history together. I imagine you've figured that out already."

"Yes, she told me about it."

"I'm sure she did." His eyes went cold. "You'd be wise not to believe everything you hear."

"I never do."

"Mark Terry asked where I was when I left the sunroom during Coach's performance that day. I assume you'd like to know that, too?"

I sat still, hands demurely folded in my lap. "If you wouldn't mind telling me."

"I took Boss outside. He can be a bit of a handful, as I'm sure you've noticed. He was trying to bully me, and I didn't want to correct him the way he needed to be corrected with the patients and staff sitting right there. There'd already been one complaint lodged against him. I didn't want to draw any more attention our way than I had to. The doors were right there, so we stepped outside."

"Where was Kelly?"

Steve looked surprised. "Pardon me?"

"How come you were holding Boss? Why didn't she have him?"

"She'd gone to visit the ladies' room. For obvious reasons, Kelly didn't want to drag the dog all through the building with her. Or be dragged by him, as the case may be. I told her I'd watch him for a minute."

I watched the play of expressions across Steve's face. He was speaking slowly, thinking about his words before he said them. Mark Terry might have asked where the trainer had been, but clearly he hadn't asked the follow-up question.

Maybe Steve hadn't even thought about it himself. But he was now, and he was already formulating excuses. "She was only gone a minute or two," he said. "No time at all, really."

Two minutes might have been enough, I thought, with everyone else's attention diverted elsewhere.

"Did you happen to notice whether anyone else left the room?"

Steve shrugged. "People were coming and going all the time. Stacey might have disappeared for a bit. And Paul did, too, I believe. But nothing about anyone's activity seemed particularly ominous to me. Including yours."

"Mine?"

"You were the only newcomer to the group. The only thing that was different on that visit was your presence. It's hard not to wonder . . ."

"What?" I asked, though I could already guess where he was heading.

"Whether the fox is investigating the chickens, so to speak."

The best defense was a good offense. Clearly, Steve had figured that out.

"So you have nothing to hide?"

"I wouldn't say that exactly," Steve countered. "But murder Mary Livingston? Not me. Why would I? I have no motive."

"Nor, seemingly, does anyone else," I said. "That's the problem."

Steve stood up to show me out. "Your problem," he said silkily. "Not mine."

23

It was only a short drive from New Canaan back to North Stamford. I took the back roads rather than the parkway and was home in no time. To my surprise, as I drove up in front of my house I saw that a hand-lettered sign had been taped to the front door.

I parked the Volvo in the driveway and got out. Sam must have written the note with a thick black marker because I could read it from where I stood. DON'T COME IN, it said.

Well, that sounded ominous.

I was standing there wondering what to do next, when Sam came strolling around the side of the house. I noted with relief that he looked calm and composed. His hands were slipped nonchalantly into the pockets of his shorts. He looked as though he might simply be out for a walk on a sunny Saturday afternoon.

What he didn't appear was unduly alarmed or half crazed—like I might have looked if I had had a good reason to be barring people from their own home.

"I thought I heard a car drive up," he said. "Did you have a nice morning?"

"I had a fine morning." My gaze slid over to the sign on the door. "Until now."

"Problem?" Sam asked innocently.

Davey had been known to give me exactly the same look when he knew he was in trouble. Bob, too, come to think of it. Maybe it was a male thing—that wide-eyed, who me?, I-haven't-done-anything-wrong look that had the immediate effect of putting every woman in the vicinity on her guard.

"I don't know," I said. "Why don't you tell me?"

"Everything's under control here."

Sam linked an arm through mine and began walking again, heading back around the house toward the fenced yard. I was towed smoothly in his wake like a tugboat escorting a barge to the harbor.

"Sam?" I said sweetly.

"Hmm?"

"Why aren't we going into the house?"

"There's been a minor complication."

"Minor?"

"Exactly." His stride never faltered.

"Involving the *whole* house?"

We were approaching the gate, which Sam had shut and locked behind him. That meant that the Poodles were within the enclosed yard—so they weren't in the house either. I'd only been gone two hours. What could have gone so wrong in the meantime?

"You know how it is," said Sam. "Sometimes even a little problem has to be treated in a forceful way. Nipped in the bud, so to speak, before it can escalate into something bigger."

What escalation? I thought. Complications were bad enough. Now we were worried about escalation?

Sam held the gate open, and I slipped through in front of him. The Poodles gathered en masse around my legs, a sea of wriggling bodies and wagging tails.

"Exactly what little problem are we working on?" I asked.

Sam said something under his breath. Or maybe he just coughed. It was hard to tell, and either way I was none the wiser. He looked at me brightly, as though he were happy to have cleared things up. Which, of course, he hadn't done at all.

"Pardon me?" I said.

Sam mumbled again. It sounded as though he might have said, "Please," which made no sense. Please what? Please stop asking? Please go away? Please get a grip . . . ? And then it hit me.

"Oh, crap," I said out loud. "Fleas."

"Now, now." Sam's tone was soothing. "It's not that bad. I'm almost finished dealing with the situation."

Contrary to what Mr. Sunshine said, it *was* that bad, and we both knew it.

Fleas are the bane of a Poodle owner's existence. Dogs "in hair," those that are ready to be shown, are never allowed to scratch. Scratching made mats and holes in the coat. It played havoc with the all-important mane hair. It could keep a Poodle out of the show ring for weeks.

And if a dog wasn't allowed to scratch, then it followed that his owner must never allow him to become itchy. So fleas were definitely out. One of Aunt Peg's favorite lectures had to do with how two small fleas, left untreated, could quickly lead to a whole infestation. And once a battalion of fleas got inside your house, there was nothing left to do but . . .

"You bombed the house," I said.

Sam nodded. "About an hour ago. I had to run out and get some stuff or I'd have started sooner. I treated the Poodles, too."

Several years earlier, that would have meant dipping or powdering each dog. Both processes were deadly to show coats, unless the flea preparations were immediately washed out, rinsed clear, and the hair blown dry; and that often meant that the products weren't as effective against the fleas as they needed to be. Now, thankfully, there were products on the market that could do the same job while only causing minimal havoc.

Still, it was a big job, and an annoying one, and a totally unnecessary one if precautions were taken against letting the dogs be exposed to fleas in the first place. Which I thought I'd been doing. So where had I gone wrong?

Sam's Poodles were newly in residence, but he wouldn't have brought me fleas. Tar was as much at risk from the pesky intruders as Eve was. Besides, Sam had been the one to discover the problem. If his dogs had had fleas before moving in, presumably he'd have found them earlier and dealt with them.

Still simmering with annoyance, I looked around the small backyard. To be certain of wiping out the infestation, we'd need to treat that area, too. My gaze skimmed upward to the top of the cedar fence. Considering my frame of mind, it was probably a good thing that no cats were perched up there at the moment, waiting to heckle us. Maybe with all the Poodles out in the yard, they hadn't liked the odds . . .

Sam was watching me closely and following my train of thought. He knew the moment I figured out what had happened.

"Damn!" I spun around and headed back toward the gate.

"Wait." Sam grabbed my hand, and I slid to a precipitous halt. "Where are you going?"

As if he didn't know.

I simply stared. He got the point.

"It wasn't Amber's fault," he said.

"Her cats have fleas."

"Apparently so."

I crossed my arms over my chest. "Whose fault is that?"

"She didn't know."

Like that helped. "Then she didn't care."

"She's not the one who let her cats into our house," Sam pointed out.

Right. That had been Davey. I'd deal with him when he got home. In the meantime, I was itching to go and blow off some steam at the new neighbor. In fact, now that I knew we had fleas in our house, I was itching all over.

"Besides," said Sam, "I already talked to her about it."

"And?"

"She didn't realize there was a problem. Now she does. She's going to treat all the cats and get rid of the fleas."

"And maybe try keeping them home once in a while?"

Sam shook his head sadly, as if he were dealing with someone who was a little slow on the uptake. "I don't think she'll go that far."

"Her cats are trespassing."

"I don't believe there's a law against that."

"There are leash laws for dogs."

"Cats are different," said Sam.

"Tell me about it," I snapped, but my anger was beginning to fade.

In my absence, Sam had not only found the problem, he'd dealt with it. Maybe that was why I was so anxious to complain, I hadn't had to do any of the work. I ought to be grateful, not snapping at him.

"Thank you," I said belatedly.

"You're welcome."

"And she's really going to treat those cats so this doesn't happen again?"

"Already done," said Sam. "I picked up some products for her when I got ours."

I gazed up at him. My smile was luminous. "My hero."

"Don't you forget it," said Sam.

As if.

Sunday afternoon I loaded Faith in the car and headed down to Greenwich for the weekly visit to Winston Pumpernill.

It was a beautiful spring afternoon; I had the car windows open and the radio volume cranked up for the drive. Any responsible person will tell you that it's not safe for a dog to ride with its head sticking out of a car. Faith and I both knew that as well as anybody. But she was having so much fun— her mouth open, tongue lolling, black-fringed ears flapping in the breeze—that I didn't have the heart to stop her. In fact, if I hadn't had to steer, I might have been tempted to join her.

Now that two weeks had passed since Mary Livingston's death, things seemed to have quieted down once again at the facility. Loss was not, after all, an entirely unexpected occurrence there. And if the circumstances surrounding Mary's demise had been somewhat unusual, it looked as though the staff and administration would just as soon forget all about that small aberration and move on.

Our group assembled out front as usual. Lynn, the Director of Volunteers, greeted us at the door. Any reservations she might have harbored the previous week about our group's visit had since been set aside. She thanked us for coming, walked us through the wide corridors to the sunroom, and left us at the door.

Jay, the orderly who'd been manning the entrance during our last visit, was inside the room this time. He was chatting with Sandy Sandstrum and several other patients whom I hadn't yet met. Our group dispersed and headed in different directions. I spied Mrs. Ellis sitting in the sun that slanted in through the long windows, just as she'd been during Faith and my first visit.

Windows *and* French doors, I thought. Faith and I headed that way.

Mrs. Ellis had been staring out the window, but she turned slightly as we approached. Most of the patients smiled when they saw Faith coming their way. The big Poodle certainly did her part to look appealing; she wagged her tail and tipped her head winningly to one side.

The effect was lost on Mrs. Ellis, however. Her

stern expression didn't change when I pulled up a chair and sat down. Faith's offer of a front paw was pointedly ignored. Being a big believer in positive reinforcement, I shook the paw myself, then placed it back on the ground and patted the Poodle for making the effort.

"Well?" Mrs. Ellis barked.

"Well what?" Not the best comeback I'd ever delivered, but she'd caught me by surprise.

"Why are you back?"

"The group comes every Sunday." I tried not to sound defensive. "Most of the residents seem to enjoy it."

"That's their business. Maybe you should go entertain them."

"I'm sorry," I said, starting to rise.

"Quitter." Her lip curled. "Pansy."

"Pardon me?"

"For starters, you can stop being sorry for every damn thing."

"Yes, ma'am."

Her brow lifted, but she didn't comment. Instead, after a minute, she said, instead, "Sit."

I sat. Faith did, too. Mrs. Ellis looked pleased by our obedience.

"You're Melanie," she said, pointing a gnarled finger, "and that's Faith."

"That's right," I agreed, then shut up. It seemed safer to let her lead the conversation.

"Most people learn their lesson on the first try. Nobody ever comes back to see me a second time. Yet here you are again. So, which are you, brave or stupid?"

"I guess I'd have to say I've been known to be both."

"Hopefully the former more than the latter." Mrs. Ellis stared down at Faith. "I still don't like dogs, you know. At least yours isn't all touchy-feely. There's nothing worse than a dog that wants to lick your face."

Faith was a pretty accomplished face licker. But she knew better than to press unwanted attention upon strangers. Sitting upright beside my knee, she was the very model of Poodle decorum. How anyone could prefer a cat to that, I had no idea.

"You want to talk about Mary Livingston," Mrs. Ellis said.

She was right, but I wasn't sure I wanted to admit it. "What makes you say that?"

"I've got eyes and ears, don't I? What do you think? When you youngsters go home we old folks go into limbo until your return? Well, guess again. We sit around and talk about you. It's not as if we have a million other things to do."

I supposed not.

"Sandy told me what you were up to last week. Asking questions about Mary and that long-lost son of hers. You aren't some sort of police detective, are you?"

"No."

"Didn't think so." Mrs. Ellis thumped the arm of her chair with satisfaction. "The staff's been pretty careful about keeping them out. Though you might have slipped through anyway, seeing as how you look pretty innocent."

"I do?"

The older woman nodded. "Like butter wouldn't melt in your mouth. Trust me, you can use a look like that to fool a lot of people. I sure did in my day. So what have you got to tell me about Mary's murder?"

This wasn't a conversation; it was more like a runaway train. And I was no more than an unwitting passenger clinging to the side of a careening car.

"I thought I was going to be the one asking the questions," I said.

"You thought wrong."

Case closed.

"There's a reason why the administration has been trying to keep information from you. Nobody wants the residents here to be unduly alarmed."

The thought made Mrs. Ellis sneer. Or maybe she was smiling. It was hard to tell. "Do I look like the kind of person who's apt to become unduly alarmed?" she demanded. "Well?"

"No."

"At my age, what have I got left to be frightened of? Death? It's already staring me right in the face. It may be coming, but it hasn't gotten here yet. And until that happens, I fully intend to use what little time I have left. Now go on ahead and tell me what happened to Mary."

"She was smothered by a pillow while she was asleep in her room."

Mrs. Ellis waved a hand in the air. "That's old news. Grapevine around here has had *that* for ten days. Tell me what else you know."

So I did. I laid out the facts as I knew them and watched Mrs. Ellis puzzle over each new revelation. At the end, I said, "I was hoping that since you were sitting over here by the doors that day, you might have noticed if anyone went in and out."

"You mean sneaked in and out?" She didn't miss much.

"Precisely."

"There's a problem with that."

"What is it?"

"The reason I sit over here when your group shows up is that I don't want to be involved. I don't *want* to pay attention to the silly antics and goings-on. So I don't. Plus . . ."

I waited, and after a minute, she continued.

"It's a sad fact that I'm more likely to remember what I wore to a ball sixty years ago than I am to remember what I had for breakfast this morning. You're asking me about people I don't know, who were doing things I didn't care about at the time."

Entirely too true. I should have realized this probably wasn't going to work out.

"If you want to investigate something, I'll tell you what you ought to be asking questions about."

"What's that?" I asked. Even Faith pricked her ears.

"Things have been going missing around here lately. Even more so than usual."

"What kinds of things?"

"Big stuff, little stuff. You name it. I lost some money myself. Not a huge amount, just something I had tucked away in my jewelry box for a rainy day. I went looking for it the other day and it was gone. Now where did it go, can you tell me that?"

"Did you report the theft to anyone on the staff?"

"Not much point, is there? In the first place, cash is cash, and I'll never see it again. Second, at my age they'll probably think I just misplaced it. And third, the way the whole administration's been acting so skittish, I'm not about to be the one who adds to their worries."

"If you like," I said, "I'd be happy to talk to someone about it."

"Talk is cheap," Mrs. Ellis snapped. "I'd rather see some action."

"I'll try," I said.

Just one more thing to add to the list.

24

I left Mrs. Ellis and went to stand beside Jay. He'd positioned himself in a back corner of the room to observe the proceedings unobtrusively. Security might have been downgraded at Winston Pumpernill since my last visit, but it hadn't disappeared entirely.

"Can I talk to you for a minute?" I asked.

"Sure thing." The big man leaned down and greeted Faith. One hand stroked the top of her head; the other shook her paw solemnly. Then he straightened and looked me in the eye. "What's up?"

"I've heard some things . . ."

"Uh-oh, bad sign," Jay said, but his dark eyes were twinkling. He didn't look like a man who had anything to hide.

"I was told that if someone wanted to smuggle something into Winston Pumpernill, you'd be the person to see."

"You were, were you?" He still didn't look unduly dismayed. Jay gazed around the room. "Got to say something for these old folks. They mean well, but not a single one of them can keep a secret worth a damn."

"So then it's true?"

"I guess it might be under certain circumstances. But let's be clear on what we're talking about here. In my whole life, I've never done anything that would cause somebody harm, and I'm not about to start now. The fact that an eighty-five-year-old man wants to enjoy a smoke every now and again? Frankly, I can't see how that hurts. And those Twinkies for Mrs. Boardman? They may not have been on the approved diet plan, but they made her as happy as I've ever seen her all year."

"I hadn't heard about the Twinkies," I said.

"Did Mr. Beamish tell you about his stash of girlie magazines?"

I shook my head, and Jay grinned.

"Maybe I better just shut up then before I incriminate myself any further."

"Actually, the only thing I'm interested in is a note."

"You want me to pass someone a piece of paper?" Jay sounded incredulous, and with good reason. He was probably wondering why I couldn't manage that feat myself.

"No. I'm talking about a note you already delivered. Probably about three weeks ago. It went to Mary Livingston."

He thought for a minute, then slowly shook his head. "Nope. Didn't happen."

"It was from her son, Michael," I prompted.

"Sorry. Never met the man."

"Maybe he had someone else give it to you?"

"But I would have delivered it to Mrs. Livingston?"

"Right."

Jay was still shaking his head. "I'd have remembered something like that, especially in light of what happened and all. Nobody ever gave me anything and asked me to take it to her. And she never asked me to bring anything in to her. I'm afraid I don't know what you're talking about."

Well, that rearranged things, didn't it? I'd assumed Jay knew about the note. I'd been hoping he might have been there when Mary had opened and read it. I knew it was a long shot, but I'd wondered if he might have had some idea of its contents.

Now I was back to square one and faced with a whole new set of questions. If Jay hadn't delivered Michael's note to Mary, then who had?

"Thanks for your time," I said.

"No problem. I guess I wasn't much help. Seems to me, if you want to know something about Mrs. Livingston, you ought to try talking to Mr. Grey and Mrs. Reeves. Those were the two people she was tightest with. Near as I could tell, those three were great friends."

He'd directed me to Borden and Madeline, the two people Mary had been sitting with the first time we'd met. Borden had been among the group that had pointed me toward Jay, but he'd also freely admitted that he never remembered much of what happened from one minute to the next. Maybe Madeline would have a lead for me. At any rate, it couldn't hurt to talk to both of them again.

"I'll do that," I said.

I scanned the room and located the older woman among a cluster of people gathered around Mark and Reggie. There was no point in interrupting her, so I looked for Borden. For a minute, I

didn't see him at all. Then the door to the sunroom opened and he came shuffling through. With
Faith by my side, I moved quickly to intercept him
before he could join a group of friends.

"Hi, Borden," I said brightly. "I'm Melanie.
Remember me?"

"I never forget a pretty lady," Borden said with a
practiced smile. He reached out and patted my
arm in greeting, but his eyes remained frustrat-
ingly blank.

"We met a couple of weeks ago. Mary Livingston
introduced us. Then we spoke again last week when
you were playing bridge with Sandy and Harry."

"I know who you are." The light was slowly beginning to dawn, and Borden, accustomed to covering for his faulty memory, was loathe to admit
that things had ever been dark. "You're the lady
from the obedience group who has the big Poodle."
He glanced down at Faith and was pleased to see
his guess confirmed.

"Exactly."

"So this must be Sunday," Borden said happily.
"I knew there was a reason why Nurse Sims sent me
to the sunroom."

"It was to enjoy a visit from the dogs." I placed
my hand on top of his and led him to a plump,
overstuffed chair.

Borden sank down into the cushion and patted
his knee. "Here, girl," he said to Faith. "Come on
up and say hello."

The Poodle obliged him by hopping up and
placing her front legs across his lap. Gently, he fin-
gered the silky hair on her ears. "Like down from a
pillow," he said. "I never saw a dog this soft in all
my life."

I settled in a chair opposite him. "Her hair gets

blown dry after she has a bath. That's why it's so plush and smooth."

"Blown dry?" Borden looked startled. "Like with a hair dryer?"

I nodded. "A really big one, on a four-legged stand. It takes a really long time to do. Faith usually lies down on the grooming table and goes to sleep."

"Sounds like a lot of work to me."

"It is."

"So why do you do it?"

I thought for a minute. "So she can be beautiful, I guess. Once you get used to seeing a Poodle look this way, it's hard to let them go back to being scruffy."

"I never had anything but scruffy dogs myself," Borden said. He leaned down and inhaled Faith's clean scent. "Mutts and retrievers and the like. I always heard Poodles were supposed to be the smartest dogs."

"They are."

That answer was easy. Anyone who'd ever lived with a Poodle would tell you the same. Lots of dogs are smart, however, so it wasn't just the innate intelligence of the breed that made them a joy to live with. It was their desire to please and to communicate with people that set Poodles apart.

"I don't know if that's such a good thing." Borden's hand continued to stroke Faith's neck, and she leaned into the caress. "I wouldn't want to have a dog that was smarter than I was. She know any tricks?"

"Just the basics: sit, stay, come, shake."

"Seems to me—though maybe I'm mistaken, that happens to me a lot these days—that somebody brought a dog to visit us once that could do all sorts of things. Jump through hoops and the like."

"That was Minnie." I gestured toward a nearby couch where she and her Standard Schnauzer were holding court. "She and Coach gave a demonstration a couple of weeks ago."

Borden nodded, but I got the impression that he was being polite rather than actually recalling the incident.

"As it happens, I wanted to ask you a question about something that happened around the same time," I said.

"Same time as what?"

I'd expected this to be slow going, and it looked like I'd been right. I took a deep breath, moderated my impatience, and backed up a couple of steps.

"You remember your friend, Mary Livingston?"

Borden sat up straight, shifting Faith abruptly to one side. "Of course I remember Mary! Nicest lady you'd ever want to meet. Known her for years. How could anyone forget someone like that?"

"Do you remember when we spoke about a note she'd received from her son, Michael, shortly before she died?"

"Mary's passed on?" Borden thought about that for a minute, processing the information. Then finally he nodded. "That's right, I remember. Maddy and I went to her memorial service."

"Yes, you did. And then last week when you were playing bridge with Sandy, the two of you told me about a note Mary had received from her son who wanted to come and visit her. Whatever the note said made her very upset."

"Never play cards with Sandy Sandstrum," Borden stated firmly. He stared off into the distance. "The man cheats, and that's a fact. He thinks he can slip all sorts of things by me, but I'm as sharp as I ever was."

For Borden's sake, I really hoped that wasn't true.

"Do you remember the note I'm talking about?" I persisted. "Sandy and Harry thought that Jay had delivered it to her, but he didn't."

"No, he didn't." Borden shook his head.

Now we were getting somewhere.

"Do you know who did?"

He stared at me. "Now how would I know something like that?"

"I just thought that maybe since you knew it hadn't come from Jay . . ."

"Of course I knew it didn't come from Jay." Borden's voice rose. "You just told me that, didn't you?"

Damn. I'd misunderstood. He'd been agreeing with me, not offering new information.

"I'm sorry," I said gently. "I didn't mean to upset you. Let's just forget about the whole thing."

"Too late for that," Borden announced. "I suppose if you're going to keep asking about these things, they must be important. And if they're important, that means I probably have something written about them in my files."

"Your files?"

"Right here." He reached up and tapped his chest. "That's where I keep all the things I need to remember these days. Right next to my heart. That way I always know where they are."

He reached inside his sports coat and withdrew a small notebook. "Maddy, now, she makes fun of me for taking notes. But I say, hell, why not? It's no different than keeping a diary." He peered over at me. "You ever keep a diary, journal, something like that?"

"I'm afraid not."

"You ought to give it a try. It's a good habit to have. And when you get to be older like me, it helps you to keep things straight in your mind. Now let me see, when is this we were talking about?"

"It would have been about three weeks ago. That was when Mary first found out that her son was in town."

Borden flipped back through the pages, stopping every so often to check the dates on the top. Faith, realizing she was no longer the center of his attention, hopped down from his lap and came over to sit beside me. I pushed my fingers into her thick hair and rubbed her shoulders.

"You're very organized," I said to Borden.

"I ought to be. I used to be an accountant. I'll bet you didn't know that, did you?"

"No. I have an ex-husband who's an accountant."

Time was passing and we were making small talk. Once again, I had to try to curb my impatience. Borden continued to thumb through the pages of his small notebook, stopping every so often to read an entry that caught his eye. I wondered if he even still remembered what he was looking for.

Finally, he looked up. "Here we are."

I leaned forward. It was all I could do to keep from snatching the pages out of his hand. "What does it say?"

"Looks like I wrote down that Mary's son, Michael, was back in town."

"Yes."

"He'd been gone for a long, long time."

"Twenty years," I said.

"That's a long time," Borden repeated. "Mary was excited that she was going to get to see him."

So far, he hadn't told me anything I didn't already know. Maybe I'd been crazy to think that he would.

"Does it say how Mary knew that Michael was back in Greenwich?"

"Let me see." Borden licked his finger and slowly turned the page.

Inching closer across the distance that separated us, I could see the rows of aimless scribbling. Even right side up, I knew I'd have a hard time deciphering Borden's script.

"He got a message to her, even though her family didn't want him to. He had an old friend deliver it."

"What old friend?" I asked. "What did the message say?"

He chewed on his lip and consulted his notes. "The message said that Michael needed to see her right away; that it was important. I remember that now. Mary was upset because she'd had no idea that her son was in Connecticut, much less right here in Greenwich. Of course she wanted to see him, and the sooner the better. She was mad as blazes when she got that note and found out that her relatives had tried to keep them apart."

I sat back in my seat, feeling deflated. So the note itself hadn't contained anything inflammatory. What had upset Mary Livingston, and justifiably so, was her family's meddling.

Almost as an afterthought, I said, "Did you happen to write down who the friend was who brought the message to Mary?"

"Sure did. It says so right here." Borden lifted his eyes and gazed around the room. "It was that lady sitting right over there."

I looked in the direction he indicated. The middle of the room was filled with people, patients, and dog handlers alike. Borden and I had been talking for so long that the groups were beginning to break up. It was time for our visit to end; staff members were starting to escort the residents back to their rooms.

I saw a nurse heading toward us and quickly turned back to Borden. "Which lady are you talking about? Who brought Mary the message?"

"That one." He lifted a finger and pointed. "The nice one with the silky little dog with the big ears."

Silky little dog . . . big ears . . . Bubbles the Papillon. It had to be.

"You mean Stacey Rhoades?"

"If you say so," Borden said vaguely. He closed his book, replaced it in his pocket, and smiled at the approaching nurse. "You here for me?"

"That's right, Mr. Grey. It's time to take a walk."

"Glad to hear it." He slipped her a wink. "I'm always happy to take a walk with a pretty lady."

25

I tried to have a word with Stacey as the obedience club regrouped by the door and was escorted out. She and Bubbles were near the front of the party, however, and Stacey was engrossed in conversation with Kelly. Faith and I, having lingered that extra minute to talk to Borden, were near the back, and the corridor was filled with too many people for us to walk around and catch up.

While waiting to try again when we were outside, I mulled over what Borden had told me. When Michael had needed to get a clandestine message to his mother, he'd entrusted the delivery to an old friend. It was interesting that I hadn't heard anything about this friendship before. Not from Michael, not from Paul, and not from Stacey herself.

Although now that I thought about it, it occurred to me that I'd never questioned Stacey about her relationship with the Livingston family. Mostly because it hadn't crossed my mind that she had one. Of course, there was always the possibility

that Borden, with his memory lapses and his scribbled notes, was mistaken. But either way, I needed
to get some answers.

By the time Faith and I reached the parking lot,
Stacey was already unlocking her car. She opened
the door, lifted Bubbles up, and placed her carefully on the front seat. The Papillon scampered
across to the other side and waited expectantly.
Faith and I hurried over before Stacey could slide
in the car herself.

"Excuse me, do you have a minute?"

"Maybe one." Stacey turned and looked back.
"I'm kind of in a hurry."

"I'll be quick. I was just wondering how well you
knew Mary Livingston."

Immediately, Stacey's expression closed down.
Her eyes grew wary. The change was almost imperceptible, but I deal with kids all day; I can read eva-
sive body language at ten paces. And in the space
of a heartbeat, I'd lost her.

Damn, I thought. Wrong question.

"Not very well at all," she replied. "That it?"

"No, I—"

Stacey slipped inside her car. She quickly
slammed the door shut. Now there was a window
between us. I hoped Stacey might lower it, but she
didn't. Instead, she reached down and fitted her
key into the ignition.

"Sorry." Her voice, muffled by the glass, was
barely audible. "Got to go."

It was a good thing Faith and I moved to one
side, because the car was already backing up. I got
the impression that even if we'd continued to stand
in the way, she wouldn't have hesitated.

"Watch your toes," Julie said. Her SUV was
parked in the next space, and she and Jack came

up behind us. "When Stacey's ready to roll, heaven help the person or dog that tries to stop her."

"I just wanted to ask her a question," I said as Stacey's car sped out of the lot.

"Don't take it personally. Stacey's always like that after a visit to this place."

"Like what?"

"You know, furtive, edgy, in a hurry. Like she can't wait to get out of here. Haven't you ever noticed that before?"

"No." I angled Faith to one side as Julie opened her door and the Doberman hopped up onto a seat. Immediately, Julie reached in and cracked all the windows. "But I haven't been here that many times."

"Oh, that's right," Julie said, nodding. "To tell you the truth, I don't know what Stacey's story is. But something about this place must creep her out. At first I thought that maybe being around all these old people made her uncomfortable. But if that's the case, why would she keep coming back? Nobody's forcing her to make these visits."

"Did you ever ask her about it?"

"Once. She blew me off, much like she just did with you. So I figured, hey, it's none of my business."

Words to live by, I thought. Too bad I'd never been able to.

"Some people aren't good at answering questions," I said. Then stared pointedly.

I might have been remiss in not talking with Stacey earlier, but I hadn't made the same mistake with Julie. The problem was, even though I'd spoken with her, I hadn't managed to learn anything.

Julie stared back. She looked faintly annoyed but also a bit amused.

"Go ahead," she said. The words came out sounding like a challenge. "Take your best shot. What do you want to know?"

Mindful of the fact that I'd overlooked the possibility of a relationship between Mary and Stacey, I led with the same question I'd asked a minute ago. "How well did you know Mary Livingston?"

"Not at all. Aside from seeing her here periodically and hearing bits and pieces about the family from Paul, nada, zip. Which, by the way, if you're keeping track, and I assume you are, means I couldn't possibly have had a motive for murder."

"I guess not," I said agreeably. Some days I'm in Bad Cop mode. Today, I was feeling more like Good Cop. "I am curious about one thing, though."

"What's that?"

"I heard you had some skeletons in your closet."

Caught by surprise, Julie laughed out loud. Actually, she guffawed. I hadn't realized I was that funny.

"That's what's bugging you? You think *I* have something terrible to hide?"

It was hard to remain serious when she continued to laugh in my face. "Do you?"

"Doesn't everybody?" Julie took a deep breath and got her amusement under control. "I mean, *come on*. Is there anyone in the world who would like their life to be an open book?"

Now that she mentioned it, I didn't have anything to hide. At least nothing I could think of quickly. Maybe that meant I hadn't led a very interesting life. Either that, or all my secrets were already on display. Come to think of it, either alternative was pretty depressing.

"Are you going to tell me who pointed you in my direction?" Julie asked.

"No."

"Fine, then I'll guess. It's not terribly hard to figure out. It was Minnie, right?"

I didn't nod or agree in any way. Still, Julie went on as though I'd confirmed her guess. "Did she tell you what it is I'm supposed to be hiding?"

"If she had, would I be asking?"

Oops. Belatedly, I realized that confirmed the part about Minnie.

Julie didn't seem to notice. "It really isn't any big deal," she said.

I kept quiet and waited her out. She turned around and checked on Jack. Luckily for me, the Doberman wasn't offering any excuses. Like the well-trained dog he was, Jack sat patiently in the SUV. He appeared perfectly content.

"I joined the army right out of high school," Julie said after a minute. "I wanted to go to college and become an engineer, but I didn't have the money. The army offered to educate me, and I decided to let them."

The armed forces also taught people how to kill, I thought idly as I waited for her to continue. Not that Mary's death had needed much skill on the part of her murderer, but it had required a particular mind-set: the determination of someone who'd been taught how to approach an unpleasant job and see it through to the end.

"I don't know why I even ever told Minnie this," she continued, frowning. "But you know how it is when a bunch of women get together. There's a pitcher of margaritas on the table, and next thing you know you're sharing life stories."

I nodded because it was the response she seemed to want. Most of the time I'd spent with groups of other women seemed to involve juice boxes, lost shin guards, and a host of shrieking kids. But maybe that was just me.

"So I did my time and got my degree and everything was copacetic. Or at least as copacetic as it can be when you don't make most of your own decisions and your life isn't really yours to run. Let me give you the short version. The army and I had irreconcilable differences."

"How irreconcilable?"

"The AWOL kind." Julie held up a hand to stop my next question. "Not that I didn't have my reasons. Good ones, too. Even they eventually had to admit that. You remember back when all the branches of the armed forces were having problems with sexual harassment? Tail Hook, stuff like that?"

"Tail Hook was the navy," I pointed out.

"Doesn't make any difference. It was going on all over. I got pretty fed up with the situation and the attitudes I had to deal with and took what you might call a self-authorized extension on a three-day pass. Stupid, I know, but I was young and foolish. It's the only excuse I've got."

One that most people could probably sympathize with, I thought.

"Of course," Julie continued, "as soon as I stopped and thought about what I'd done, I realized I wasn't about to spend the rest of my life running away. When I went back, I found out I was facing a court-martial. So I told them to go ahead, but chances were they weren't going to like hearing the kinds of things that were going to come out in open court. It took a while and some legal wrangling, but eventually they decided just to discharge me, and I got the heck out."

"And?" I said.

I tried not to sound too hopeful. Because, so far, based on that story, I had diddly. So Julie had gotten in trouble with the military when she was younger. I couldn't see what any of that had to do with Mary Livingston's murder. Or why Minnie had pointed me in Julie's direction. Unless Minnie had simply been trying to get me off her own case.

"And nothing," Julie said flatly.

"Minnie seemed to think differently." It was a shot in the dark, but I threw it out anyway.

She rolled her eyes in disgust. "Minnie's a drama queen, pure and simple. Haven't you figured that out yet?"

Sometimes being the new kid was a real pain.

Once in the car, I called Sam and told him I was running late. He asked if I needed any help, told me he'd coordinate with Bob for getting Davey back home, and wanted to know how I felt about grilled chicken for dinner. How could I ever have thought that marriage to this man would complicate my life? Aside from a few small technical glitches, so far it had done nothing but make me deliriously happy.

The next call I placed was to Michael Livingston. "I'm in Greenwich," I said. "Do you have a few minutes to spare? If you want to give me directions, I can come to you."

"No need for that," Michael replied hastily. I wondered if he was embarrassed about his living arrangements. "Why don't we meet in a restaurant on Greenwich Avenue?"

"Sorry, I can't. I've got a dog with me, and it's too warm to leave her in the car by herself."

We settled on Bruce Park as a place that would

work for both of us. Faith and I arrived first. I took the Poodle for a walk past the tennis courts and around the lake while we waited for Michael to show up. She chased squirrels and scrambled up and down the big rocks for ten minutes before I called her back to my side.

When we returned to the parking lot, Michael was waiting for us. He'd left his car and was sitting at a picnic table under an old elm tree. Faith and I were both happy to sit down in the shade.

"That's a pretty fancy looking dog," Michael said.

Faith had been freshly groomed in anticipation of the visit to Winston Pumpernill. Her thick black coat—bathed, blown dry, and scissored the night before—looked luxuriously plush. The pompon on the end of her tail was perfectly round and full. Add to that the fact that she was probably larger than most of the Poodles Michael had ever seen. I've grown so accustomed to the way Sam's and my dogs look, that it takes a fresh eye to make me stop and appreciate how truly striking they are.

Faith preened at the compliment. She might not have understood every word, but she was great at picking up nuances. Deciding Michael was a new friend, she sat down next to him and offered him her manicured paw.

"She just learned that," I said. "You don't have to play if you don't want to."

"I don't mind." He shook the paw briefly. "Your dog has better manners than most people I know in this town. Since we're here, I'm guessing you have a message for me from my family."

"Actually, I don't," I admitted. Then I stopped and thought about what he'd said. "You mean they still aren't speaking to you?"

"Not if they can help it. I thought my mother's death might have brought about some sort of rapprochement, but instead they're treating it as if the last link between us has been severed. So the hell with it. I don't need their money, and I don't need their acceptance. I'll be heading home to Colorado in a few days. I'm just as glad you called today. It gives me a chance to say good-bye."

26

"Good-bye?" I echoed faintly. "How can you leave now?"

"Why would I stay? Now that my mother's gone, there's nothing left for me in Greenwich anymore. Believe me, that's been made abundantly clear."

"What about Mary's will . . . ?"

It was a rude question. I didn't quite have the nerve to finish it. But I let the topic dangle in case Michael wanted to contribute. Fortunately, he did.

"The will said just what I expected it to. Most of my mother's money was tied up in the family trust. She had a bit on the side, and that came to me."

In a family that had been manufacturing widgets for decades and for whom great wealth was the norm, even "a bit on the side" could add up to a substantial amount.

Michael must have been reading my thoughts. "It's not about the money," he said. "It was never about the money. It was about family and belonging and having a chance to see my mother again before it was too late."

He stopped and sighed. "None of that happened. And now, obviously, the chance has been lost forever. I've made a good life for myself, one that doesn't need to involve my relatives. So I'll be going home in a day or two. Actually, it will be a big relief to get out of here."

I supposed I could understand that, but the thought that his family would be lost to him forever seemed infinitely sad to me. "Did you ever talk to your relatives about your illness?"

"No, I never had the chance. And, frankly, under the circumstances, it wasn't any of their business. If that's what it would have taken—the knowledge that I might die soon—to make them welcome me back into the fold, then I'm afraid I'm just not interested."

In his place, I'd have probably felt the same. I wondered whether the police had counted Michael as a suspect in his mother's murder and how they felt about his leaving town. He laughed in reply when I asked.

"If the police are thinking about detaining me, they certainly haven't let on. I checked in with Detective O'Malley a couple of days ago. All he told me was that the investigation was proceeding, whatever that means. I don't think my presence here makes a difference. I'm sure the Livingston clan has enough clout to keep law enforcement working diligently."

Two weeks had already passed, I thought. If the police had turned up any viable leads, they hadn't been reported in the newspaper. Which brought me to the topic I'd come to broach.

"Do you mind going over a few more things with me?" I asked.

Michael shrugged. "Sure, why not?"

"When you first came back to Greenwich . . . when was that, by the way?"

"Last month. Which is another reason why it seems like time for me to go. My lease is just about up, and I don't plan on renewing."

I nodded. "Upon your arrival, how did you go about getting in touch with your mother?"

Michael thought back. "I started by calling the house. You know, the phone number she had the last time we'd spoken, which, admittedly, was a while ago."

"You didn't know that Mary was living at Winston Pumpernill?"

"I didn't know anything about her life, which was just the way the family wanted it. Unfortunately, she'd decided to accede to their wishes, or maybe she'd been browbeaten into agreeing. Anyway, when that didn't work, I tried calling my cousin Sylvia and ended up talking to Paul. He made it perfectly clear that my presence was neither needed nor wanted here."

"Did he tell you where your mother was?"

"He did give me that much." Michael's tone was bitter. "I guess he felt pretty secure in the family's ability to keep us apart. And as it turned out, he had good reason to feel that way. Before I'd even placed my first phone call to Winston Pumpernill, the administrators knew who I was. None of my calls was put through, and when I tried to visit, I couldn't even get inside the front door."

"You must have been feeling pretty frustrated."

"Frustrated isn't the word. I was about ready to kill someone." He stopped abruptly. "It's a figure of speech."

"I know," I said. "I'm not above using it myself."

Faith, having grown bored listening to our con-

versation, was now stalking a pair of squirrels that
were racing up and down a nearby tree. If I'd
thought she had even a hope of catching one, I'd
have called her off. But she seemed to enjoy the
chase more than the kill, so I left her to her game
and turned back to Michael.

"And then?"

"Then I got lucky. It was the last thing I expected. I was walking down Greenwich Avenue
one day and I ran into someone I used to know.
Her name was Stacey Quillan back then. We went
to high school together."

Stacey Quillan then, Stacey Rhoades now. The
woman hadn't been an old friend of Mary's, she
was an old friend of Mary's son. That made more
sense.

"But that's not the amazing part," Michael continued. "It turned out that Stacey knew my mother
was at Winston Pumpernill. She'd been visiting
the home once a week with some sort of dog
group."

"I know," I told him. "I'm a member of the therapy dog group, too. That's how I met your cousin,
Paul."

"So you've already spoken to Stacey about this
part?"

"Actually, no. That's why I wanted to hear it
from you. You wrote your mother a note and had
Stacey pass it to her during one of the visits, didn't
you? That's how Mary found out that you were in
Greenwich and wanted to see her."

Michael nodded. "It went like clockwork. I told
my mother that I'd been prevented from getting
in touch with her directly. I wrote that she had to
initiate the contact herself. I gather she went back

to the family and raised holy hell. Which was pretty gratifying under the circumstances."

"I'll bet."

Faith came racing back, warm from her exertions, tongue lolling out of the side of her mouth. She'd done her job; the squirrels had vanished. She flopped down on the cool grass feeling like a hero.

"The funny thing is," I said, "Stacey never mentioned to anyone that she knew your mother. And when I asked her about it earlier, she denied there was any connection."

"That doesn't make sense," Michael said.

"I agree." I reached down and stroked Faith's long back. "And here's something else that's odd. Apparently Stacey finds the visits to Winston Pumpernill pretty stressful. I've been told that she always seems agitated and in a hurry to get away."

Michael looked up sharply.

"What?" I asked.

"Probably nothing." He looked away.

"But maybe it's something."

"I shouldn't be telling tales."

"Why not? We're talking about people you haven't been in touch with for twenty years. People who pushed you out of their lives."

"It wasn't like that with Stacey," Michael said. "She and I were close in high school. Boyfriend and girlfriend for most of senior year. We even went to the prom together. But then we both went off to college, and you know how it is. You begin to grow in different directions."

"Been there, done that," I said.

I could remember my high school boyfriend's name, but the details of his face were a little hazy.

We'd broken up when we both came home over Thanksgiving break of freshman year. The parting was mutual, and I hadn't thought about him in years.

"Anyway," Michael continued, "what you said a minute ago about Stacey wanting to make a getaway just jogged something in my memory, that's all."

I hadn't phrased things quite that way, but I wasn't about to correct him. This sounded interesting.

"Back when we were teenagers, Stacey had a bit of a problem. You know what it's like growing up in a town like Greenwich. Kids get given way too much, way too early. And when everything comes to you that easily, maybe you begin to look in inappropriate places for a quick thrill."

"Are we talking about drinking?" I asked. "Drugs?"

"Oh, no, nothing like that," he said quickly. "At least nothing beyond the usual teenage experimentation. This was something else entirely. I can't say that I ever really understood what it was about, but Stacey liked to steal things . . . you know, shoplift? She'd stuff a blouse in her purse or a scarf under her sweater. She'd take things she could easily afford to buy, stuff she didn't even need. Someone dared her once to steal a watermelon from the supermarket and damned if she didn't manage to get it out of there without paying for it."

"Wow," I said under my breath. I wasn't admiring her technique, I was pondering the implications. And they were pretty big.

"She was good all right." Michael obviously had misunderstood my comment. "Scary good if you know what I mean. I'm not much of one for psychobabble, but, trust me, this was some sort of addiction. It was like she couldn't stop. Sometimes I'd make excuses not to go places with her because you never knew what she might make off with."

"You were worried about getting caught?"

"Hell, yes! It might have been a kick for her, but it scared me silly. I tried talking to her about it, but she just laughed and told me not to worry; that it wasn't a big deal and she knew what she was doing."

"And nobody ever caught her stealing?"

"Maybe once or twice, but don't forget, this was twenty-five years ago and things were totally different then. The store manager would give her a lecture rather than calling the police. Her parents would come down and pay for whatever she'd taken, and that would be the end of it."

I thought of all the items that had gone missing recently at Winston Pumpernill: Madeline's ruby brooch, the leather backgammon board, and Mrs. Ellis's cash. There had to be a connection. I wondered whether things had started disappearing when the visits from our group began, and if they'd all been misplaced on Sunday afternoons.

Michael was right. Times *had* changed, and the stakes were totally different now. Security was tighter everywhere, and people who got a thrill from stealing could expect to be arrested and prosecuted if they were caught.

Unless, that is, they happened to stumble across the perfect locale in which to indulge their bad habits. One where security precautions were scarce and missing items would most likely be ascribed to the forgetfulness of their elderly owners.

"What?" Michael demanded, staring at me across the table. "You're thinking something. What is it?"

"I'm wondering whether, in all those intervening years, Stacey ever got help for her problem, like therapy or counseling."

"I wouldn't have any idea."

"I know," I admitted. "I guess I'm just thinking out loud."

"What difference does it make?"

"I'm not sure. But things have been disappearing recently at Winston Pumpernill. Little things, the kind of stuff that would be easy to snatch and stash away."

"The sorts of things Stacey might be lifting if she were still looking for a quick thrill," Michael said.

He wasn't slow, I'd give him that.

"Did she take anything from my mother?"

"I don't know. Mary and I never spoke about it."

"My mother wouldn't have put up with it if she had." Michael's fingers curled into a fist. He looked as though he wouldn't have minded hitting somebody with it. "You know, I hadn't thought about any of this stuff in years. When I left Greenwich, I thought I had left it all behind."

I leaned closer. "All what?"

"Back then . . . my mother knew about Stacey's problem. I think a couple of the mothers had been discussing it by the pool at the club. I'd kind of forgotten this, but that was one of the reasons Stacey and I broke up. My mother brought some pressure to bear. She didn't think it was right for me to be associating with that sort of person."

Gossiping around the pool at the club? Worrying about associating with *that sort of person*? How very "old Greenwich." And yet . . . it sounded as though Michael might be onto something.

Abruptly, he shoved back the bench and stood up.

"Where are you going?" I asked.

"Somewhere, anywhere. I don't know. I need to process this and think things through."

"Fine," I said. "Let's walk."

Faith liked this form of entertainment even better than lying in the shade. The park was mostly empty, so I didn't bother putting her back on a leash. The Poodle gamboled on ahead several steps in front of us as we started down the hill and around the lake.

"Tell me what else you know about Stacey," I said.

"She was never a violent person, at least not back when I knew her. But she was an opportunist."

With a hobby like hers, she'd have to be, I thought. What was it I'd said when I was talking to the other club members about Mary's murder? That with the distraction provided by Minnie and Coach, the killer must have seen his shot and taken it?

"Are you thinking that Stacey might have felt threatened by your mother?" I asked Michael. "Maybe by what your mother knew about her?"

That was what I was thinking, at any rate. It would have been nice to have my ideas seconded.

"Possibly . . ." Michael stopped and shook his head. "It's looking like this is all my fault."

I stopped, too. Faith, circling past us, skidded up short. "What is?"

"Don't you see? My mother was fine, everything was fine, until I came back to Greenwich and started this whole chain of events. I'm the one who gave Stacey the note to deliver. I'm the one who sent her to my mother. I came back into my mother's life, and now she's dead as a result."

"That's not true—" I said, but Michael wasn't listening. Instead, he was moving again, faster now, and heading back toward the lot where we'd left our cars. Faith and I hurried to catch up.

"Paul said I was nothing but a bad luck charm, and it looks like he was right. I've made a mess of everything. There's only one thing I can do now."

"What's that?" I asked, pretty sure that I wasn't going to like his answer.

"I have to fix things," Michael said.

27

"Fix them how?" I asked.

Michael didn't answer. That might have had something to do with the fact that he was still two steps ahead of me and he'd already reached his car. He unlocked the door and yanked it open.

"Where are you going?"

He glanced at me briefly over his shoulder as he slid onto the seat. "To see Stacey. To figure out what the hell is going on."

Good idea, I thought. It was the kind of thing I might have wanted to do myself. Except that I would have been tempted to stop by the police station on the way to tell Detective O'Malley what we'd figured out.

Michael didn't look like he was going to be stopping anywhere first. He looked mad enough to spit nails.

"Do you know where she lives?" I thought the question might slow him down, but it had no discernible effect at all.

Instead, Michael reached down and started his

car. "Hell, yes," he said through the window. "I know where to find her."

I cupped a hand around Faith's muzzle and pulled her swiftly out of the way as the car began to back out of the space. As soon as he was clear, I released the Poodle and sprinted toward the Volvo, which was parked several spots down. I had no idea what Michael was planning to say to Stacey, or what she might do in return; but whatever was about to happen between them, I had no intention of missing any of it.

Faith liked this new game of spin and run that we were playing. She beat me to the Volvo and jumped up to plant both front feet on the door. I beeped the locks and let us in.

Luckily, Michael was a cautious driver. Before he'd even left the park, we'd fallen in neatly behind him. Michael never glanced in his rearview mirror; I doubted he even knew we were there. I tailed him up onto I-95, heading east toward Darien. Faith, riding shotgun, sat upright on the seat beside me and kept him in her sight.

As I drove, I pulled out my cell phone. I called Aunt Peg and quickly brought her up to speed on all the latest developments.

"Not Stacey Rhoades," she said incredulously. "The woman with the Papillon?"

"Bad owners happen to good dogs," I replied, watching Michael edge his car into the right-hand lane. He turned on his signal and prepared to exit, so I did the same.

Aunt Peg harrumphed. "You said she didn't seem serious about obedience training. Maybe after she found out about the visits to Winston Pumpernill, coming to class was just an excuse."

"Quite possibly," I agreed.

"Where are you now?"

"Darien. I believe I'm on my way to Stacey's house."

"Don't you *know?*"

"Not exactly. I'm following Michael."

"I hope you're not following him right into trouble."

Poppycock. I knew Aunt Peg better than that. She thrived on trouble. And there was nothing she liked more than knowing I was, once again, right in the thick of things.

"Give me the address," Peg said, and I did. Up ahead, Michael was pulling over to the curb and parking his car. "Maybe I should call the police and send them your way."

"We should be fine," I said. "All I'm planning to do is watch and listen when these two get together and see what shakes out. I'll call Detective O'Malley afterward."

"Call me, too," Aunt Peg said. I snapped the phone shut and tucked it away.

The neighborhood Stacey lived in was not unlike my own—rows of neatly kept smaller houses on quarter-acre lots. We'd headed south toward the shore when we left the thruway, and although I couldn't see Long Island Sound, I could smell the tang of salt in the air.

Halfway down the block, I found a tree to park beneath. I rolled all four windows part of the way down and told Faith to stay. She looked disappointed but resigned. Chin resting on the top of the open window, she settled down to await my return.

By the time I joined Michael on Stacey's front step, he'd already rung the doorbell. He looked at me in surprise. "Where did you come from?"

"I've been following you since you left Bruce Park."

"You have?"

The man really was oblivious.

"Yes."

"Why?"

"Because I want to talk to Stacey, too."

"Me first," said Michael. He looked as though he thought I might want to fight him for the privilege.

So he wouldn't get the wrong idea about that, I took a step back. At that moment, Stacey opened the door. Her eyes widened. Mouth slightly agape, she stared out at the two of us. Bubbles, standing on the floor beside her, began to bark. The little Papillon bounced up and down in place.

"May I come in?" Michael asked.

He didn't wait for her to answer. Instead, he simply pushed past Stacey and walked into the house. Precedent set, I followed suit. It was nice not to have to be in charge for a change.

"Melanie?" Stacey asked, sounding confused. "What are you doing here?"

"Following Michael," I said. How simple was that?

She closed the door and turned in place. Michael had kept going; he was heading toward the living room. "You two know each other?"

"We met a couple of weeks ago, after Mary Livingston died."

Stacey seemed frozen in place, stuck in the hall next to the door, as if she was hoping that Michael would come back and she could open it and push the two of us out. Since that didn't seem likely to happen, I decided to continue following his lead.

I walked into the living room; reluctantly, Stacey came after us.

"I wasn't expecting visitors," she said.

I wondered if that was supposed to be a comment about her housekeeping. Compared with my place, her home looked immaculate.

The living room was decorated in Early American, with dried wreaths on the walls and a hooked rug on the floor. The curtains were sprigged cotton, and the upholstered furniture was covered in denim. The fireplace had been neatly cleaned for spring; logs and andirons had been replaced by a big brass urn that held a spray of dried flowers. There were knickknacks on the mantelpiece and on nearly every other surface in the room, mostly Hummel figurines and small vases holding more dried blooms.

The place must have been a bitch to dust.

"Don't worry," said Michael. "We won't be here long."

I clasped my hands behind my back and smiled. This really was rather pleasant, I thought. I didn't have to do any work at all.

"I want the truth," said Michael. "And I want it now."

He sounded ominous. Stacey began to look a little concerned.

"What the hell happened between you and my mother?"

"Oh, dear." Stacey collapsed into a nearby chair.

Michael was unimpressed by her dramatic turn. "We'd like some answers," he said.

At least, I noted, he'd begun including me in the discussion. Maybe he was hoping I might have something to contribute. Not that I needed to. Things seemed to be going pretty well without me.

"Maybe you should sit down." Stacey gestured toward a dark blue love seat with plump, overstuffed cushions. "Would you like some coffee?"

"No," Michael snapped, answering for both of us. "What I want is for you to tell me what's really going on here. I thought we met up by accident that day on Greenwich Avenue. What a bit of serendipitous good fortune it seemed like at the time. Now I'm thinking maybe it wasn't an accident at all."

"Of course it was," said Stacey. "Just a bit of good luck, that's all."

"Then how is it that I find myself wondering why you didn't seem nearly as surprised to see me as I was to see you. And while you're explaining that, you might want to rethink your claim that you had remained friends with my mother all these years. Even at the time that struck me as odd considering that she never liked you."

Stacey's eyes blazed. "She did too like me! I told her once that I thought you and I were the perfect couple. That when we got married, our children were going to be beautiful, and she agreed."

Michael raked a hand through his hair. "My mother always agreed when people said outrageous things to her; it was just her way of trying to be polite. It didn't mean anything."

"I wasn't being outrageous! I was telling her the truth."

"Except that we didn't end up getting married," Michael pointed out. "And we don't have any children."

Stacey frowned in obvious annoyance. "There is that."

This was good stuff, I thought. Since it was beginning to look like we were going to be there a while, I went to the love seat and sat down. Bubbles ambled over and sniffed my ankles. Checking out Faith's scent, no doubt.

"How did you find out I was back in Greenwich?" Michael asked.

Stacey mumbled something under her breath.

"Pardon me?"

"Paul told me. He told half the class. That obedience club is worse than *Melrose Place* with all the gossiping that goes on. He was bitching about you coming back to try and coerce money out of his family, and I listened. Paul's young enough to be from a different generation. He didn't even know that you and I had once been—"

"Friends?" Michael supplied.

"Lovers," she corrected.

"For Christ's sake, Stacey, we were eighteen years old. I doubt that either one of us knew the meaning of love at the time."

"We were old enough to make a baby together," Stacey said quietly.

Michael stared at her for a long moment. "And mature enough to figure out what to do about that."

"It was a mistake."

"It had to be done."

Both of them seemed to have forgotten I was even in the room.

"You moved on," Michael said. "We both did. You got married."

"I got divorced."

"It happens."

Michael walked over to a nearby table and picked up a figurine, a plump shepherdess holding a lamb in her arms. "You always did like trinkets," he said.

Stacey's expression brightened. "See? Even after all these years, you remember. You might have tried to forget me, but you didn't."

"What I remember is your proficiency as a

thief," Michael said coldly. He rubbed his thumb up and down, caressing the cool china curves. "Did this come from a jewelry store in town? Did you slip it into your pocket as you were walking out the door? Or maybe you picked it up in some patient's room over at Winston Pumpernill."

Stacey shrank back as if she'd been slapped. "You don't have any idea what you're talking about."

"I know exactly what I'm saying." He nodded in my direction. "Melanie tells me there have been a number of incidents at Winston Pumpernill recently. Things have begun to disappear. Now to me, that sounds a lot like old times."

Stacey braced her hands against the arms of the chair and rose. "It's time for you to leave."

"Not yet," said Michael.

"Get out!"

She strode forward. Though Stacey tried her best to look threatening, she was smaller than either one of us. Michael could have subdued her easily. If it came to that, I probably could, too. Nevertheless, I stood up and moved to one side as a precaution. As full of surprises as Stacey was proving to be, I didn't want to be caught flat-footed.

Michael wasn't intimidated by her in the least. Instead of retreating, he walked toward her. "Did my mother catch you in the act?" he demanded. "Or did she hear her friends complaining about things that were missing and put two and two together? Either way, I'll bet she confronted you. That's just what she would have done. Once a thief, always a thief, right, Stacey?"

She glared at Michael venomously. Stepping suddenly sideways, she whipped a poker out of the stand of tools beside the fireplace. Stacey spun back around swinging the weapon in a wide arc.

Michael jumped back just in time to prevent the heavy metal bar from smashing into his side. Even though it was several feet from me, I jumped back, too. My reaction was reflex coupled with a quick reassessment of the situation.

Momentum from Stacey's powerful swing carried the poker into a lamp. It flew from an end table and crashed into the wall. The base and the bulb both shattered; shards of glass sprayed toward us.

Michael looked at the carnage, incredulous. "Are you crazy?"

"Of course not. I asked you to leave my house, and you didn't. You were yelling at me. I was afraid for my life and I acted in self-defense." Stacey's gaze shifted my way. "You heard him. You saw how he was behaving. I was acting in self-defense."

Not by my book, but I wasn't about to offer any commentary.

Michael had gone very still. His face was white, his lips drawn in a thin line. "I didn't really believe it before," he said. "I couldn't imagine it was true. But it is, isn't it? You killed her, didn't you?"

"You don't know anything," Stacey snapped.

"Tell us what happened," I said quietly.

"Yeah, right. So you can go running straight to the police?"

"We're going to the police anyway," Michael said. "And we're taking you with us. You may not have to tell us anything, but you will have to talk to them."

He advanced toward her. Stacey had lowered the poker. Now she raised it again and took a step back. "Stay away from me!"

"Like hell."

She reached around behind her and grabbed the nearest object, a dainty vase filled with dried flowers. Stacey flung the vase and it hit Michael's shoulder. She had quite an arm. The blow stopped him in his tracks.

"Don't come any closer," she said, snatching up a china statue.

Michael reached up and rubbed his shoulder. The vase lay broken at his feet. Bits of dried petals and stems clung to his sweater. He brushed them away.

"Why?" he asked.

"Your mother was going to tell on me." Stacey lobbed the statue. Michael ducked to one side. It broke against the wall behind him. "She was going to have me arrested. I would have been booked and prosecuted. And for what? For helping myself to a few small items that none of those old people needed anyway?"

"You should have tried to reason with her," said Michael.

"I did, but she wouldn't listen. You have no idea what she was like. She said I'd been a wicked girl, and now I was a wicked woman. Who the hell did she think she was to talk to me like that?"

Stacey swept up another figurine and sent it flying. Michael, distracted, didn't get out of the way in time. It struck him a glancing blow to the forehead. Blood beaded up on the spot; he didn't seem to notice.

Bubbles was pressed up against my legs. Now she began to whine anxiously. I reached down and scooped her up so she wouldn't step on any broken glass.

"Why?" Michael asked again. He still sounded as if he couldn't believe what he was hearing.

"She was old," said Stacey. "She had a weak heart. Her life was almost over anyway, what difference did it make? She'd ruined things for me once already, all those years ago with you. I wasn't about to let her ruin my life again."

"You don't even sound sorry," I said.

Stacey glanced over and saw me holding her dog. The little Papillon was shaking in my arms. Stacey sighed, and her shoulders drooped. She dropped the poker and held out her hands. I placed Bubbles in them.

"Of course I'm sorry," she said. "But it still had to be done."

28

Once my hands were free and the china had stopped flying, I pulled out my phone to call the police. It turned out to be unnecessary. You know Aunt Peg. She couldn't not meddle if her life depended on it. Of course, she'd already contacted the authorities and directed them to Stacey's house.

Only minutes passed before a knock sounded at the door. By that time, Michael and Stacey had started arguing again. At least they weren't throwing things. I stepped carefully through the debris and went to let the officers in.

There were two of them, unusual in a small town like Darien, and both looked wary. I knew they could hear the yelling behind me. They exchanged a glance.

"Domestic dispute?" asked one. The older of the two, he looked barely mature enough to shave.

"No," I said. "Murder."

The younger officer—short, stocky, blonde—cracked a smile. "You're kidding, right?"

I took a breath and told myself to bear with them. Darien was a lovely, quiet town. These two probably had no experience with violent crime. Maybe they didn't even watch crime dramas on TV.

"A woman named Mary Livingston was murdered at the Winston Pumpernill nursing home in Greenwich two and a half weeks ago," I told them. "The woman who lives in this house just confessed to that murder. The man inside with her is the murdered woman's son."

"Holy shit!" breathed the younger patrolman.

I have to admit, it felt good to exceed someone's expectations for a change.

The other officer's hand dropped to his holster. "Are either of them armed?"

"Only with a fireplace poker and a whole lot of breakable china."

As if to punctuate my point, we heard a crash from within. It sounded as though another Hummel had hit the wall.

They looked at each other again. "We better call for backup."

"Your choice." Now that I'd reported what I knew to the proper authorities, none of this was my problem anymore.

I slipped around them and down the steps. Looking down the block, I could see Faith sitting in the Volvo, waiting patiently for my return. She spied me through the windshield, stood up, and began to wag her tail. Her whole body wiggled with the effort, and my heart lifted. Being loved by a dog does that to you. It's an oasis of sanity in a sometimes crazy world.

I called out Faith's name and ran the last few steps between us. As I opened the door, she launched herself into my arms, knocking me back a step before I could steady myself. I buried my face in her warm coat and felt restored.

Once in the car, I called Aunt Peg and filled her in. Then I reminded her about Bubbles and told her there was a good chance the little dog would need short-term rescuing. She thanked me for the heads-up and promised to get right to work. There's nothing she likes more than a project.

Midweek, I paid another visit to Winston Pumpernill. I went on my own this time as I had a debt to repay. Before leaving home, I had stopped next door. Anyone with seven cats, I reasoned, had to have at least one that was little and fluffy and cute. Thankfully, I was right.

Amber lent me a six-month-old kitten named Bosco and a traveling bag to put him in. I carried it tucked under my arm like a purse when I walked into the nursing home and nobody even looked twice. I'd called ahead, and Mrs. Ellis was expecting my visit. Even so, she didn't look pleased to see me.

"You again," she said when I knocked, then waited in the doorway of her room to be admitted.

"I'm Melanie," I said, just in case. "Remember?"

"Of course I remember." The room was large and had a sitting area on one side—two chairs with a small table between them. Mrs. Ellis was seated in one of the chairs. She'd been reading a book, which she set aside. "I'm not daft, you know. Where's the big Poodle?"

"I left her home." I slipped inside and shut the door. "I brought a different kind of visitor today."

I crossed the room and placed the bag on the

older woman's lap. When I unzipped the top, Bosco popped his head out. The kitten was the color of cream, with ears and a mask that were tipped in brown. He looked around alertly and batted at Mrs. Ellis's fingers with his paw.

"Oh, my." Her eyes softened as she gazed at the kitten. "Where did you come from, little man?"

"I borrowed him for the afternoon. His name is Bosco."

"Is he a Siamese?"

"Your guess is as good as mine. He belongs to my neighbor. She tends to be a little vague about things like that."

With a graceful leap, the kitten launched himself up out of the bag and onto the tabletop. He examined Mrs. Ellis's reading glasses carefully, then climbed up one side and down the other of her hardcover book. She laughed with delight at his antics.

"Thank you," she said softly.

"Thank *you*." I sat down in the chair opposite her.

"For what?"

"For pointing me in the right direction. Mary Livingston's murderer has been arrested. Have you heard about that?"

Holding out a hand to lure the playful kitten back to her lap, Mrs. Ellis nodded.

"I think you'll find that people's belongings are going to stop disappearing, too."

"Aha. So there was a connection?"

"There was."

Bosco skittered off the edge of the table and landed on Mrs. Ellis's legs with a gentle thump. Her gnarled fingers reached up to stroke the smooth, soft fur. The kitten arched his back and flipped his tail, then rolled his shoulders into the caress. After a minute, he began to purr, his tiny engine rumbling with pleasure.

The older woman leaned back in her chair, closed her eyes, and smiled faintly. "Can you stay long?" she asked.

"I've got all afternoon," I said.

So we traded houses with Bob. Who would ever have thought that such an unlikely idea would actually come to fruition? Certainly not me. But then, all sorts of things in my life have been coming together lately.

Maybe my karma is changing for the better. Or maybe it's Sam's doing. Or, what the heck, maybe I'm just having a run of good luck. Whatever was responsible, I'm not about to complain.

The school year is drawing to a close, but while classes are still in session, I'm keeping an eye on Ed Weinstein. I know it and he knows it, and so far his behavior has been above reproach. The minute I get an inkling it isn't, I'll shut him down so fast it will make his head spin.

Meanwhile, we still haven't met Amber's husband, James. But since Bob is now her next door neighbor and Davey is over there all the time, I imagine we will eventually. One day shortly after Bob moved in, Bosco climbed the fence, came to visit, and somehow never went home. Amber decided she had more than enough cats already, and Bob seems perfectly pleased to have a new pet. As for Davey, he couldn't be happier.

And if my son is excited about that addition to the family, I'm hoping we'll have another surprise for him soon. No, I'm not pregnant, but Sam and I are working on it. So we'll wait and see how things turn out, and maybe something good will happen.

It wouldn't surprise me at all. I'm on a roll now.

If Melanie Travis was planning on a quiet family summer with her Standard Poodle Faith, son Davey, and new husband Sam, her plans are about to turn upside down. An unexpected competition, a trip to New York, and—oh yes, a murder—later, Melanie finds herself in a choke collar of deceit and corruption.

When she receives the letter from the Champions Dog Food Company informing her that Faith has been selected as a finalist in the All Dogs Are Champions contest, Melanie is mystified—until she discovers it was Davey who entered Faith in the contest. Since he also signed the entry form that legally prohibits contestants from withdrawing, Melanie and Faith swallow their pride, tweak their top knots, and enter the ring.

The winner will be the spokesdog for Chow Down, a new—and decidedly *not poodlicious*—dog food the company is launching, and will receive a hundred-thousand-dollar modeling contract. Too bad Melanie and Faith are less than interested in winning this contest.

At the reception where they meet the other finalists—Ginger, a Brittany owned by a perky couple Bill and Allison Redding; MacDuff, a Scottish Terrier belonging to Dorothy Foyle, an older woman; Brando the Boxer, owned by Ben O'Donnell, an out-of-work actor; and Yoda, a Yorkshire Terrier who belongs to an aloof couple Suzanne and Larry Kim—Melanie immediately picks up the scent that this pack is a bone's throw away from a major dog fight.

Leaving the reception with Faith, who doesn't care for elevators, Melanie heads for the fire stairs. Above them a door opens and voices waft down followed by a blood-curdling scream as Larry Kim comes tumbling to his death. The police label the fall an accident, but something smells rotten to

Melanie, starting with the fact that no one comes forth as the person Larry talked to before he fell. Odder still, Suzanne chooses to keep Yoda in the contest despite Larry's tragic demise. With the final decision drawing near and the competition getting downright ferocious, Melanie and Faith will have to watch their backs—because Melanie's digging may well unearth a barking-mad killer who'll do anything to win.

**Following is an exciting sneak peek at
Laurien Berenson's
CHOW DOWN
coming next month wherever hardcover
mysteries are sold!**

"Let's start by introducing ourselves again," Doug said. "Since most of us are meeting for the first time, I think it would be a good idea if we each took a minute to talk about who we are, what we do, and why Champions Dog Food is important to us."

He paused and looked expectantly around the table. Everyone nodded in agreement except MacDuff who seemed to be eyeing a muffin Chris had placed next to his laptop.

"Since I'm the contest chairperson, I'll start. I'm also Vice President of Marketing for Champions Dog Food, which means that I'm the one in charge of telling the world that we manufacture the best canine nutritional products on earth."

Doug sounded as peppy as a high school cheerleader, and I found myself grinning at his extravagant job description. Nothing like a little hyperbole to get the meeting off to a good start. Then I looked around the table and realized that everyone else was taking his pronouncements seriously. Oops.

He nodded to Simone, who was seated at his right.

"Simone Dorsey," she said. Her tone was flat, modulated. "I'm Director of Public Relations. My job is to keep this company and our products in front of the public eye, so that when the time comes for people to choose a healthy, balanced diet for their dogs, they'll think of us first. This contest was my idea, and I think we've come up with five superb finalists. Any one of your dogs would make a fine representative for Chow Down Dog Food."

This time everyone smiled when she finished speaking. I was relieved to join in; finally, I was beginning to catch on to the important cues.

Chris Hovick went next. "Hey," he said, sketching a small wave in the air. "I'm Chris, more formally known as Director of Advertising. I'm the one who comes up with the specific campaigns that best illustrate to the public what our products are all about. And Chow Down is going to be big, man. I'm proud to be part of the campaign and I know you will be, too."

More cheerleading. I guessed the intended effect was to get our competitive juices flowing. If so, judging by the intent expressions I saw on the other finalists' faces, it was working.

"Cindy Burrows." The last member of the team flipped her long French braid back over her shoulder and introduced herself. "Product Manager for Chow Down and delighted to be here. I hope you all are, too. Champions Dog Food is important to me because I believe in the quality of the products." She stopped and smiled slyly, her gaze sliding around the table. "And because they sign my paycheck."

Finally, I thought, as we all laughed together. Someone who was willing to inject a small dose of reality into the proceedings. Doug and Simone, I noted, both joined in the merriment, but neither looked amused by the comment.

"Now you know who we are," Doug said when the laughter had died down. "It's your turn to tell us something about you."

"What do you want to know?" The rest of us had hesitated; but not Ben, he spoke right up.

"Whatever you feel is important for the selection committee to consider," said Simone.

Chris nodded. "Surprise us."

Nothing like a little pressure.

Ben, however, didn't seem to mind. He was in his element and happy to go first.

"I'm an actor," he said. "You've probably seen my work on television and on the stage. And Brando is an actor's dog. Aside from being a gorgeous Boxer, there's something else we bring to the table that none of the other finalists can. Brando and I are professionals. We won't require a lot of coaching to put on a good performance. We both know how to get the job done and to look good doing it."

"Thank you," Doug said when Ben paused to draw a breath.

The actor looked disgruntled by the interruption. Clearly he hadn't intended to give up the spotlight so quickly. "No, thank *you*. Brando and I would also like you to know that we appreciate this wonderful opportunity and that if we're the ones chosen to represent Chow Down Dog Food, we will devote the full range of our considerable talents to the project. I promise you we won't let you down."

"Excellent," said Simone. I wondered if she was responding to Ben's words or the fact that he'd been flirting with her shamelessly since the moment he'd first entered the room.

"Moving on . . ." Doug prompted. "Bill and Allison, what would you like to tell us about Ginger?"

"First and foremost, that she's a great dog," Allison said, her voice pumped with enthusiasm. "With a wonderful personality. She's been almost like a child to us . . ." She paused and a blush rose to her cheek. "I mean, not that we think she's human or anything—"

"It's all right, honey, they know what you mean," Bill took over for her. "Allison and I aren't breeders. Ginger is the only dog we own. And look what she's accomplished. She's a conformation champion, she's working on her Utility degree in obedience and she's also qualified for her field championship. Having the opportunity to own a dog of this caliber is kind of like hitting the lottery, they just don't come along every day—"

"What Bill's trying to say is that Ginger can do it all." Allison was speaking again now. I felt like we were being tag-teamed. On the other hand, I could see how the committee might find the couple's energy infectious.

Bill reached down and patted the Brittany's head. "Once you stop and think about it, I know you'll realize that Ginger is exactly the kind of dog you want representing Chow Down Dog Food."

"You might be right," Doug agreed smoothly. "Dorothy, what would you like to tell us?"

The older woman took a moment to gather her thoughts. She looked slowly around the table, her gaze pausing on each of the committee members in turn. "After listening to what other people have to say, I'm afraid maybe MacDuff and I are going to look a little shabby by comparison."

"No way!" Chris disagreed.

A small, satisfied smile lifted Dorothy's lips. That was just the response she'd been angling for, I thought.

"Now MacDuff and I, we're not as young and flashy as some of your other contestants. But I guess you'd have to say that we do have experience on our side. Those of you who go to dog shows, I bet most of you know who MacDuff is from his record in the ring."

She stopped and waited for us to nod. Dutifully, most of us did.

"This dog . . ." Her hand reached over to stroke his head fondly. "He pretty much won everything there was and then some. I retired him at Westminster in February. He'd earned his chance to do nothing but sit in the sun and snore.

"But funny thing about that. When it came right down to it, that wasn't what MacDuff wanted. He missed the excitement of being on the road all the time. Retirement just seemed to bore him silly. In a nutshell, that's why we're here. I figure I owe this old dog anything he wants that will make him happy. And if one more chance in the limelight will do it, then I'm just pleased to be along for the ride."

Wow, I thought, she was good. That appeal had to tug at the judges' hearts. In her own quiet, unassuming way, Dorothy had just moved MacDuff up to the top of the list.

Simone was writing furiously on her notepad. Chris had his laptop open. I couldn't see the screen but I assumed he was doing the same. It occurred to me that I probably didn't have to worry about Faith winning the contest. There was no way I was going to be able to top these performances.

"I'm Larry Kim and this is my wife, Lisa," Larry said from the other end of the table. Lisa inclined her head slightly. "And this lovely Yorkshire Terrier you see in my arms is Yoda. Others have told you about their dogs' lofty accomplishments. Of course I could do the same, but instead I would rather get right to the point.

"Yoda loves to eat. Yes, she is a small dog, but don't let her size fool you. This is a dog who always enjoys a good meal. We feed only Champions Dog Food in our kennel and Yoda was raised on it. She has been eating, and loving, Champions since she was a tiny puppy."

Approval wafted around the table like a smooth wave. The committee was lapping up this pitch.

"Recently we were fortunate to receive an advance sample of Chow Down. You should have seen Yoda dive right in. I barely had the bag open before she was begging for a morsel."

Seated beside her husband, Lisa was nodding as he spoke. I wondered why she didn't say anything herself. It occurred to me that she was the only one in the room who had yet to speak. Well, except for me.

"Let's be honest," Larry said. "What you're looking for is an adorable canine representative who loves your product and can sell it to others. Yoda is that dog."

Another top-notch appeal. As I listened to my fellow contestants speak, they had me half convinced to vote for them myself.

"Melanie?" Doug turned to me. "What would you like us to know about Faith?"

Oh right. My turn. Unfortunately I hadn't prepared something to say like the rest of the participants clearly had. Now I needed something fast.
Something fresh and catchy. A slogan. A sound-
bite. An irresistible anecdote . . .

And my mind was a total blank. I hate it when
that happens.

"Umm . . ." I said, "she's a Standard Poodle."

Doug smiled encouragingly. Cindy nodded.
Chris, waiting with fingers poised above his key-
board, was reserving judgment. As for Simone, she
already looked bored.

"The thing about Poodles is . . . that they're a
terrific breed of dog. It's true of Faith, but I can't
take too much credit because, really, it's true of all
of them. Poodles are just wonderful members of
the family. They're intelligent, they have a sense of
humor, they're empathetic. They're the perfect
pet.

"Whatever their owner's lifestyle, they adapt
and fit right in. That's why so many people have
owned Poodles over the years. And why others
have fond memories of the Poodles they knew
when they were children. Poodles make people
happy. They're evocative of everything that's good
about owning a dog."

"I see," said Cindy.

I don't think she really saw anything. I think she
just wanted to stop my disjointed rambling. And it
was probably just as well that she had.

"You know," Chris said, "now that you mention
it, our neighbors had a Poodle when I was little.
Smaller than yours. A Mini, I think. His name was
Chester and, man, that was some great dog. I bet
plenty of people would see a Poodle in an ad and
be drawn to it for just that reason. They might not

even know why, but seeing a Poodle would make them feel good."

"Subliminal," Simone said thoughtfully. "I like it."

"Definitely something to consider," Doug agreed.

The other contestants shifted in their seats and regarded me with wary respect. Desperate for something to say, all I'd done was describe how great Poodles were to be around. It was the committee members who had taken my idea—or lack thereof—and run with it. Unexpectedly, it looked as though I'd pulled a rabbit out of a hat.

Doug leaned forward and braced both his hands on the table. "Okay, now we know who we are and why we're all here. Cindy and Chris, why don't you tell everyone what's up next."

"As you know," the young woman began, "Chow Down is a new product for us. One we're going to be introducing to the marketplace shortly. To be perfectly honest, it's not like there's a shortage of good kibbles already available. So it's vital that we do something to set our dog food apart in the minds of the consumers.

"That's where the role of spokesdog comes in. We're looking for a dog that's every bit as much of a standout as we feel our product to be. A dog that's not only beautiful to look at, but that has personality and charisma, too. A dog that's one in a million."

"Obviously all your dogs are beautiful specimens of their respective breeds," Chris told us. "Otherwise you wouldn't be here. But now they need to show us something more. What we thought we'd do next is have you take them off their leashes and let them interact with one another. Kind of a 'free play' situation where we could observe what they're like when they're just being themselves."

Five strange dogs, all turned loose simultaneously in a small room and encouraged to be entertaining? It certainly wasn't the best idea I'd ever heard. Years earlier, I had taken Davey to a pre-school interview that had used a similar evaluation technique. That meeting had turned into a train wreck. This one, I thought, had similar potential.

"Fine by me," Doug said happily. Brando was already loose. The Boxer had been roaming freely around the room for the last ten minutes.

Allison shrugged, reached down, and unsnapped Ginger's leash. The Brittany was beautifully trained. She knew she'd been released, but even so she maintained her down-stay position.

"I'm not sure this is a good idea," said Dorothy. "Terriers can be territorial. Nothing wrong with that, it's their nature." It was also the reason why terriers were sometimes asked to spar in the show ring. MacDuff was one of the smallest dogs in the room. If he decided to pick a fight, he would be at a real disadvantage in the fray that followed.

Chris looked as though he was about to argue, but Larry Kim's voice, speaking calmly and deliberately, brought the room to a standstill. "This will not be happening," he said.

"Pardon me?" Simone sounded shocked. I was willing to bet she wasn't accustomed to having people deny her what she wanted.

All eyes at the table turned Larry's way.

"Your idea is not a good one. In such a circumstance, the smaller dogs' safety cannot be ensured, and, in fact, if something should go wrong, any one of the five might be at risk. I suggest that we find a different way for you to observe the dogs' personalities. Either that, or we take the time to carefully introduce them to each other before turning them loose."

"That won't be the same." Chris was already shaking his head. "What we're looking for is excitement, spontaneity. Something fresh and fun, and entirely out of the ordinary."

Larry's nod was curt. Yorkie still cradled in his arms, he rose to his feet. "Then what you are looking for is not Yoda."

For a moment, Lisa merely stared at him, wide-eyed. Then she scrambled to her feet as well. "It was a pleasure to have met you," she said softly, addressing the group. "But our coming here was obviously a mistake. Now we must go."

"Wait!" Doug jumped up.

The sudden movement startled Brando. The Boxer had been standing with his back to the table, sniffing the trash can next to the sideboard. Now his body stiffened as he spun around to face us. He landed with his feet braced in a pugnacious stance and jutted his jaw forward as he weighed the situation.

Instantly Ben was on his feet as well. He crossed the room quickly to stand beside his dog. "Easy boy," he said, his hand reaching down to cup Brando's muzzle.

At first glance the gesture looked like a caress. But watching a moment longer I realized he was holding the Boxer's mouth shut. And maybe muffling a low growl.

Interesting. It looked like there might be aggression issues there that Ben was trying to downplay.

Bill must have seen the same thing I did. Out of

the corner of my eye, I watched as he unobtrusively slipped a hand down and refastened Ginger's leash.

"Maybe you're right," Doug said to Larry. "We certainly wouldn't want to force any of you to place your dogs in a situation that makes you uncomfortable. This is only our first get-together, after all. We're still feeling our way here, finding out what works and what doesn't."

Larry slowly sat back down. Lisa followed suit.

"Fine," said Cindy. "Then let's try this a different way. Everybody up and out into the middle of the room. Dogs on leashes." She glanced at Ben, who quickly complied. "Now that everyone's under control, just let your dogs be dogs. Let them do what they want to do. And we'll just observe and see what happens."

All of us liked that idea much better. Each of the five contestants was well socialized, each had been to dog shows. They all knew how to behave in polite company.

Faith and Ginger had touched noses and wagged their tails. MacDuff ignored the others and sniffed around for crumbs under the table. Yoda circled the room looking elegant and composed, her blue-grey coat rippling as she moved. Brando sidled over and discreetly stole a biscuit off the sideboard, which he swallowed in one quick gulp.

Meanwhile, the committee stood together off to one side, watching the various antics and taking notes. Twenty minutes later, they decided they had what they'd wanted. Good thing because the dogs were beginning to tire. I wished I'd thought to bring a thermos of water for Faith.

"That's a wrap," Doug announced. "Thank you all for coming. Everyone was great. Chris, Cindy, Simone, and I will get together this afternoon and compare first impressions. Sometime in the next couple days, you'll receive an e-mail letting you know what the next test is going to be. Please feel free to stop at the reception desk on the way out and pick up a gift basket of Champions products."

I heaved a sigh of relief and headed straight for the door. Some of the other contestants hung back—probably wanting to curry more favor with the judges—but Faith and I had had enough. We were more than ready to go home.

I'd promised the Poodle that we'd take the stairs on the way out. Exiting the conference room, I saw that a red-lettered EXIT sign marked their location at the end of the hallway. But it was hot outside, our car would be stifling from sitting in the sun, and we were twenty minutes from home. Before heading down, I detoured into the ladies' room to get Faith something to drink.

Lacking a bowl or a cup, I filled the nearest sink with cold water. Then I hopped the Poodle's front feet up onto the porcelain rim and let her lap. I was glad I'd taken the time to stop; Faith drank thirstily.

When we emerged from the ladies' room, the hallway was empty. I pushed open the heavy fire door that led to the stairwell and Faith ran on ahead. Quickly she trotted down two flights of stairs with me hurrying to keep up. We had only one flight to go when I heard a door open above us.

The sound of hushed voices echoed through the vertical chamber. More of my fellow contestants, I guessed. I probably wasn't the only one whose dog didn't like elevators.

Quick footsteps tapped a staccato beat on the metal steps above us. Then I heard a sudden scream.

It was followed quickly by a series of thumps. Faith and I both froze where we stood.

"Hello?" I called out. No one answered. Only my own word echoed back.

A door slammed. I thought I heard someone moan.

Then I heard the patter of little feet and Yoda came flying down the steps, trailing her gossamer ribbon leash. Without even stopping to think, I leaned down and opened my arms. The little Yorkie flew right into them.

"It's all right," I said, as she pushed her tiny body into me and burrowed close to my chest. "You're going to be all right."

Damn, I thought. I really hated lying to a dog.